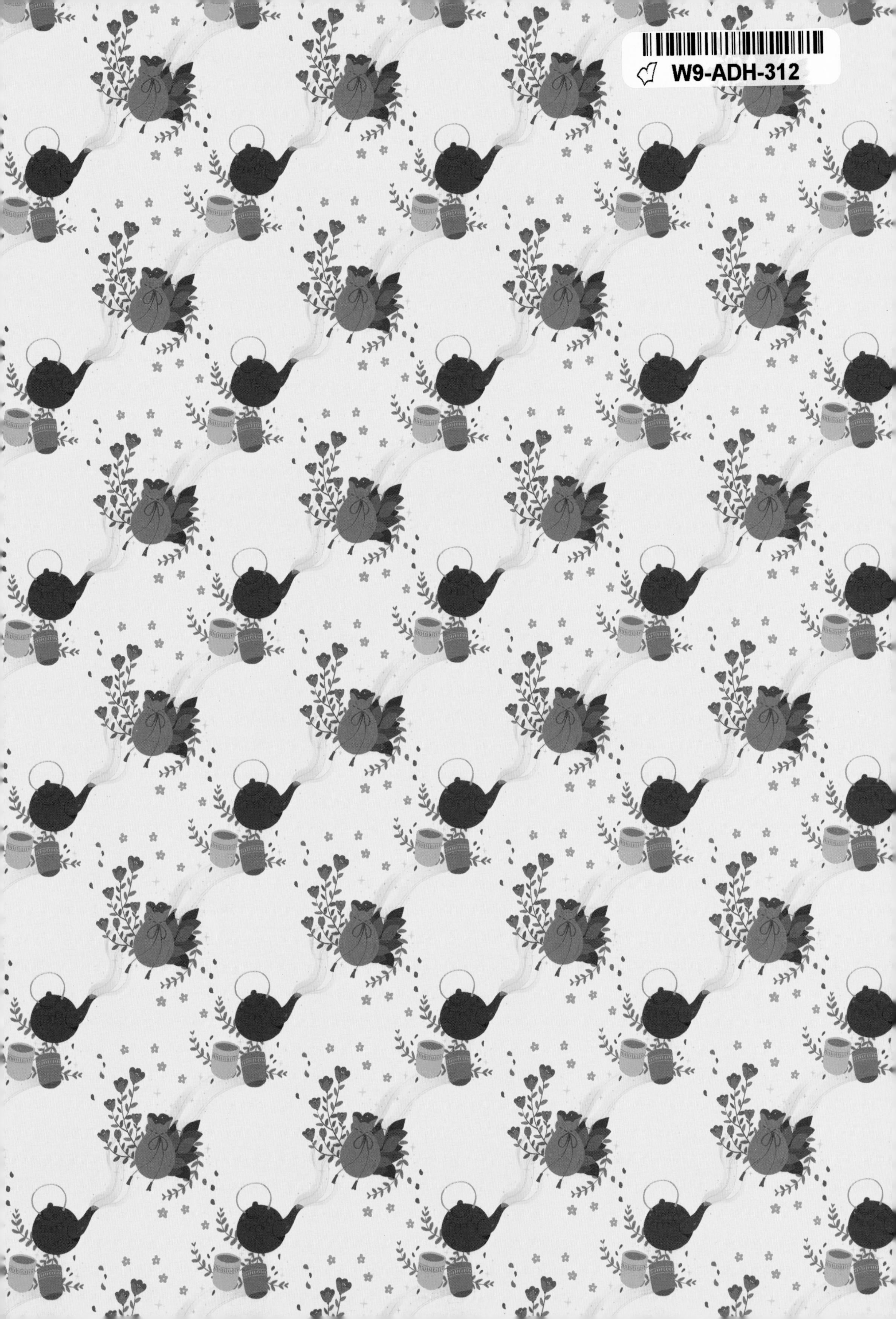

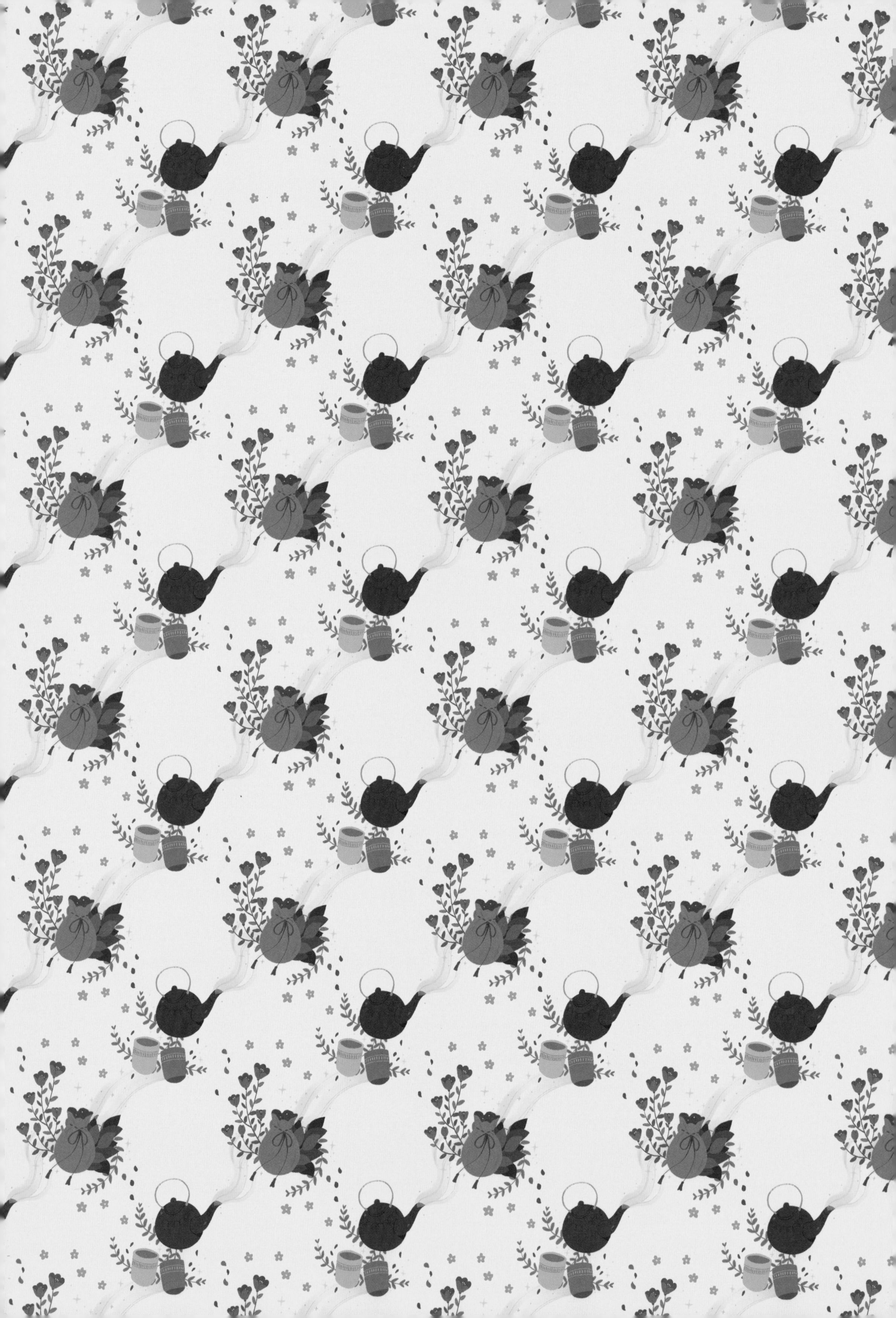

The Tea Dragon Festival

Rinn

is an aspiring cook, and they know the best places in the forest to get wild herbs and vegetables.

Aedhan

is a young dragon of the Shining Wing clan, and wants to prove himself worthy of it.

Hesekiel

is a Sylke bounty hunter, who has a talent for magic and exceptional manners.

Erik

is an experienced and hardy adventurer, always excited to use his sword, but guided by a good heart.

The Tea Dragon Festival

WRITTEN & ILLUSTRATED BY

Kay O'Neill

LETTERED BY
Crank!

EDITED BY
Ari Yarwood

DESIGNED BY
Kate Z. Stone

WITH SPECIAL THANKS TO
JENNA BEACOM AND ALEXANDREA GILL
FOR THEIR GUIDANCE

AN ONI PRESS PUBLICATION

A Note for Readers

In this book, characters use both American Sign Language and voice to communicate.

Sign language is shown like this:

Are you going out gathering?

Sign language and voice is shown like this:

I'll make a list!

Check out the back of the book for more resources about sign language!

PUBLISHED BY ONI PRESS, INC.

Joe Nozemack, *founder & chief financial officer*
James Lucas Jones, *publisher*
Sarah Gaydos, *editor in chief*
Charlie Chu, *v.p. of creative & business development*
Brad Rooks, *director of operations*
Melissa Meszaros, *director of publicity*
Margot Wood, *director of sales*
Sandy Tanaka, *marketing design manager*
Amber O'Neill, *special projects manager*
Troy Look, *director of design & production*
Kate Z. Stone, *senior graphic designer*
Sonja Synak, *graphic designer*
Angie Knowles, *digital prepress lead*
Robin Herrera, *senior editor*
Ari Yarwood, *senior editor*
Desiree Wilson, *associate editor*
Kate Light, *editorial assistant*
Michelle Nguyen, *executive assistant*
Jung Lee, *logistics coordinator*

onipress.com • facebook.com/onipress
twitter.com/onipress • onipress.tumblr.com
instagram.com/onipress

ktoneill.com • twitter.com/strangelykatie

First Edition: September 2019

ISBN: 978-1-62010-655-6
eISBN: 978-1-62010-656-3

Library of Congress Control Number: 2018964397

PRINTED IN CHINA.

3 4 5 6 7 8 9 10

Chapter One

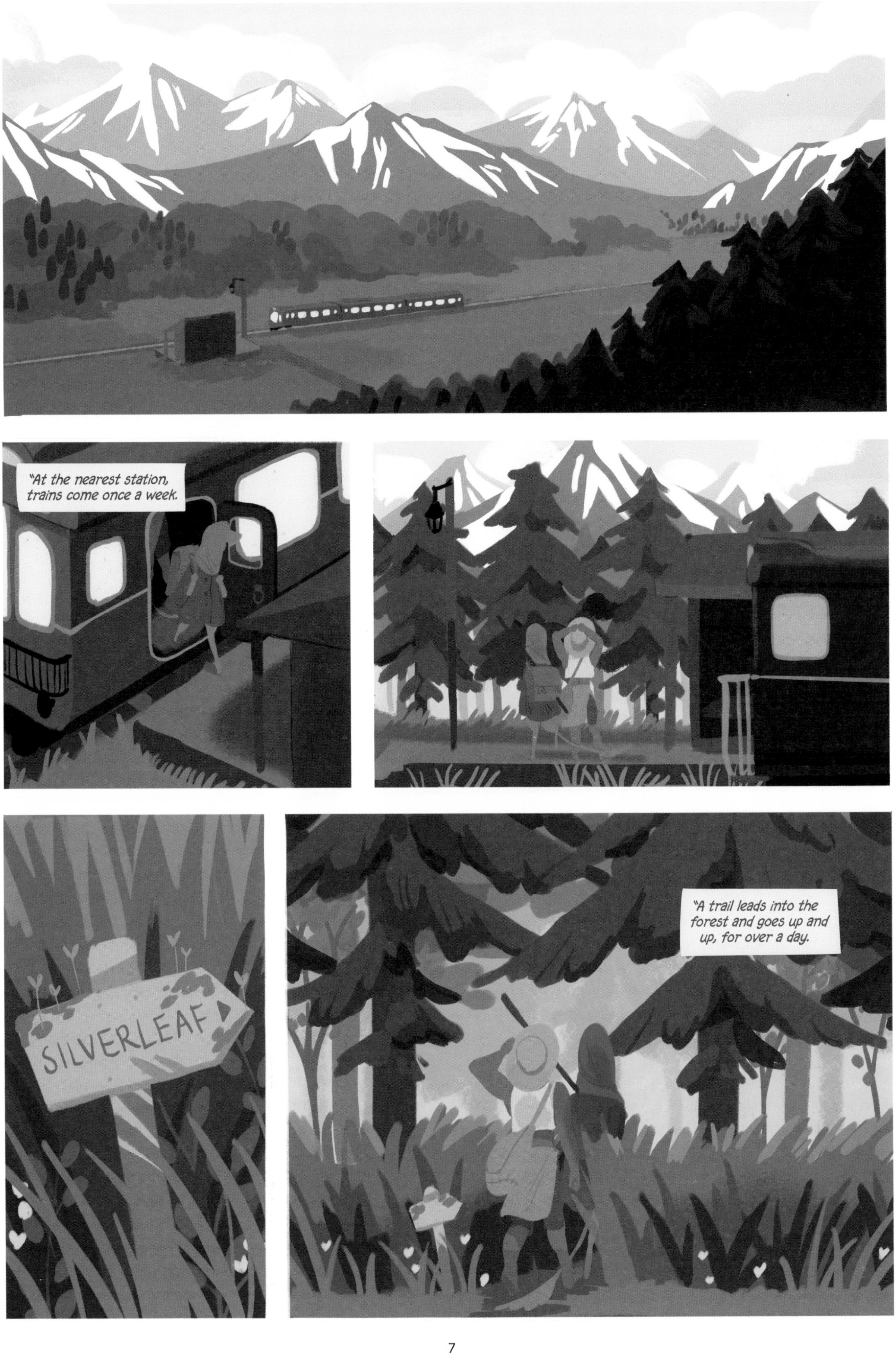
"At the nearest station, trains come once a week.
SILVERLEAF
"A trail leads into the forest and goes up and up, for over a day.

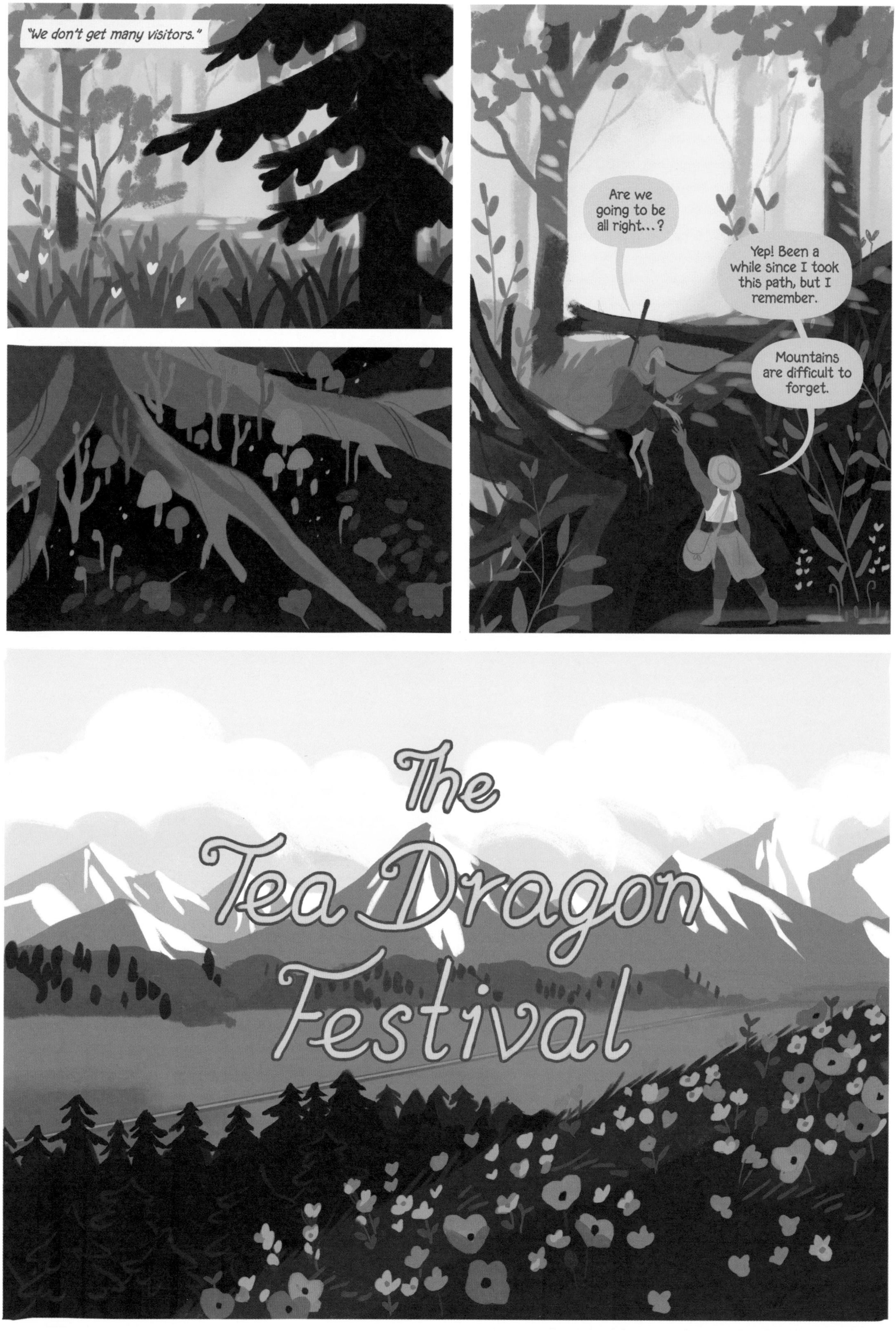
"We don't get many visitors."
Are we going to be all right...?
Yep! Been a while since I took this path, but I remember.
Mountains are difficult to forget.
The Tea Dragon Festival

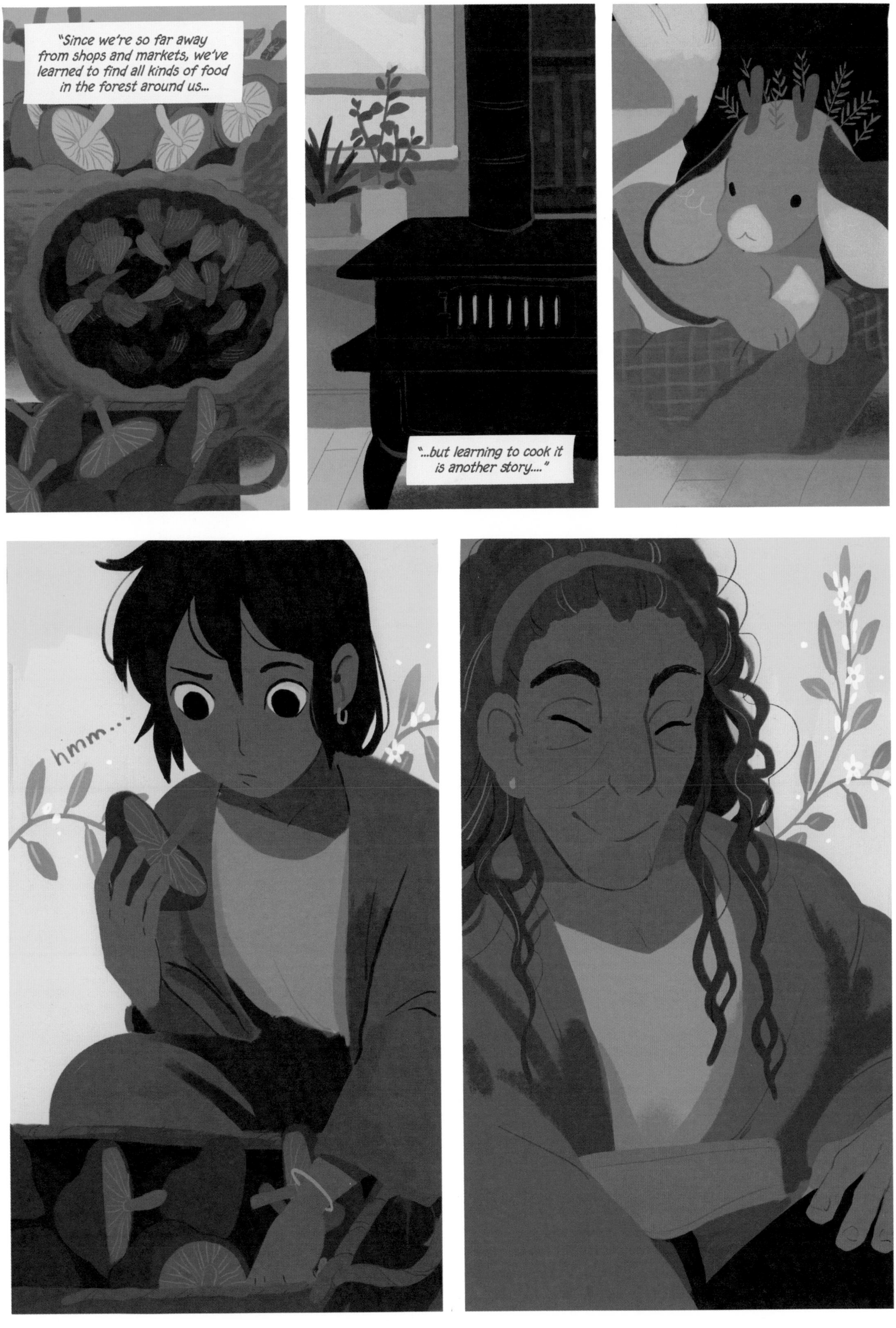
"Since we're so far away from shops and markets, we've learned to find all kinds of food in the forest around us...
"...but learning to cook it is another story...."
hmm...

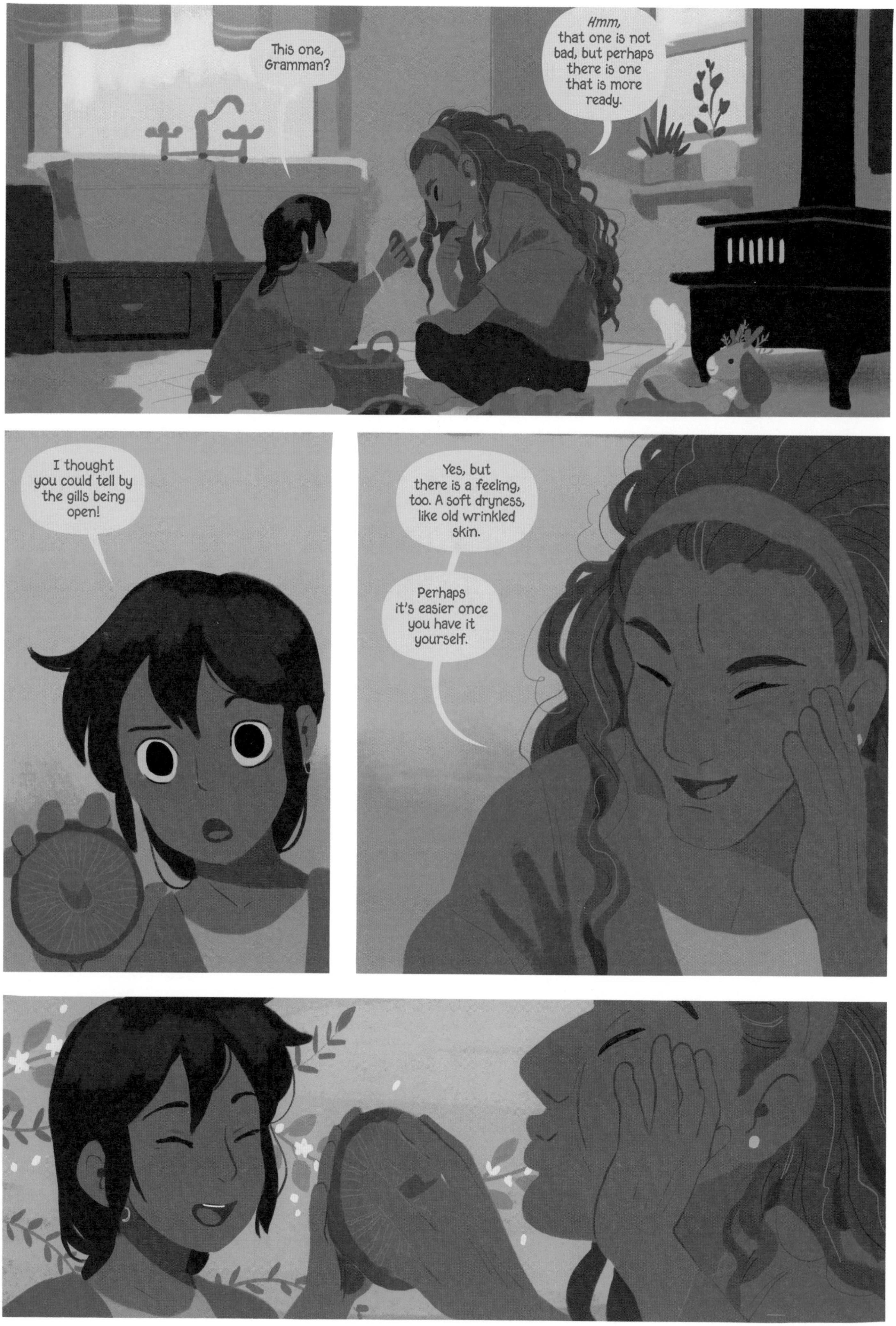
This one, Gramman?
Hmm, that one is not bad, but perhaps there is one that is more ready.
I thought you could tell by the gills being open!
Yes, but there is a feeling, too. A soft dryness, like old wrinkled skin.
Perhaps it's easier once you have it yourself.

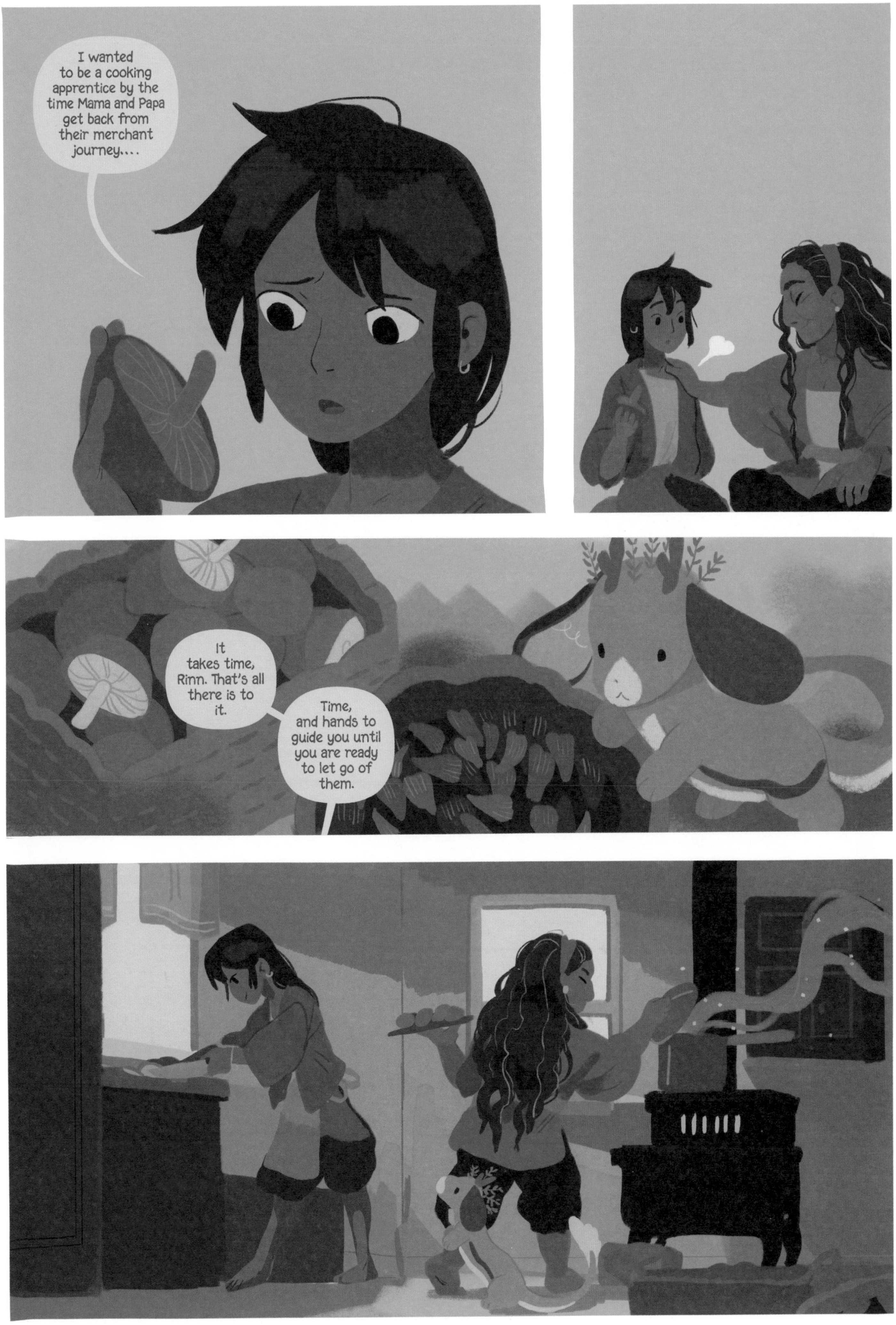
I wanted to be a cooking apprentice by the time Mama and Papa get back from their merchant journey....
It takes time, Rinn. That's all there is to it.
Time, and hands to guide you until you are ready to let go of them.

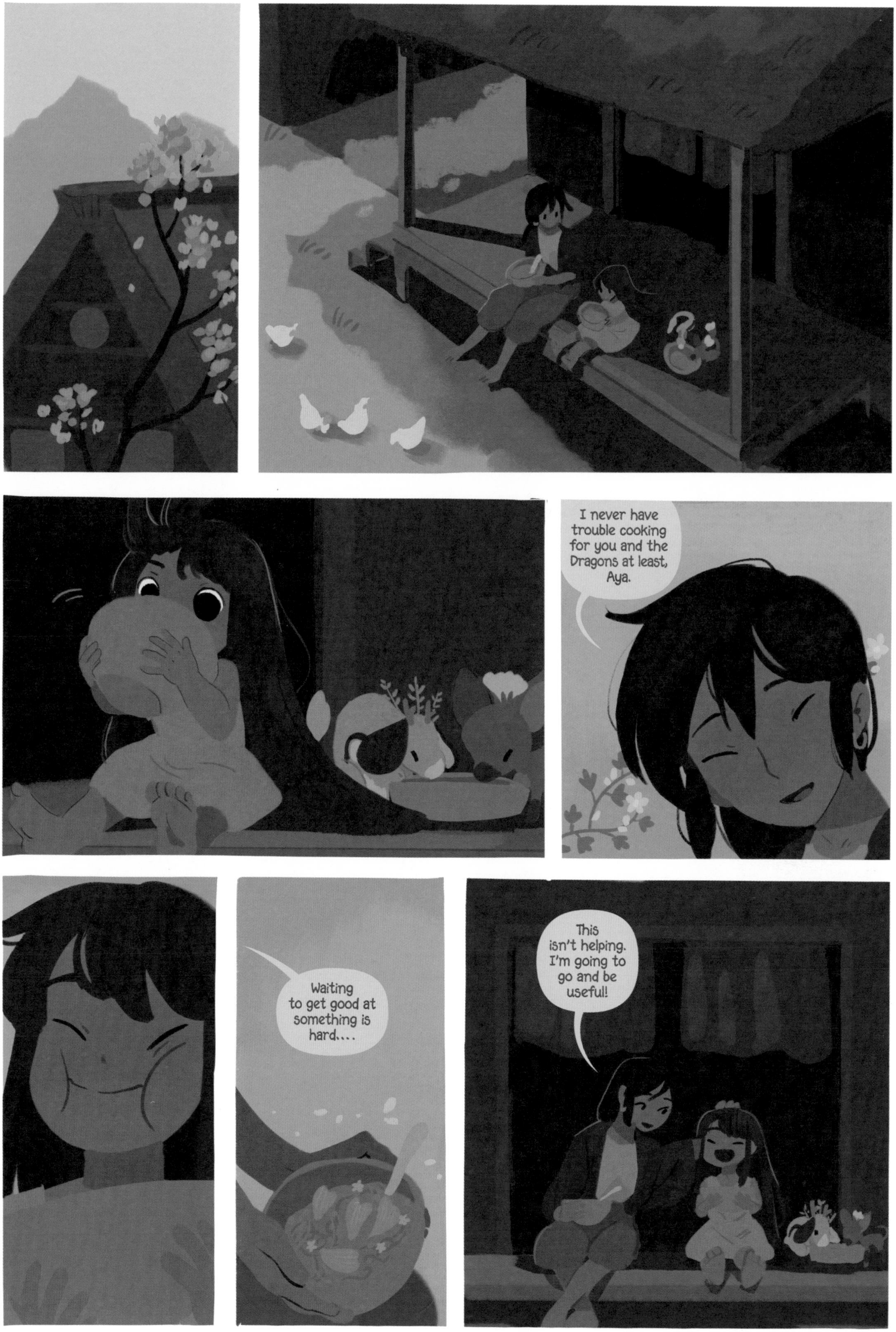
I never have trouble cooking for you and the Dragons at least, Aya.
Waiting to get good at something is hard....
This isn't helping. I'm going to go and be useful!

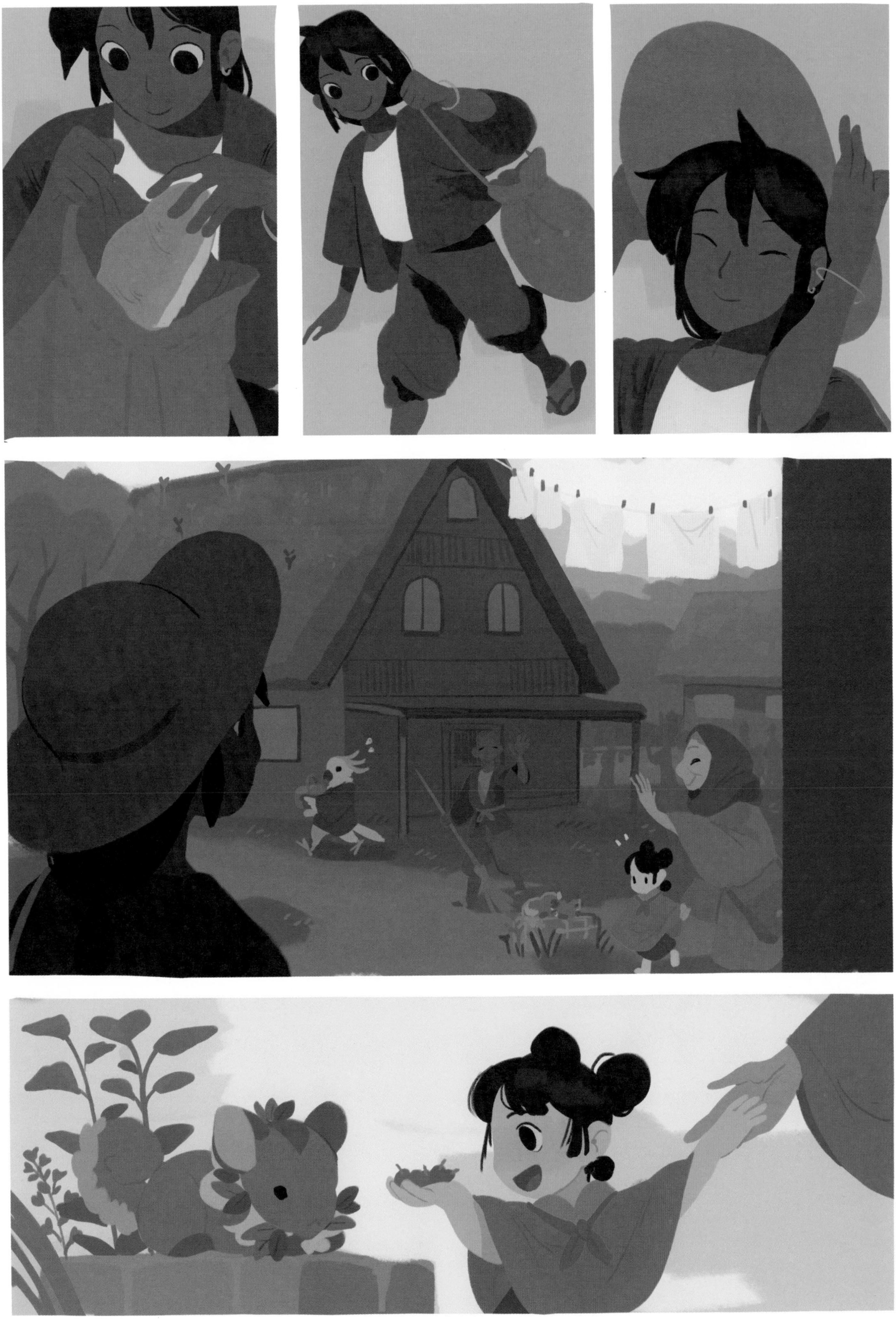

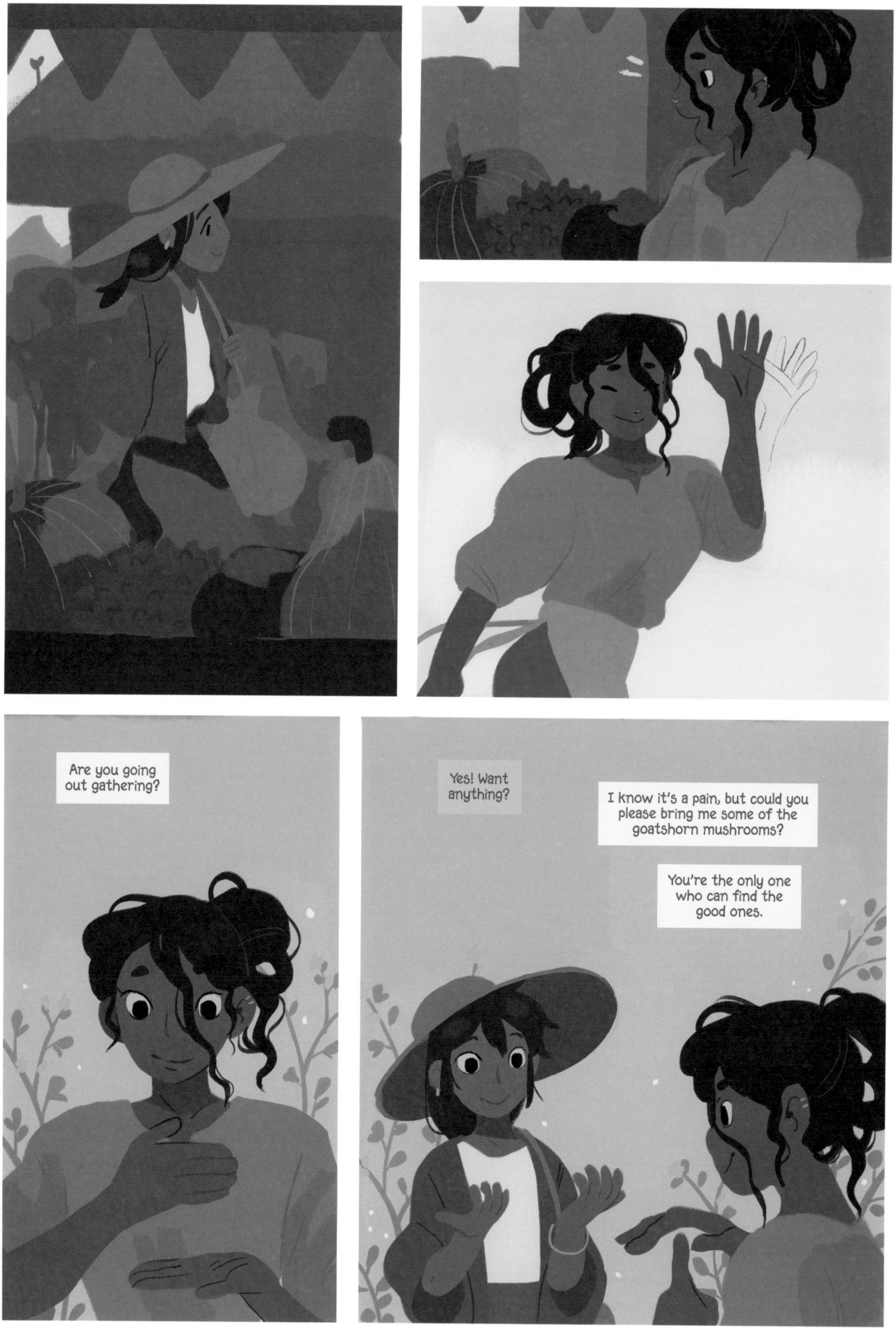
Are you going out gathering?
Yes! Want anything?
I know it's a pain, but could you please bring me some of the goatshorn mushrooms?
You're the only one who can find the good ones.

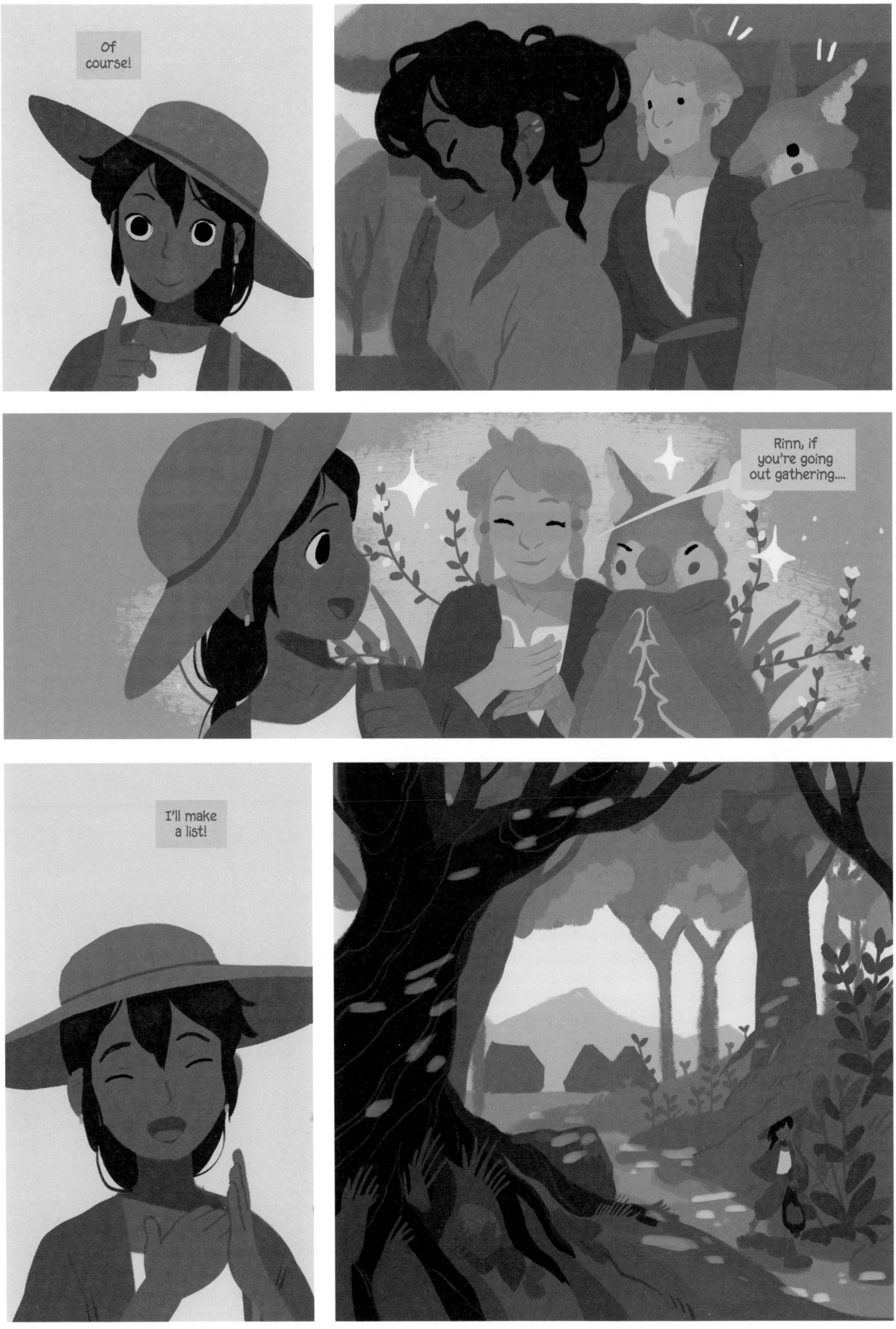
Of course!
Rinn, if you're going out gathering....
I'll make a list!

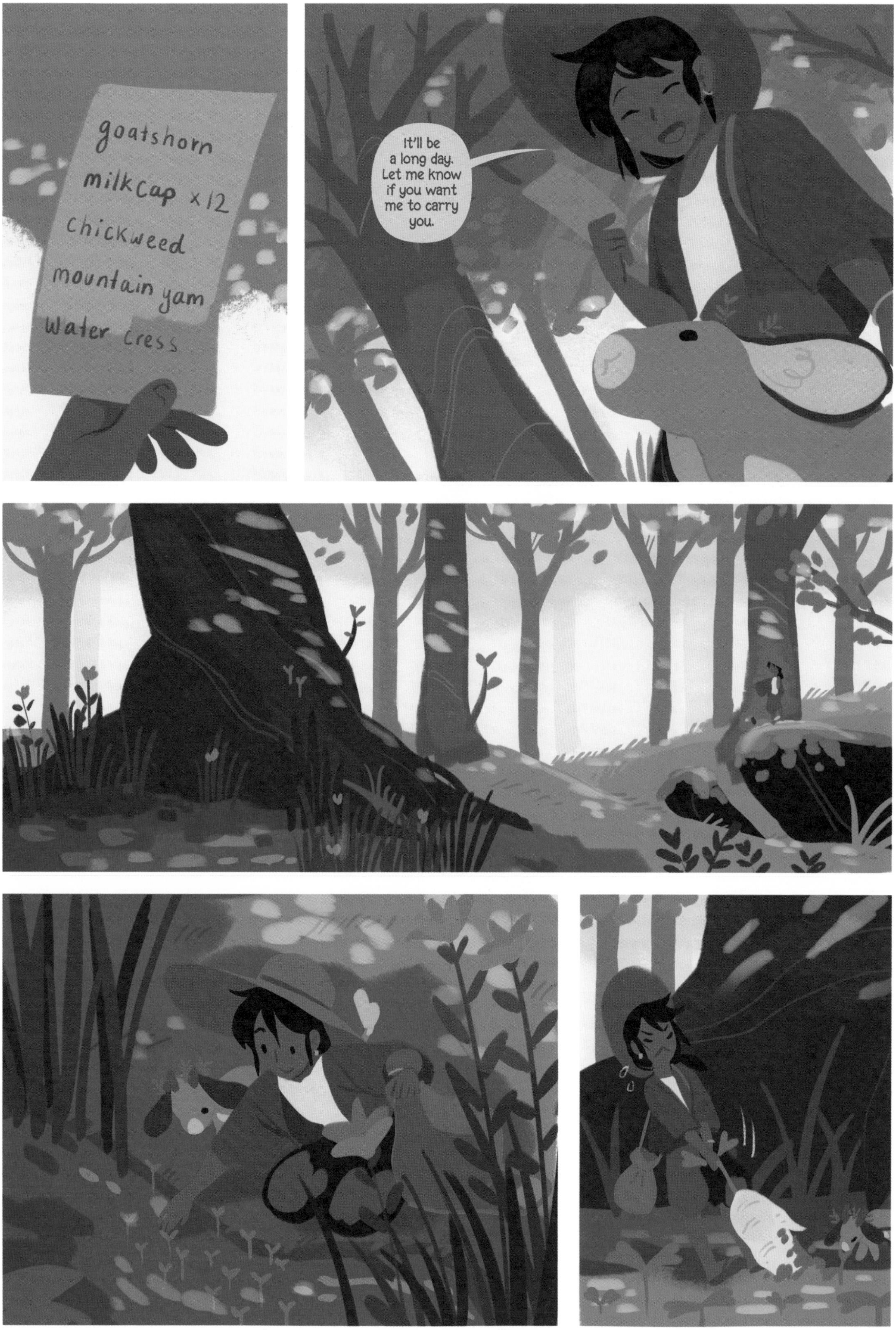
goatshorn
milkcap x12
chickweed
mountain yam
water cress
It'll be a long day. Let me know if you want me to carry you.

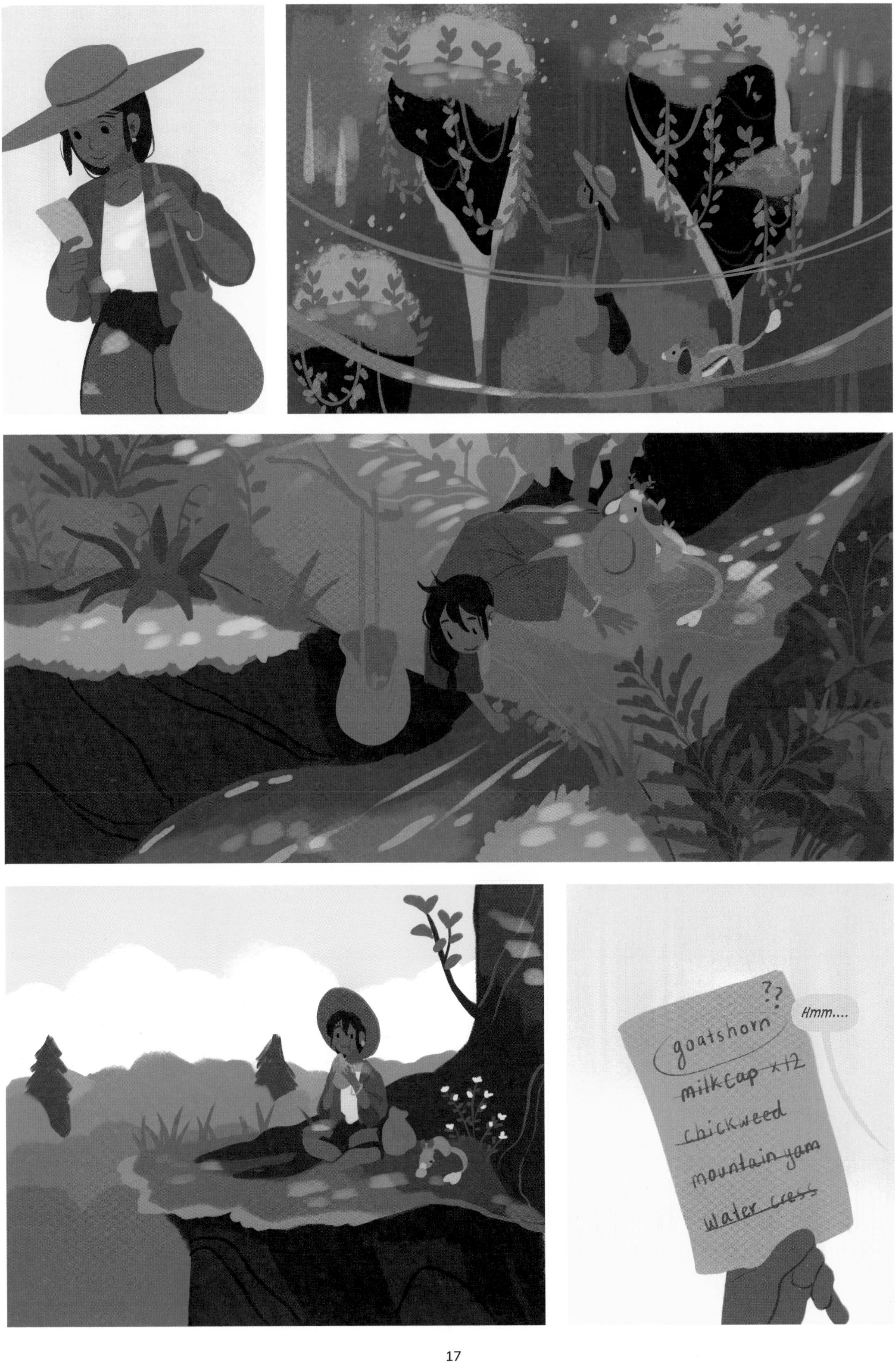
??
Hmm....
goatshorn
milkcap x12
chickweed
mountain yam
water cress

Maybe I need to cut a new path....

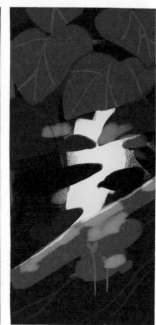

Whoa....

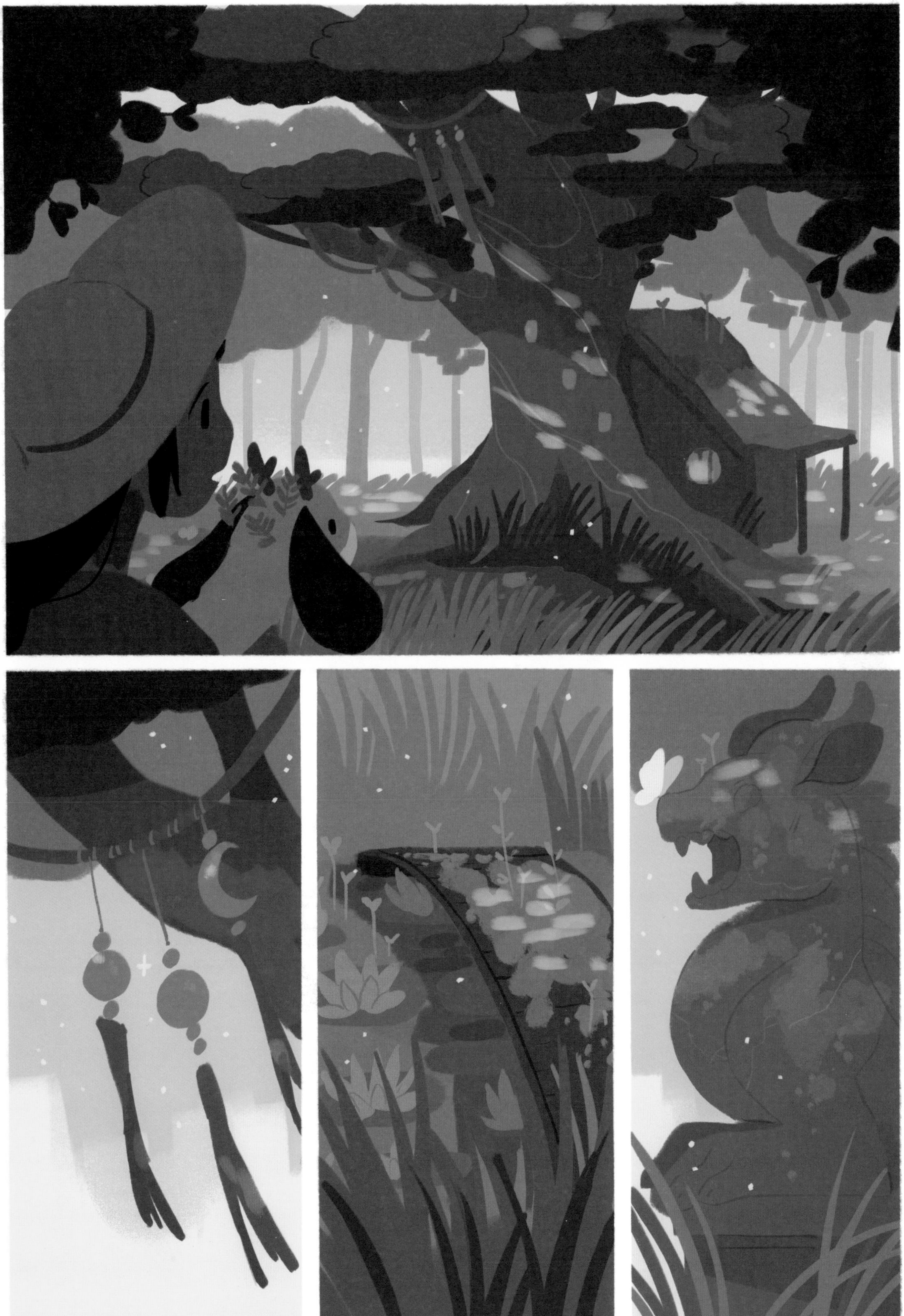

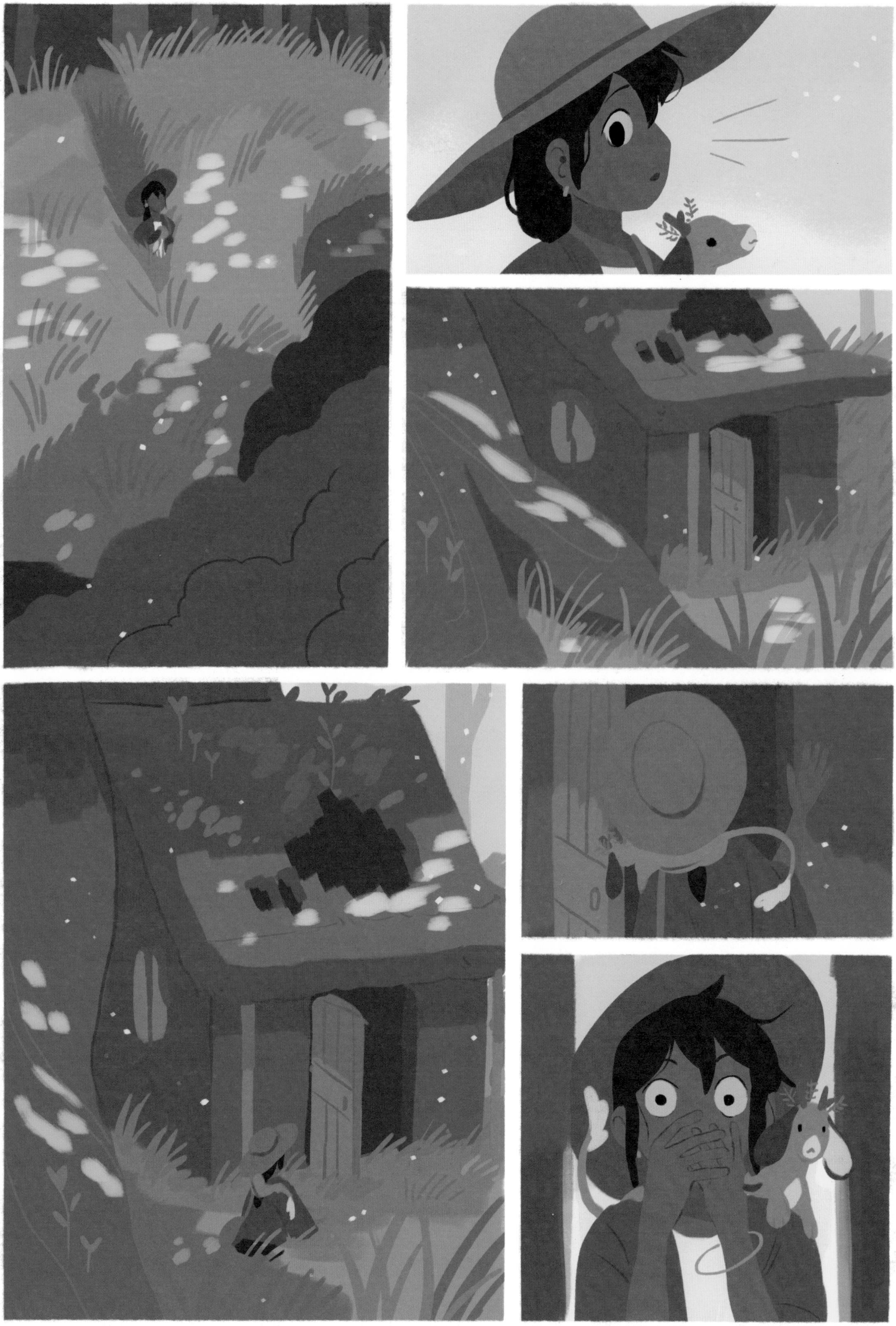

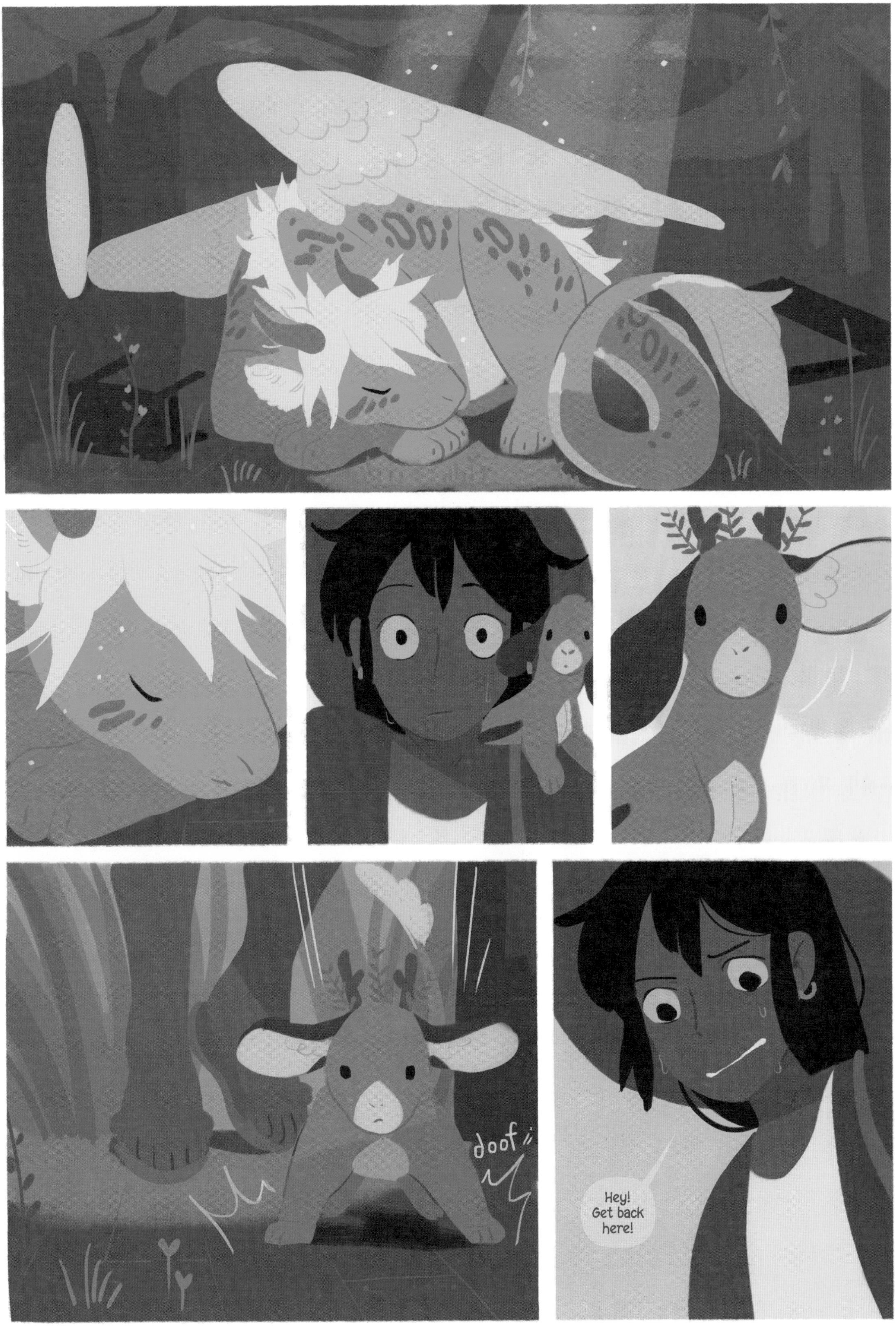
doof
Hey! Get back here!

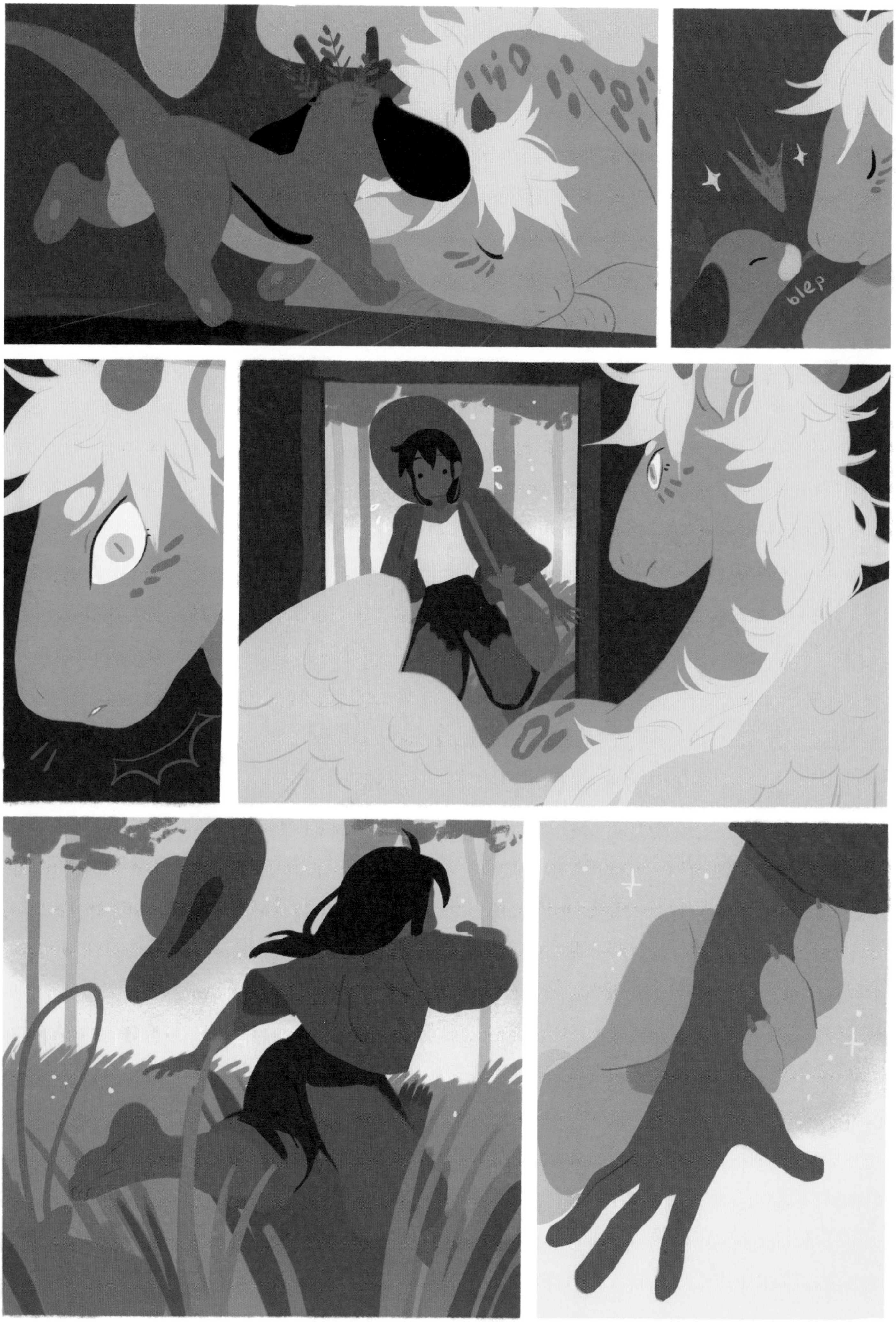
blep

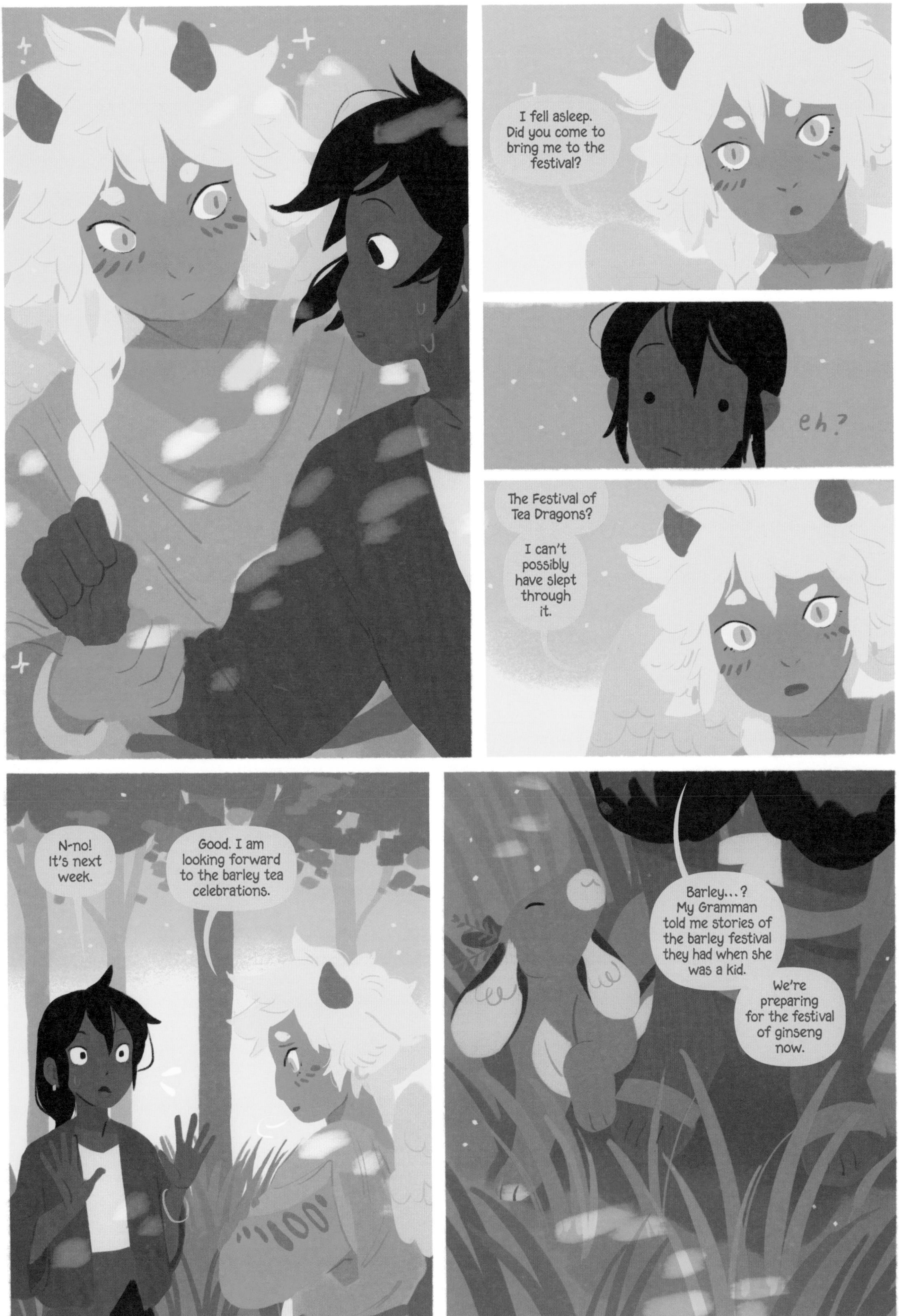
I fell asleep. Did you come to bring me to the festival?
eh?
The Festival of Tea Dragons?
I can't possibly have slept through it.
N-no! It's next week.
Good. I am looking forward to the barley tea celebrations.
Barley...? My Gramman told me stories of the barley festival they had when she was a kid.
We're preparing for the festival of ginseng now.

Her calendar must be mistaken, I can't possibly have been asleep for....

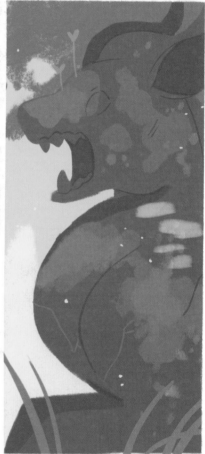

How...?

Were you living here, all by yourself?

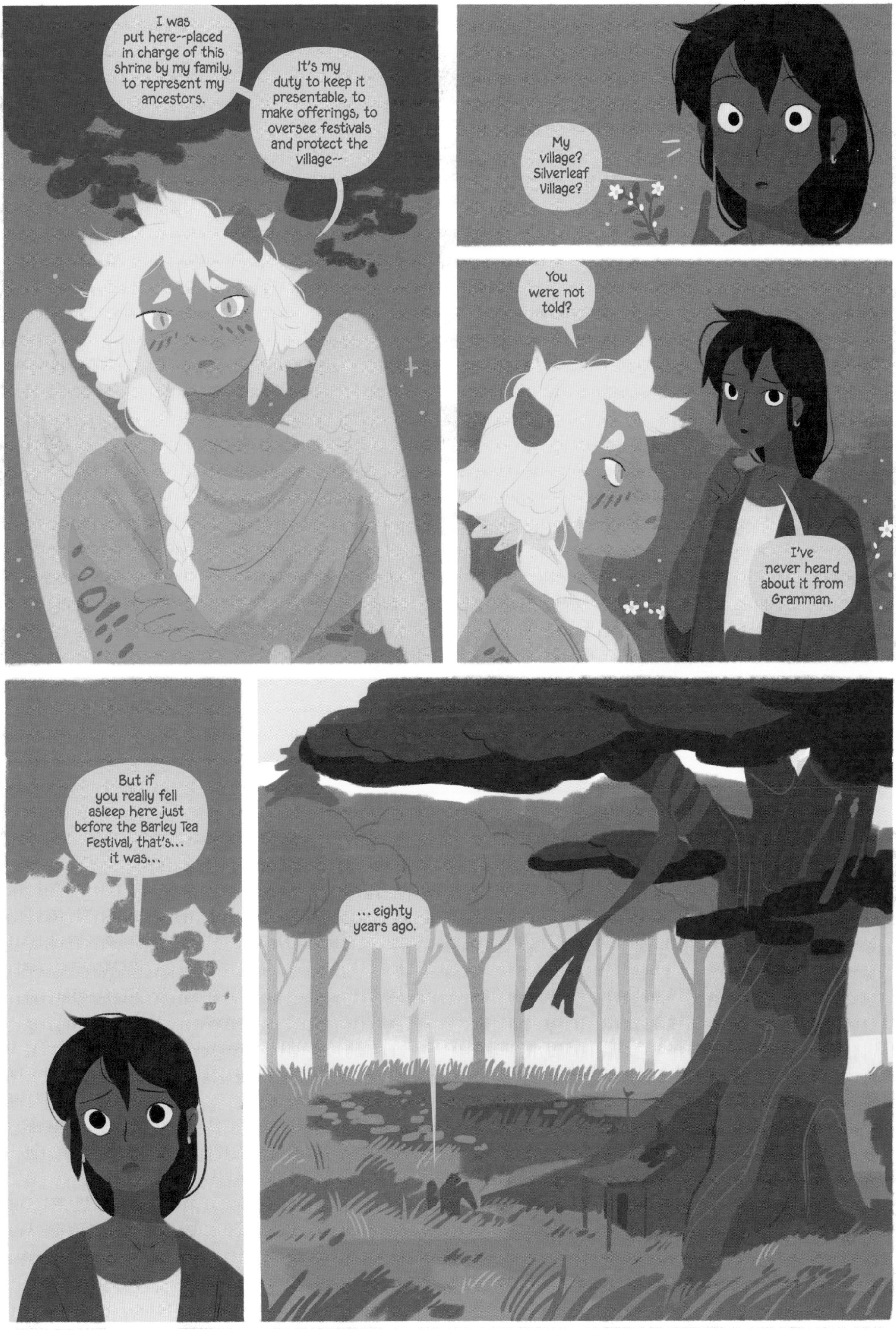
I was put here--placed in charge of this shrine by my family, to represent my ancestors.
It's my duty to keep it presentable, to make offerings, to oversee festivals and protect the village--
My village? Silverleaf Village?
You were not told?
I've never heard about it from Gramman.
But if you really fell asleep here just before the Barley Tea Festival, that's... it was...
...eighty years ago.

Chapter Two

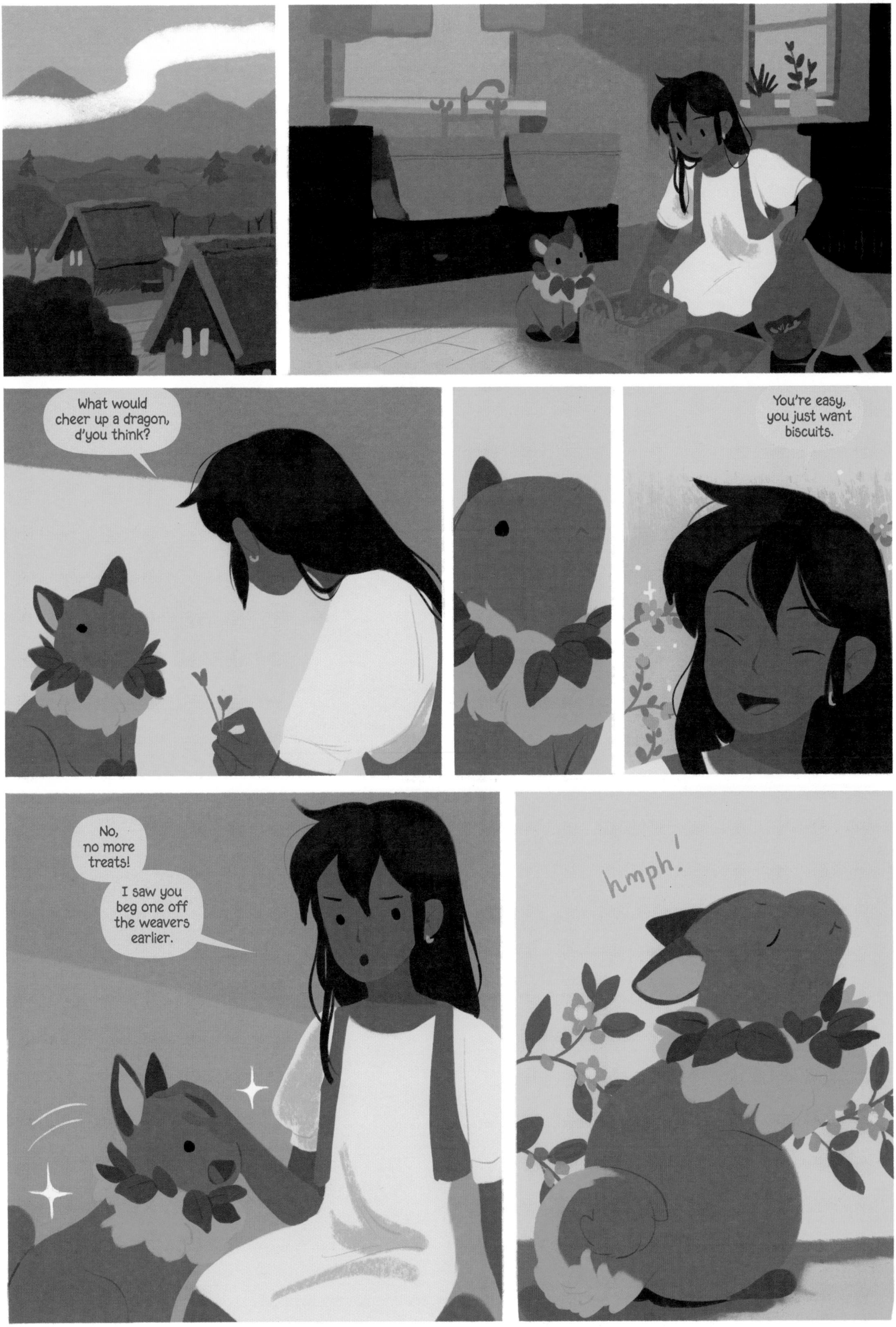
What would cheer up a dragon, d'you think?
You're easy, you just want biscuits.
No, no more treats!
I saw you beg one off the weavers earlier.
hmph!

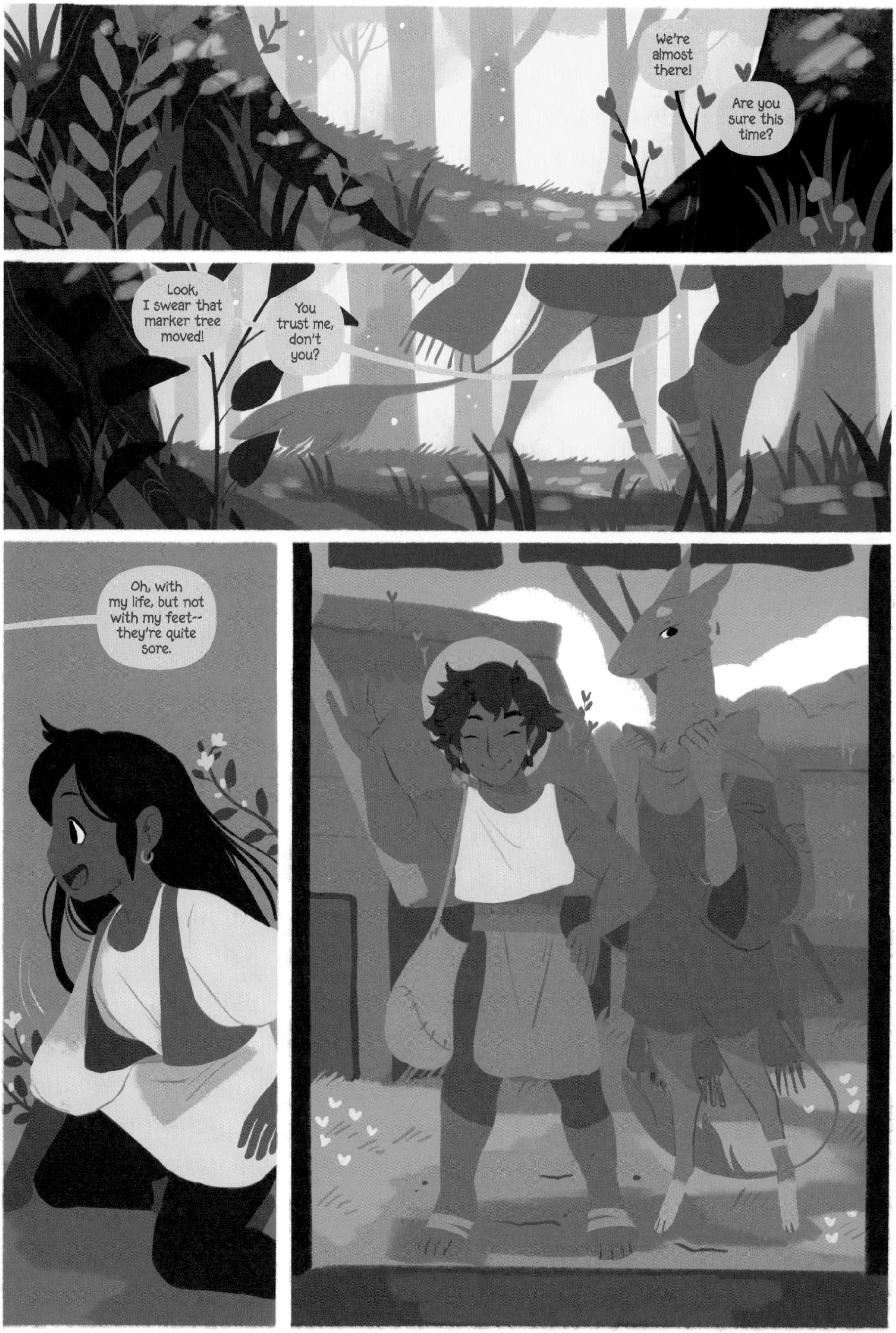
We're almost there!
Are you sure this time?
Look, I swear that marker tree moved!
You trust me, don't you?
Oh, with my life, but not with my feet-- they're quite sore.

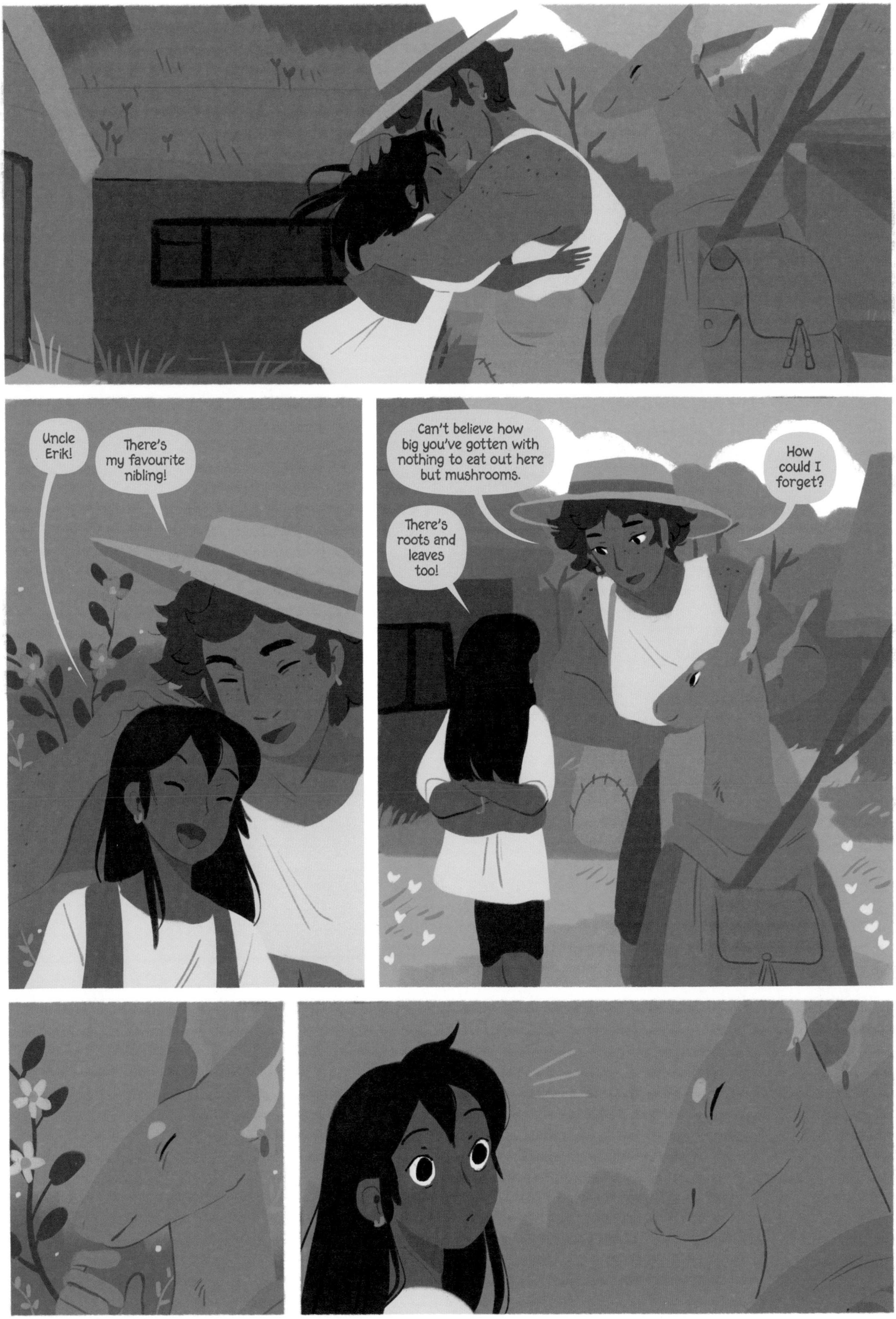
Uncle Erik!
There's my favourite nibling!
Can't believe how big you've gotten with nothing to eat out here but mushrooms.
There's roots and leaves too!
How could I forget?

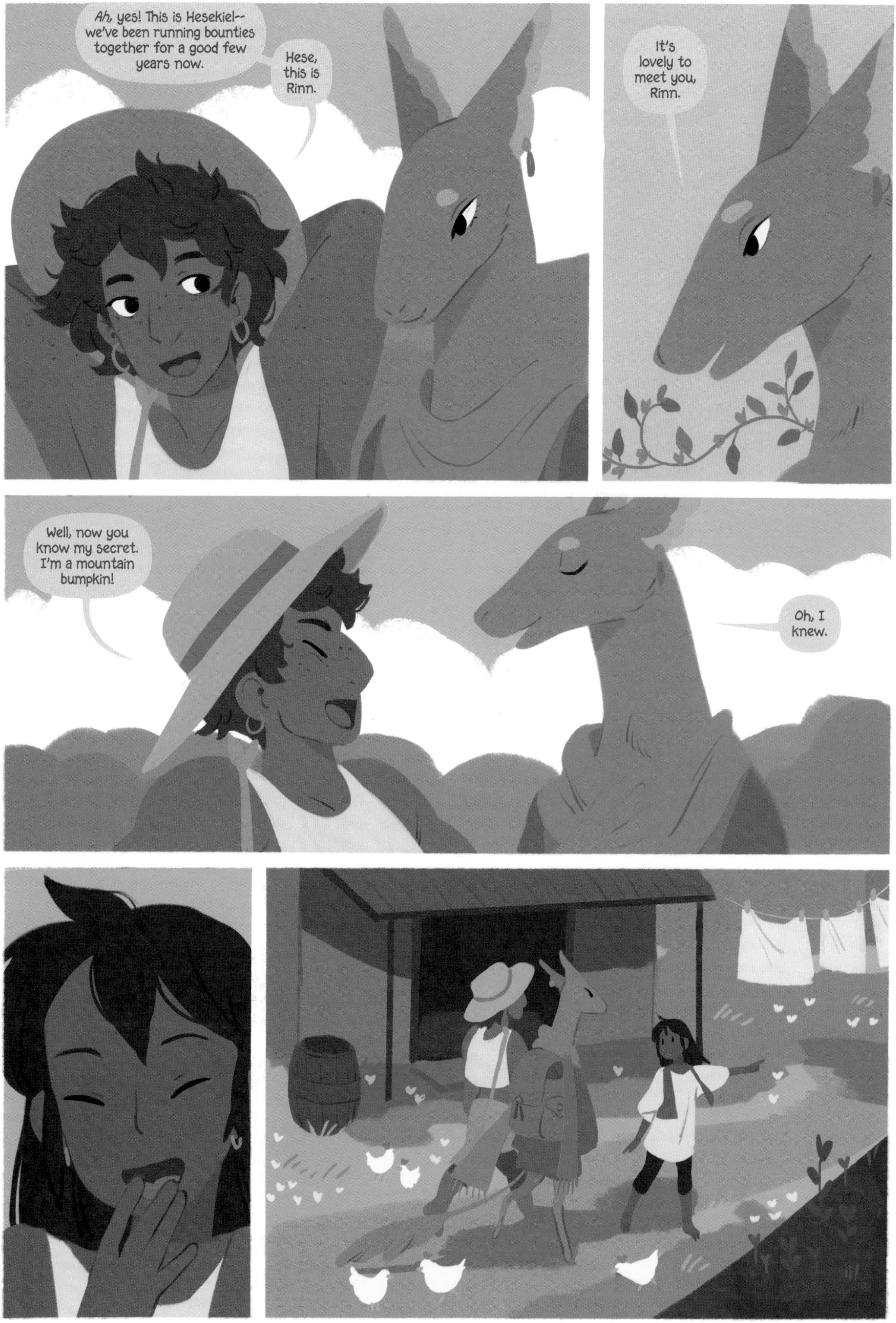

Ah, yes! This is Hesekiel-- we've been running bounties together for a good few years now.
Hese, this is Rinn.
It's lovely to meet you, Rinn.
Well, now you know my secret. I'm a mountain bumpkin!
Oh, I knew.

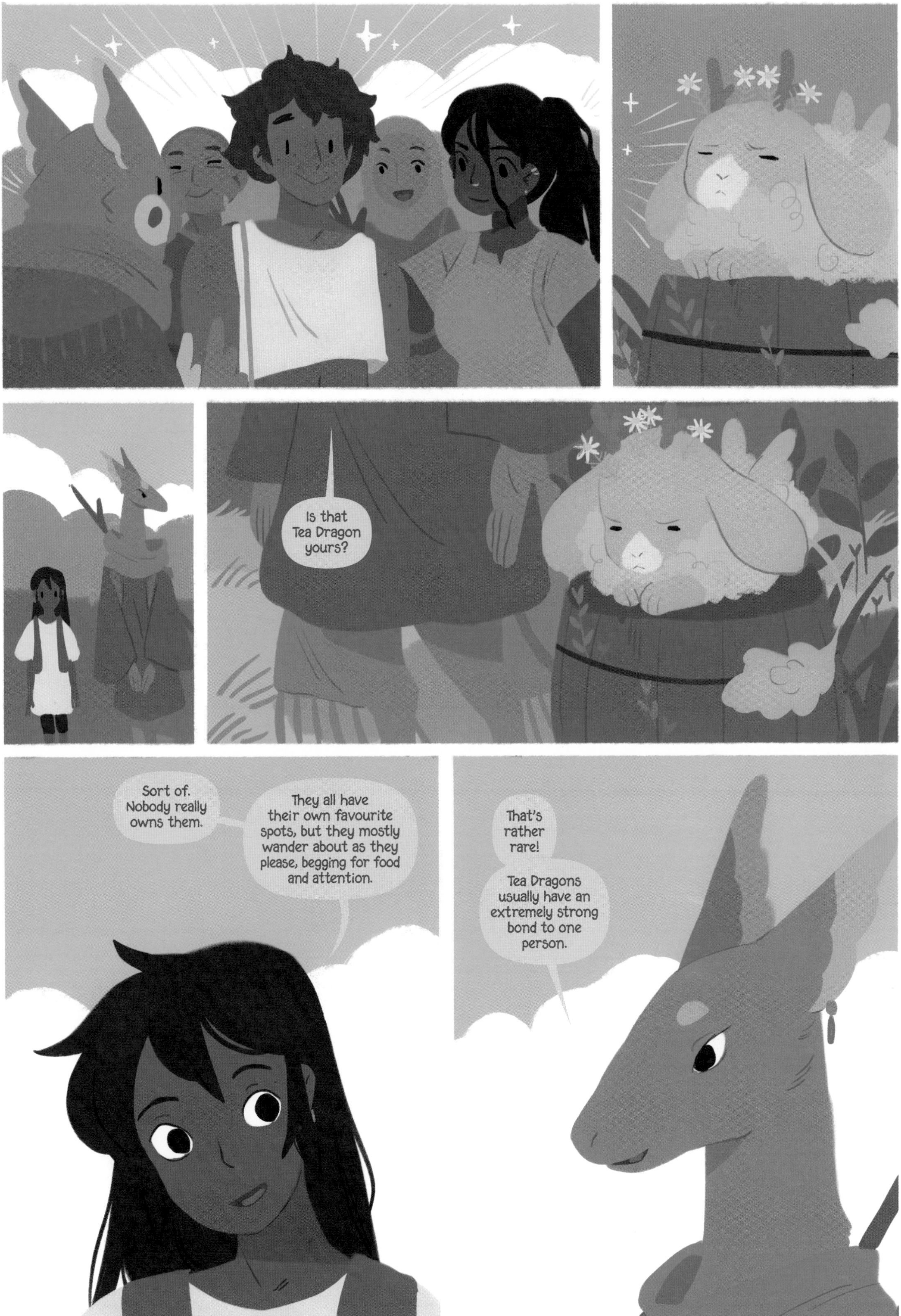
Is that Tea Dragon yours?
Sort of. Nobody really owns them.
They all have their own favourite spots, but they mostly wander about as they please, begging for food and attention.
That's rather rare!
Tea Dragons usually have an extremely strong bond to one person.

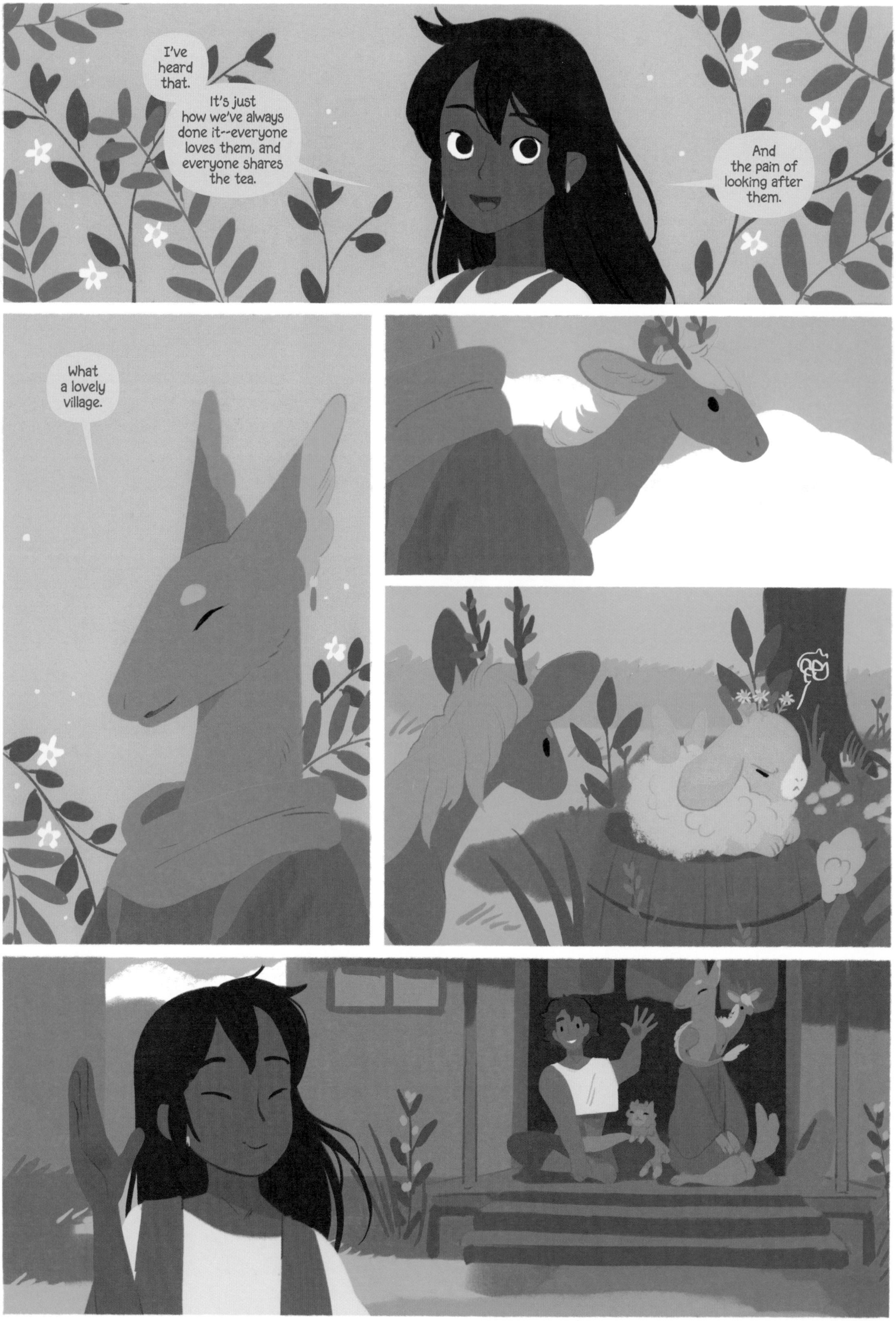
I've heard that.
It's just how we've always done it--everyone loves them, and everyone shares the tea.
And the pain of looking after them.
What a lovely village.

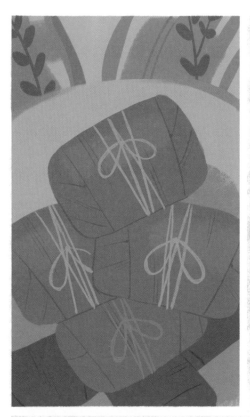

Gramman, do you remember a dragon ever coming here?

To the village?

For a short while, long ago.

He was eager to help, but after a few months he up and disappeared. I reckon he got bored.

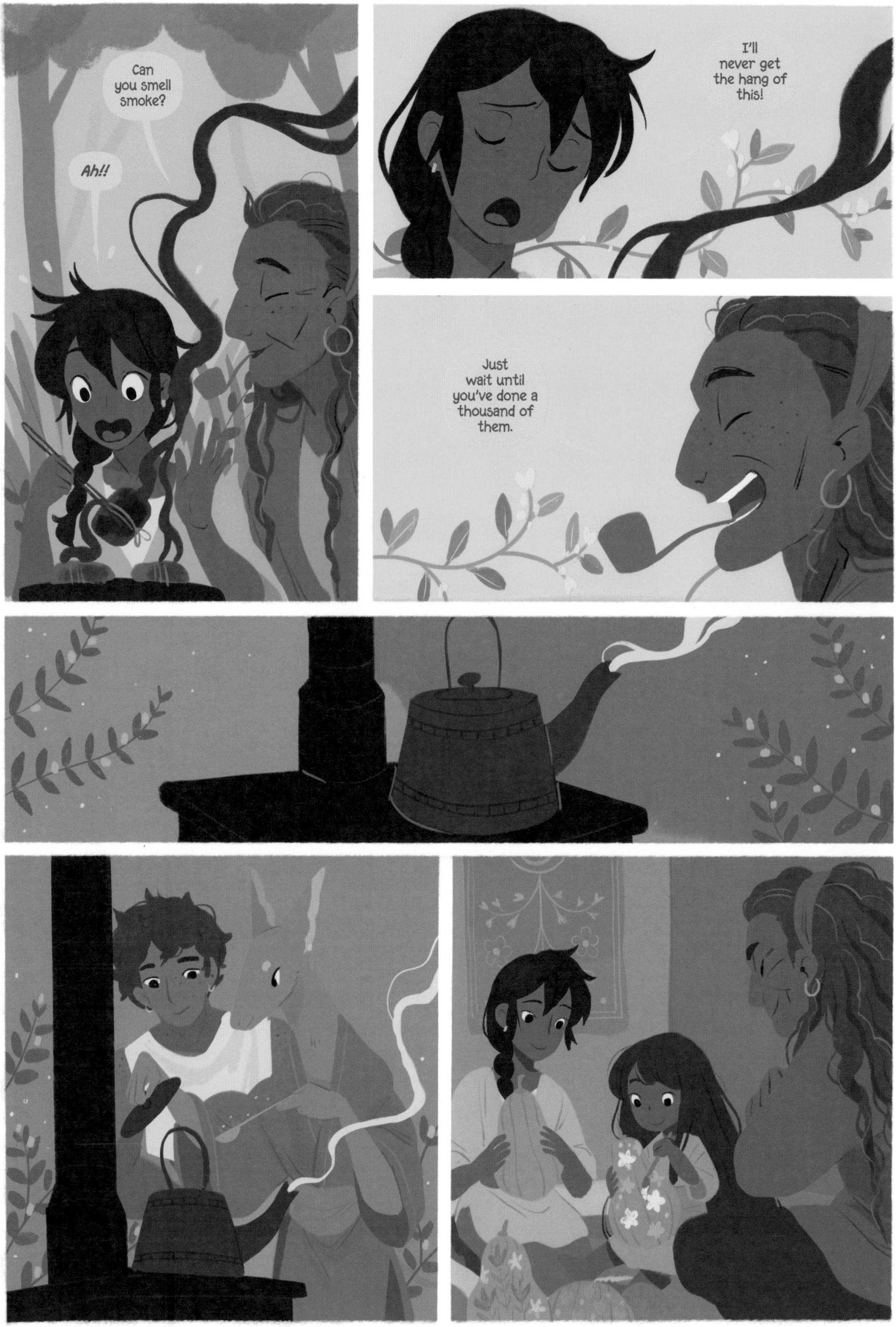

Can you smell smoke?
Ah!!
I'll never get the hang of this!
Just wait until you've done a thousand of them.

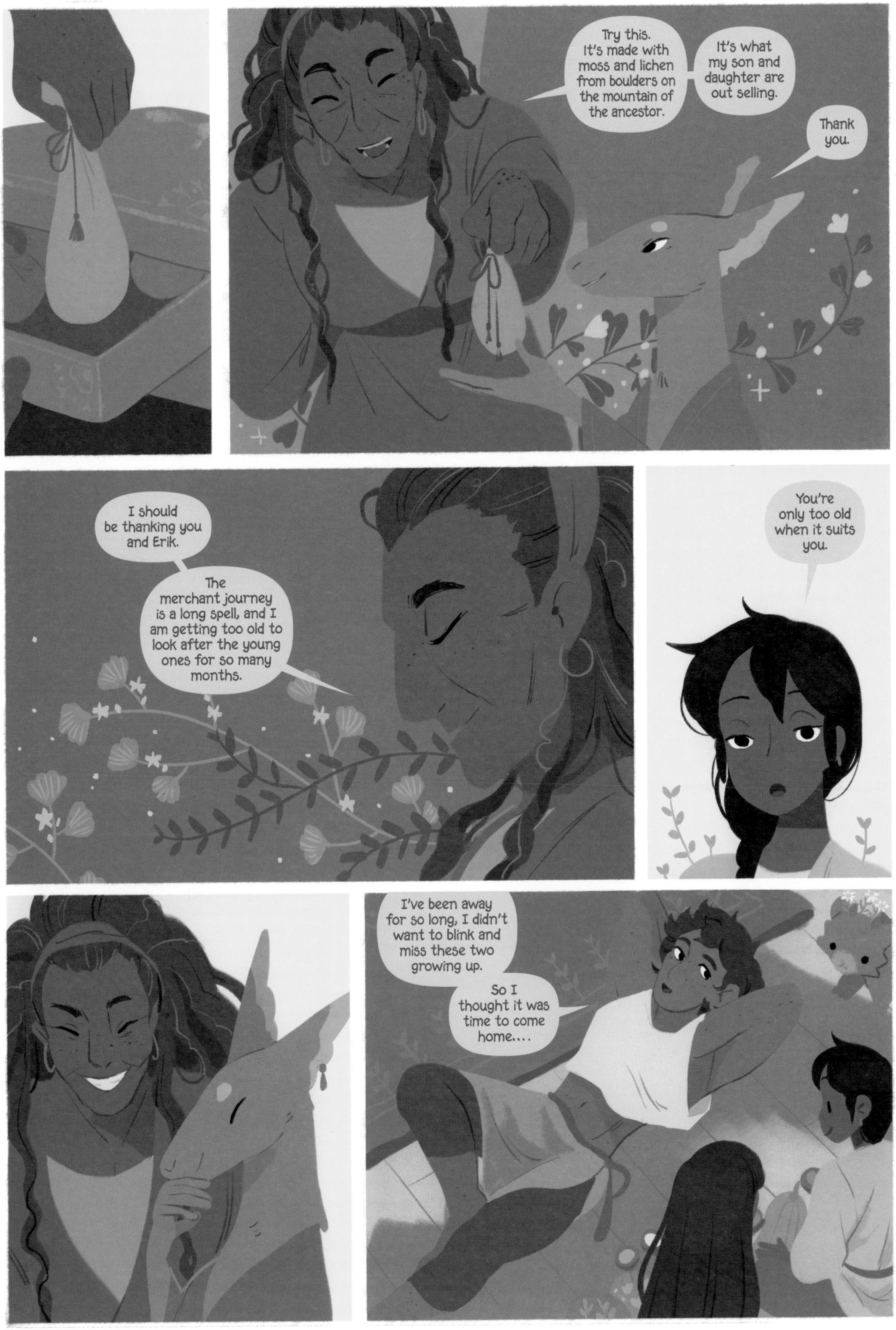
Try this. It's made with moss and lichen from boulders on the mountain of the ancestor.
It's what my son and daughter are out selling.
Thank you.
I should be thanking you and Erik.
The merchant journey is a long spell, and I am getting too old to look after the young ones for so many months.
You're only too old when it suits you.
I've been away for so long, I didn't want to blink and miss these two growing up.
So I thought it was time to come home....

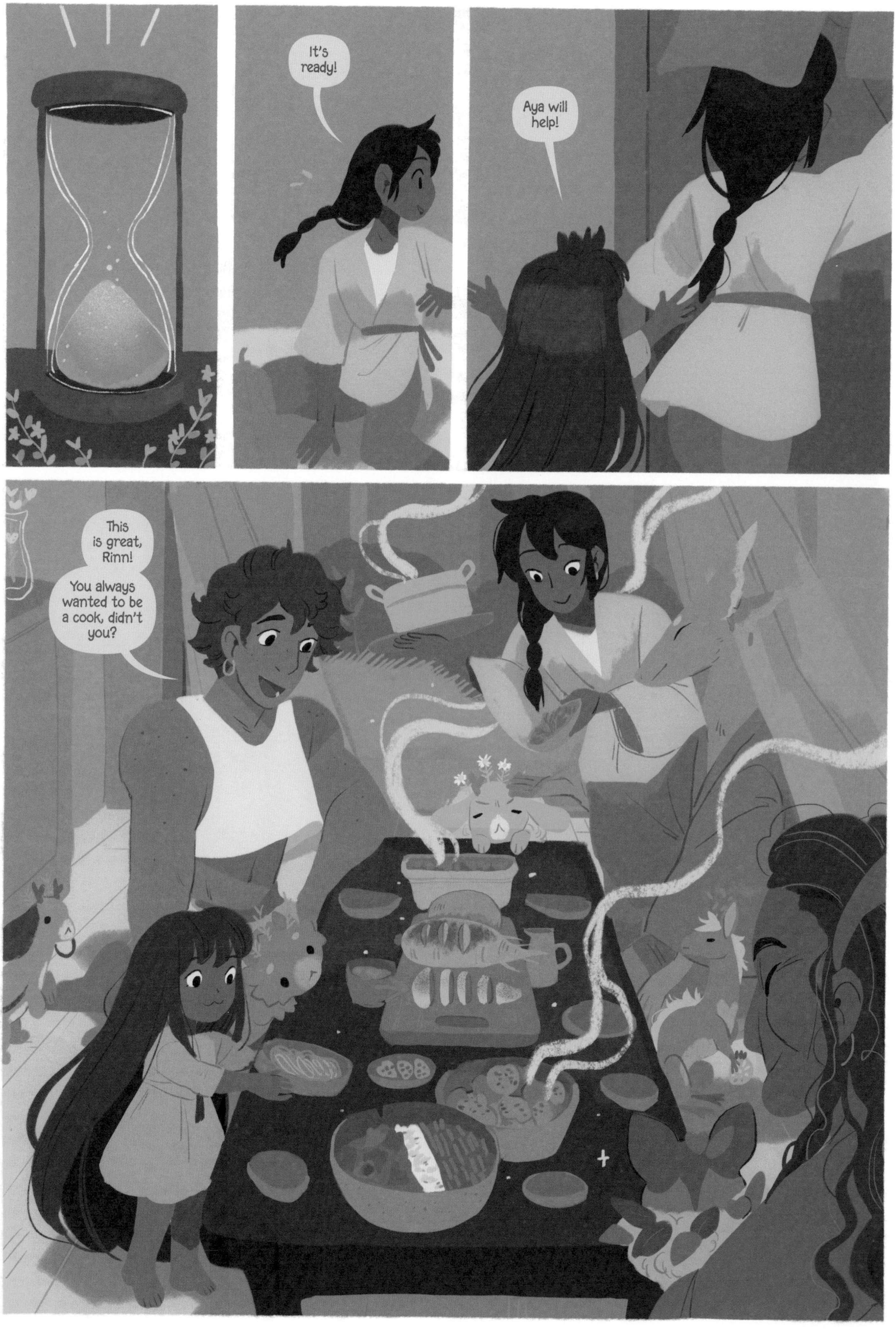
It's ready!
Aya will help!
This is great, Rinn!
You always wanted to be a cook, didn't you?

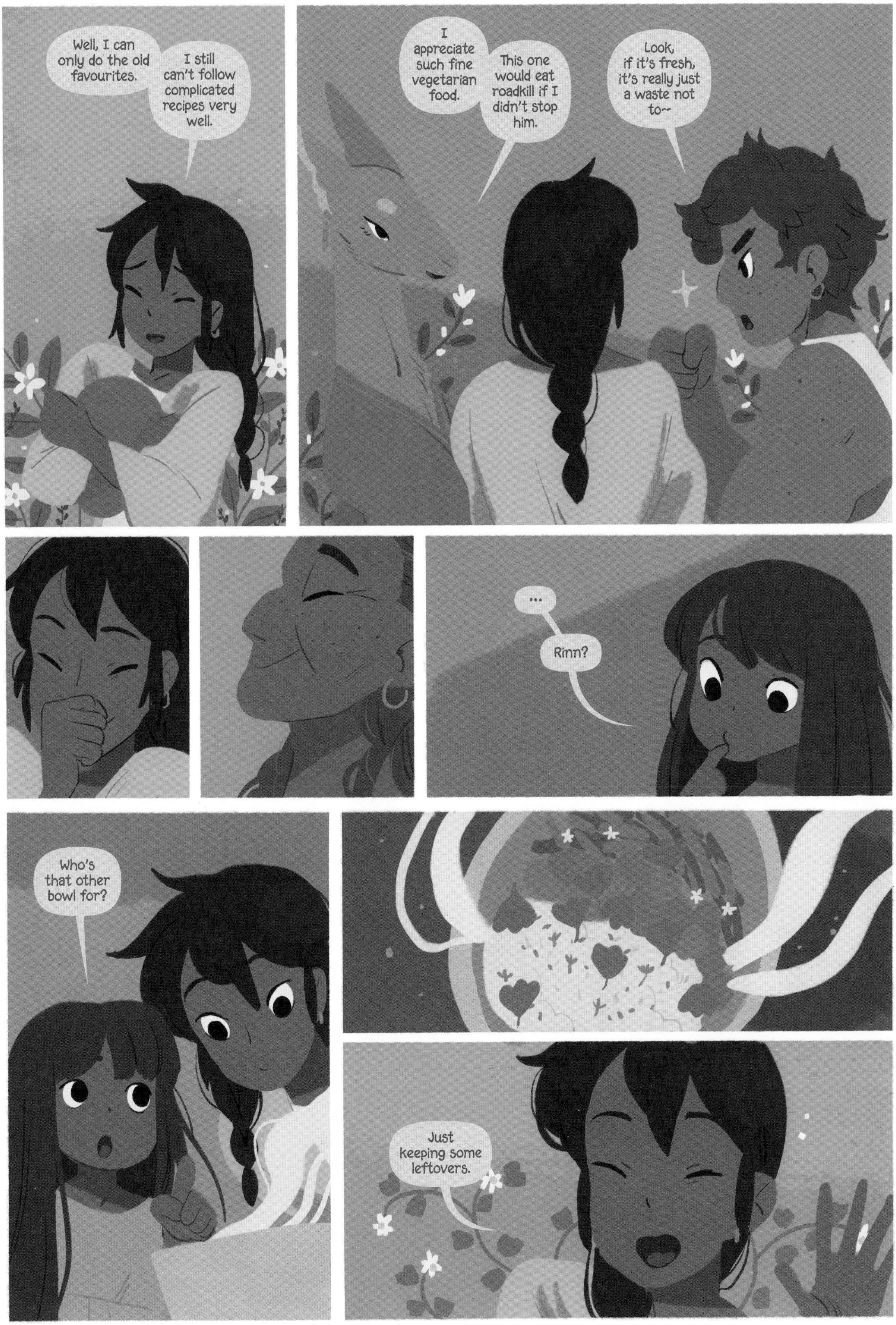
Well, I can only do the old favourites.
I still can't follow complicated recipes very well.
I appreciate such fine vegetarian food.
This one would eat roadkill if I didn't stop him.
Look, if it's fresh, it's really just a waste not to--
...
Rinn?
Who's that other bowl for?
Just keeping some leftovers.

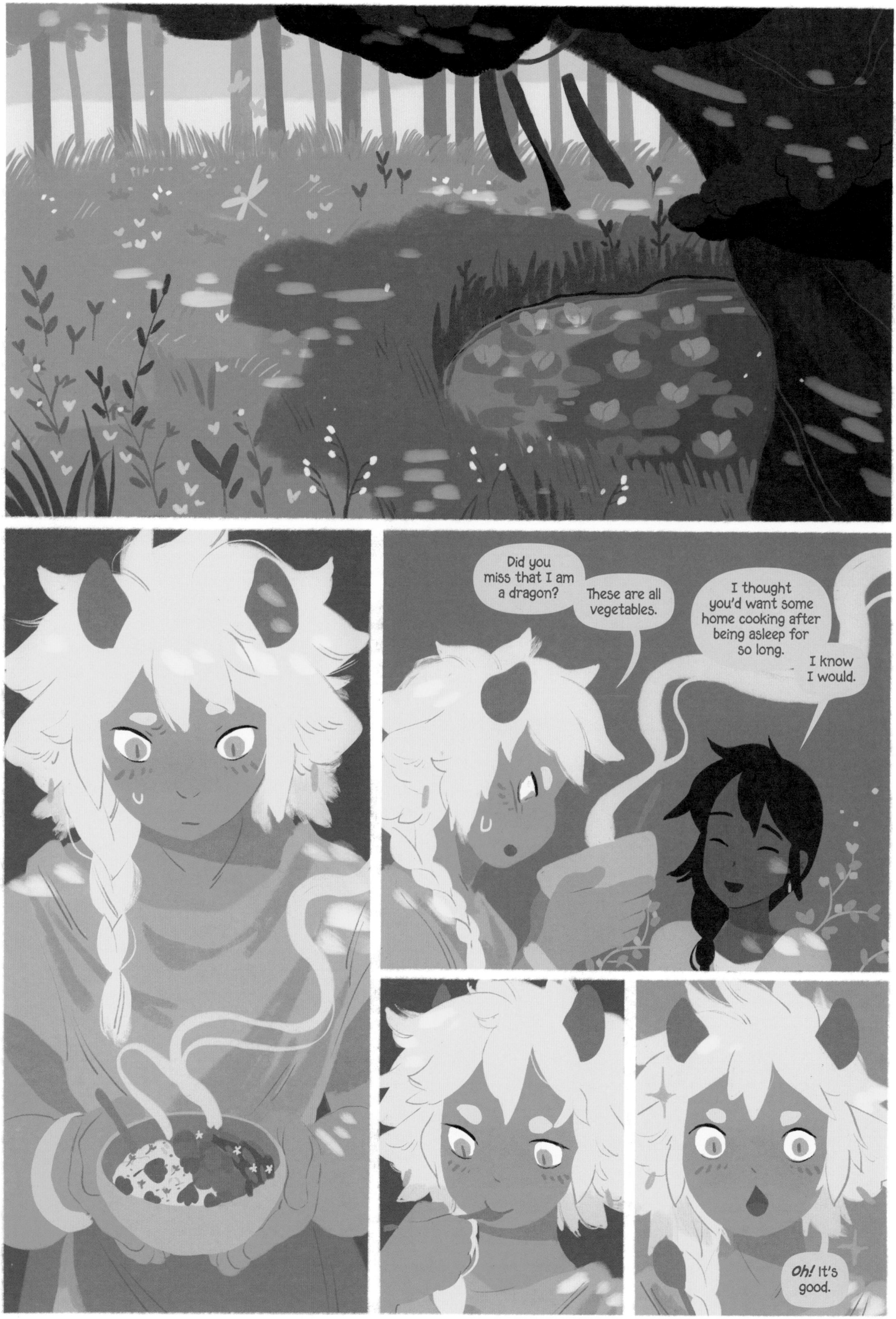

Did you miss that I am a dragon?
These are all vegetables.
I thought you'd want some home cooking after being asleep for so long.
I know I would.
Oh! It's good.

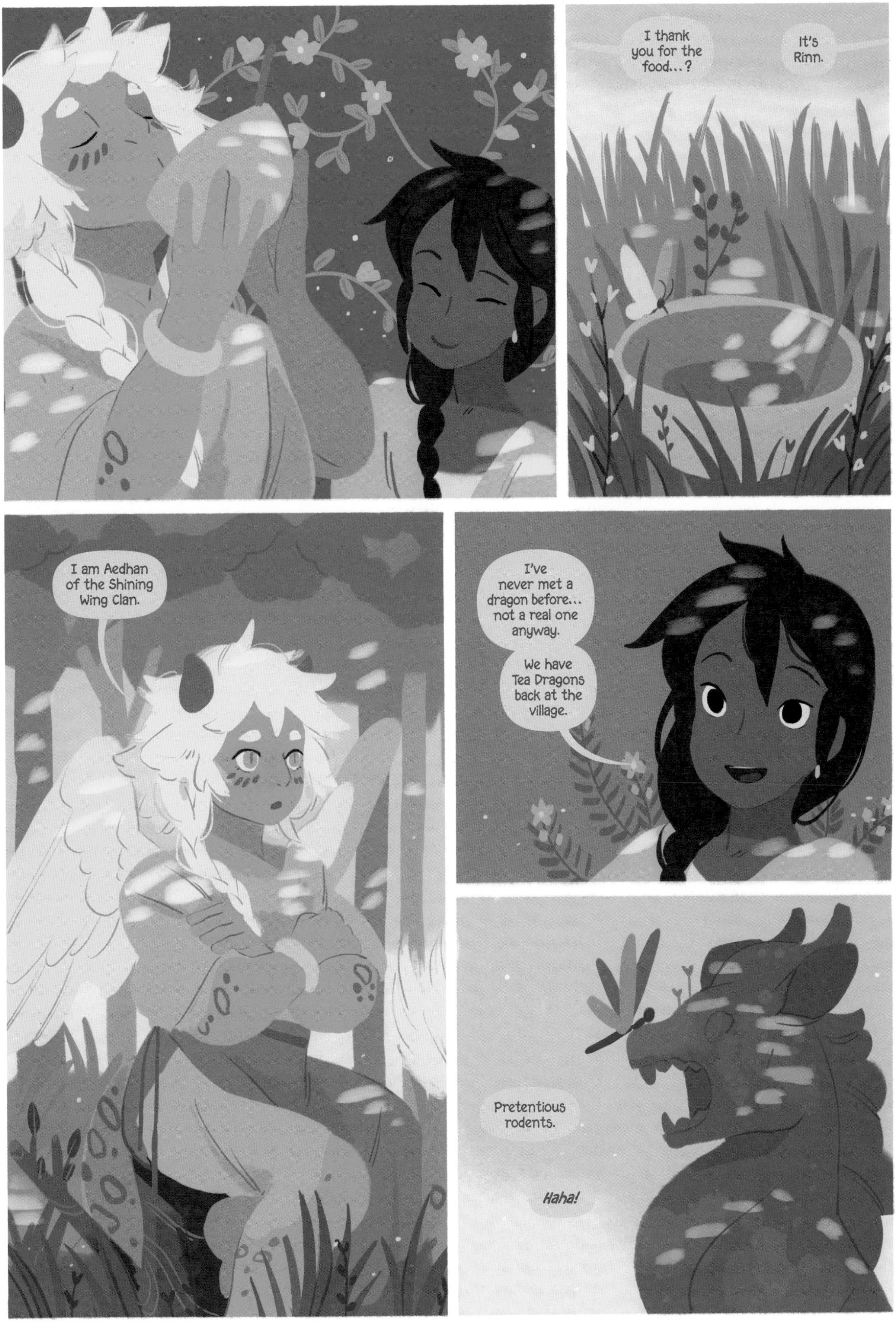

I thank you for the food...?
It's Rinn.
I am Aedhan of the Shining Wing Clan.
I've never met a dragon before... not a real one anyway.
We have Tea Dragons back at the village.
Pretentious rodents.
Haha!

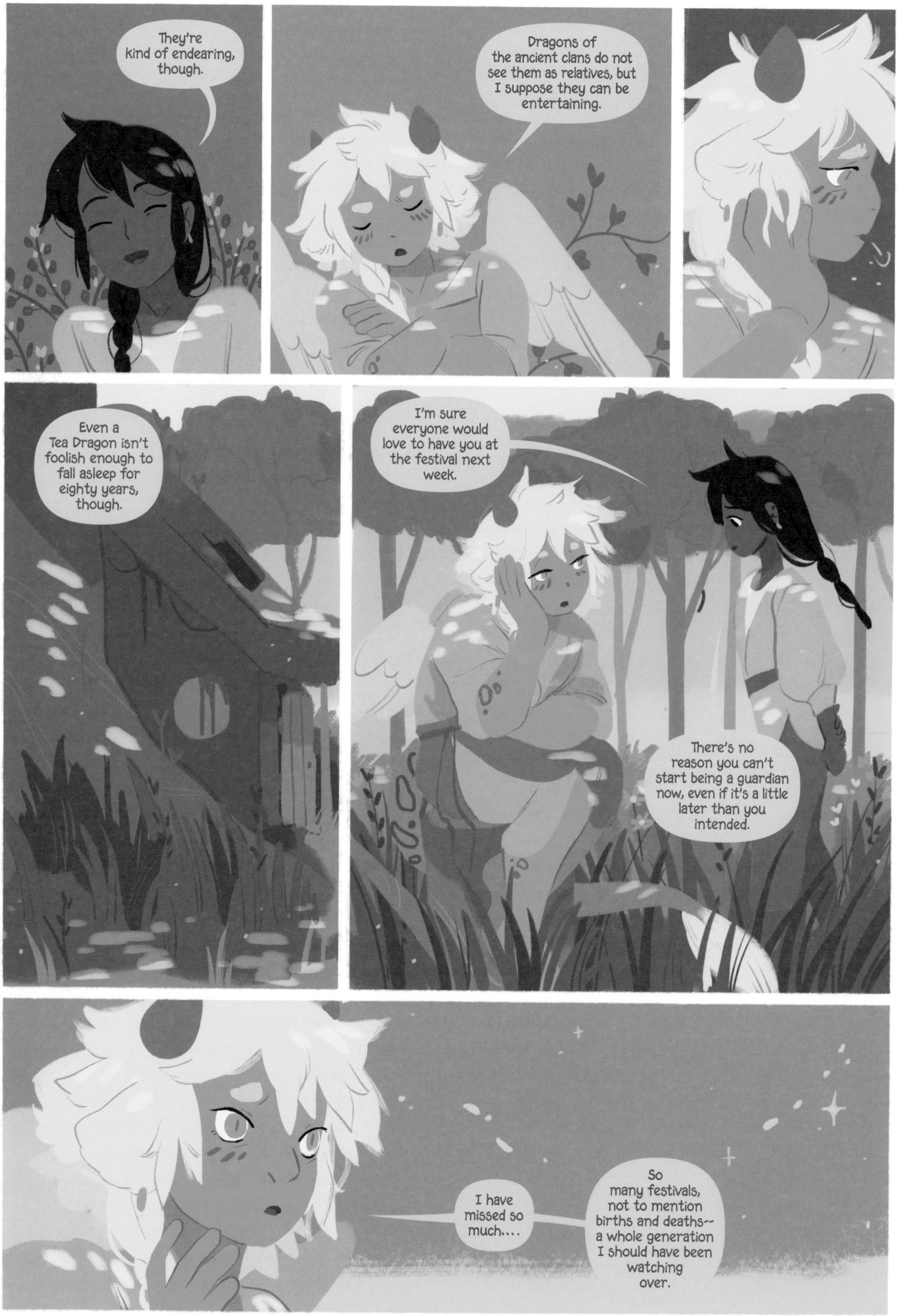
They're kind of endearing, though.
Dragons of the ancient clans do not see them as relatives, but I suppose they can be entertaining.
Even a Tea Dragon isn't foolish enough to fall asleep for eighty years, though.
I'm sure everyone would love to have you at the festival next week.
There's no reason you can't start being a guardian now, even if it's a little later than you intended.
I have missed so much....
So many festivals, not to mention births and deaths-- a whole generation I should have been watching over.

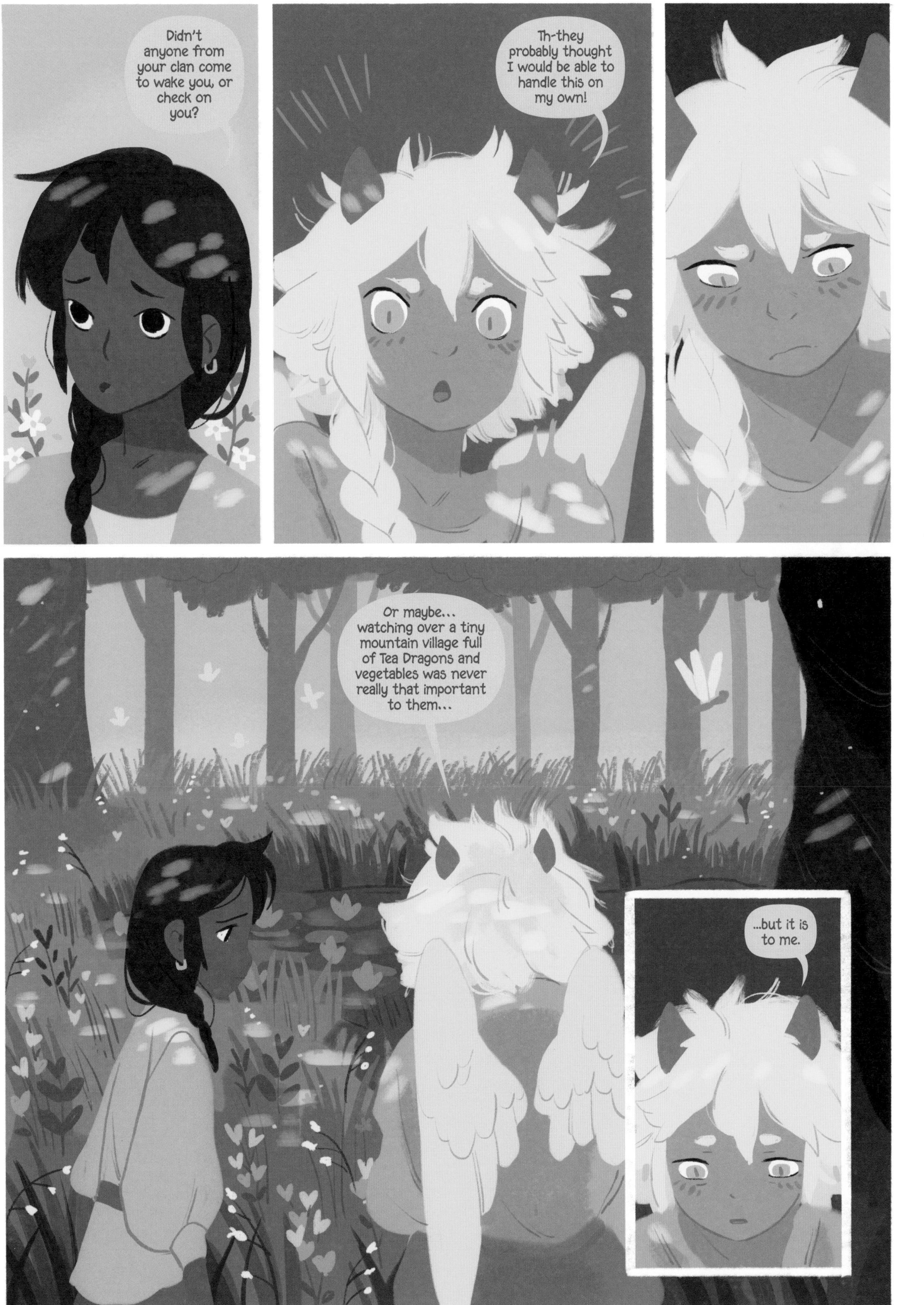
Didn't anyone from your clan come to wake you, or check on you?
Th-they probably thought I would be able to handle this on my own!
Or maybe... watching over a tiny mountain village full of Tea Dragons and vegetables was never really that important to them...
...but it is to me.

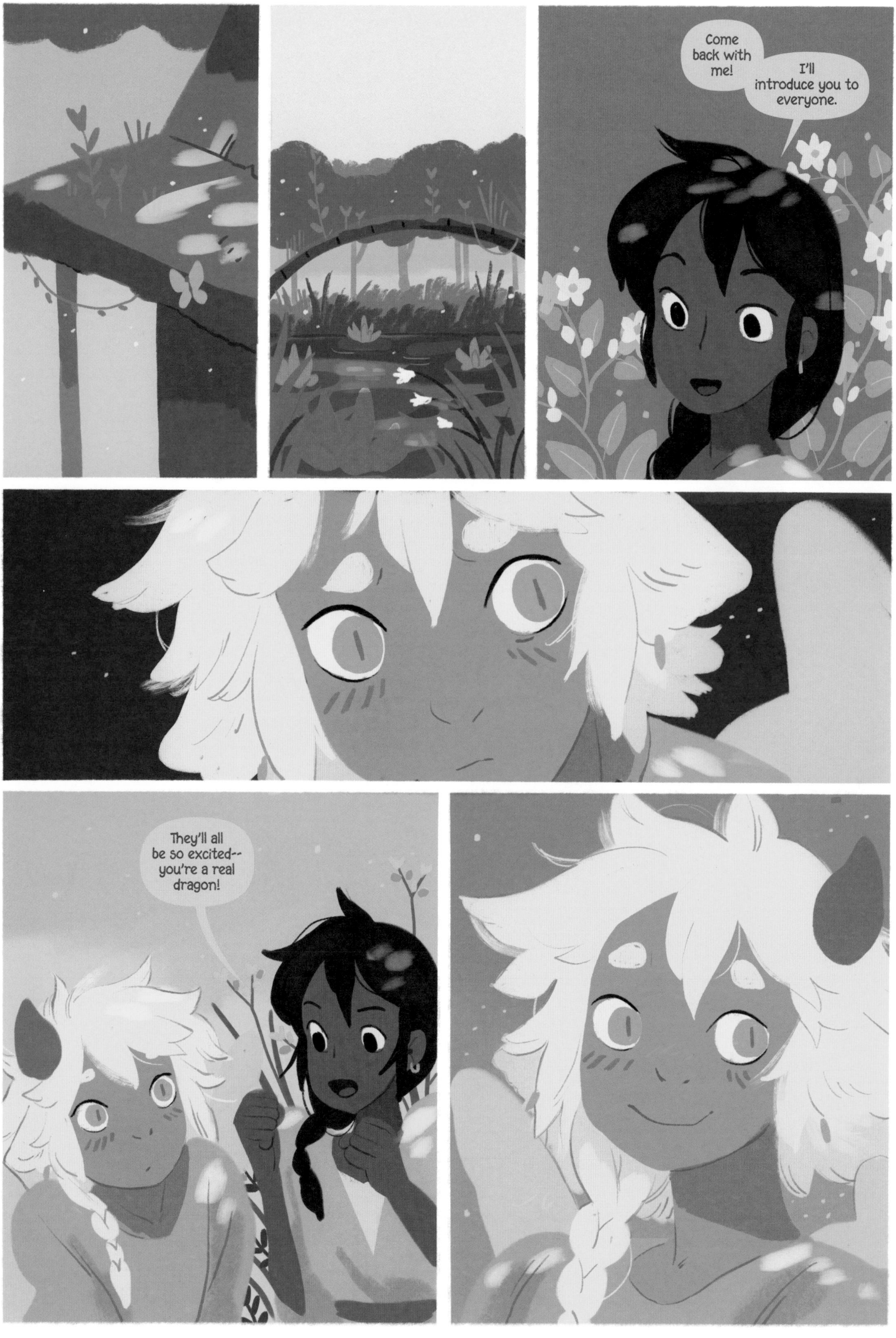
Come back with me!
I'll introduce you to everyone.
They'll all be so excited--you're a real dragon!

My name is Aedhan, of the Shining Wing Clan.

I'm Erik, of the mountain vegetable picker clan!

It's a pleasure to make the acquaintance of a descendant of the dragon Shining Wing Ashyra.

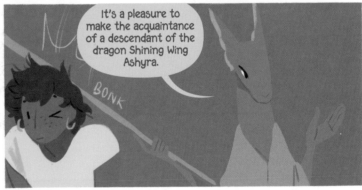

BONK

You know of her? She is my great-great-aunt!

Legends say her hoard fills fifty caverns, and she once slew a pack of vampire sloths with two broken arms--

Now that sounds like a woman I would like to have a cup of tea with!

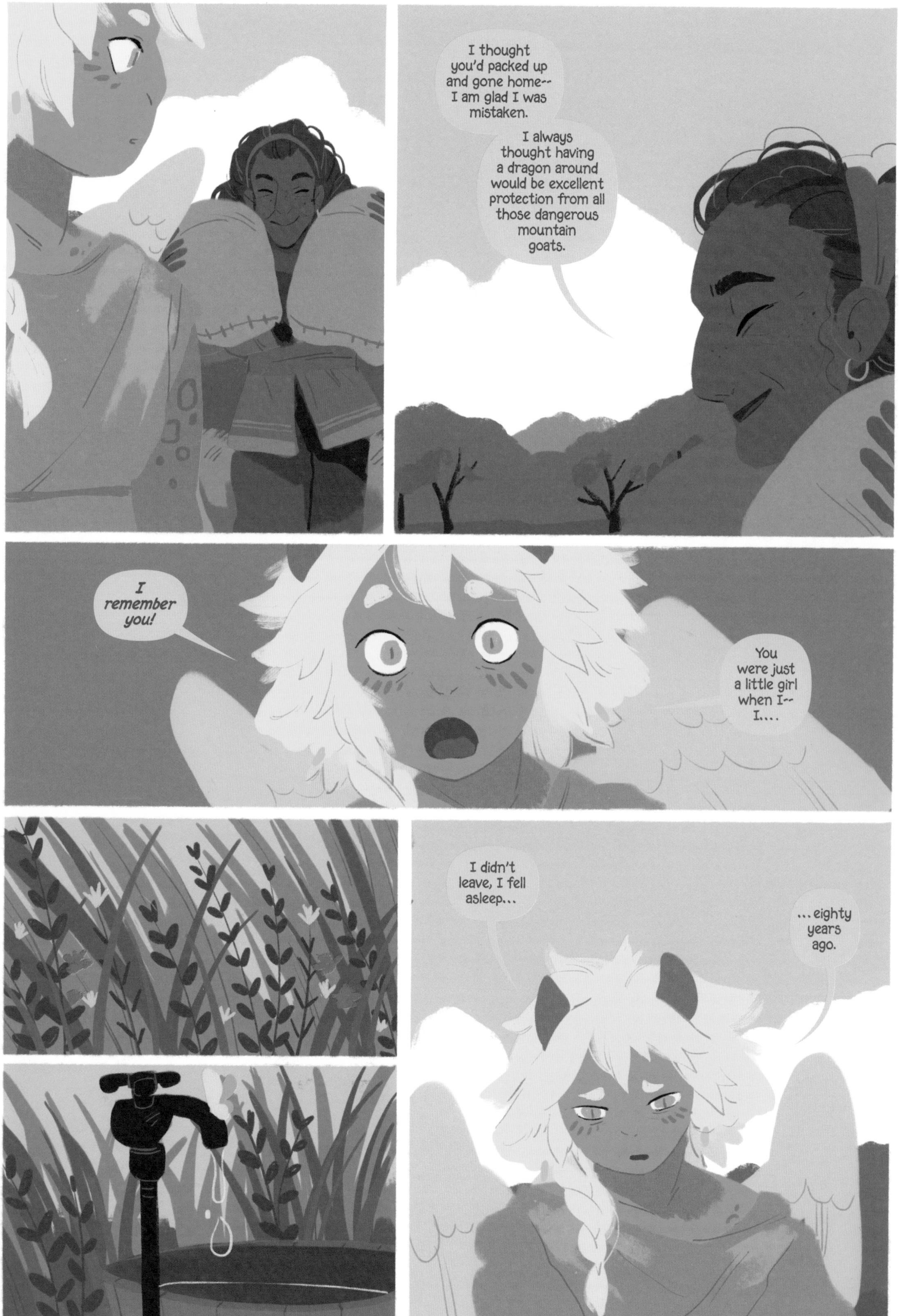
I thought you'd packed up and gone home-- I am glad I was mistaken.
I always thought having a dragon around would be excellent protection from all those dangerous mountain goats.
I remember you!
You were just a little girl when I-- I....
I didn't leave, I fell asleep...
...eighty years ago.

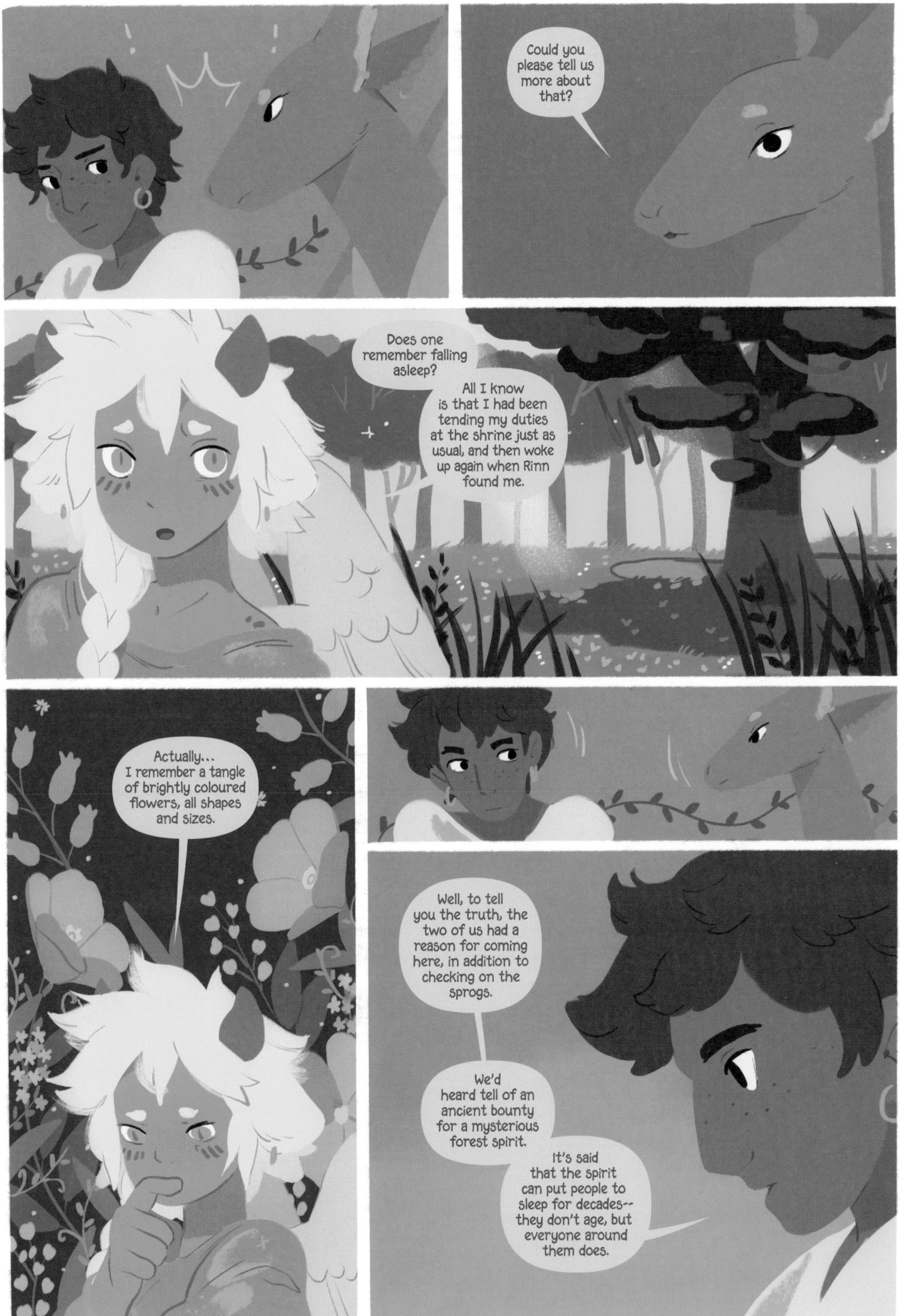

!
!
Could you please tell us more about that?
Does one remember falling asleep?
All I know is that I had been tending my duties at the shrine just as usual, and then woke up again when Rinn found me.
Actually... I remember a tangle of brightly coloured flowers, all shapes and sizes.
Well, to tell you the truth, the two of us had a reason for coming here, in addition to checking on the sprogs.
We'd heard tell of an ancient bounty for a mysterious forest spirit.
It's said that the spirit can put people to sleep for decades-- they don't age, but everyone around them does.

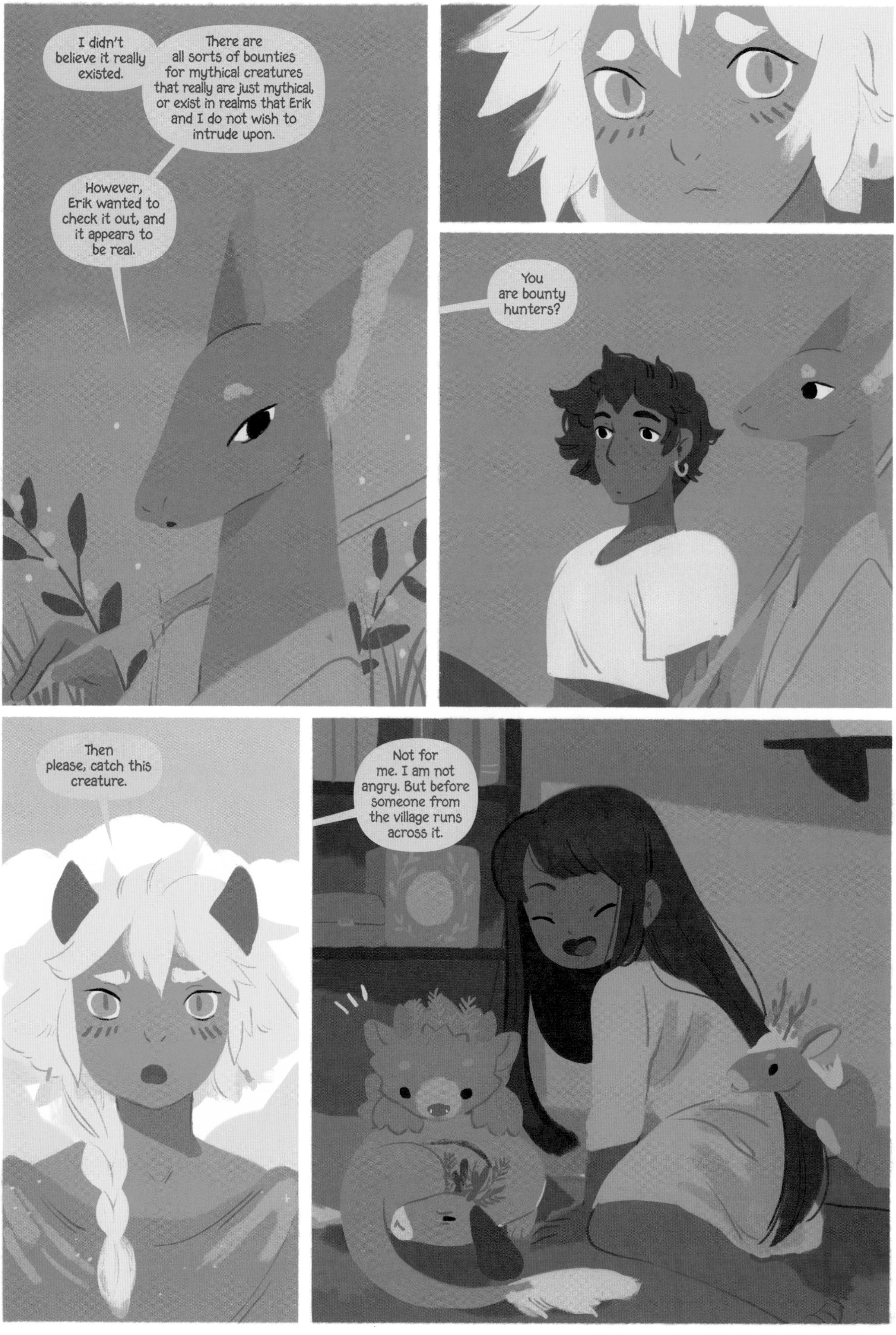
I didn't believe it really existed.
There are all sorts of bounties for mythical creatures that really are just mythical, or exist in realms that Erik and I do not wish to intrude upon.
However, Erik wanted to check it out, and it appears to be real.
You are bounty hunters?
Then please, catch this creature.
Not for me. I am not angry. But before someone from the village runs across it.

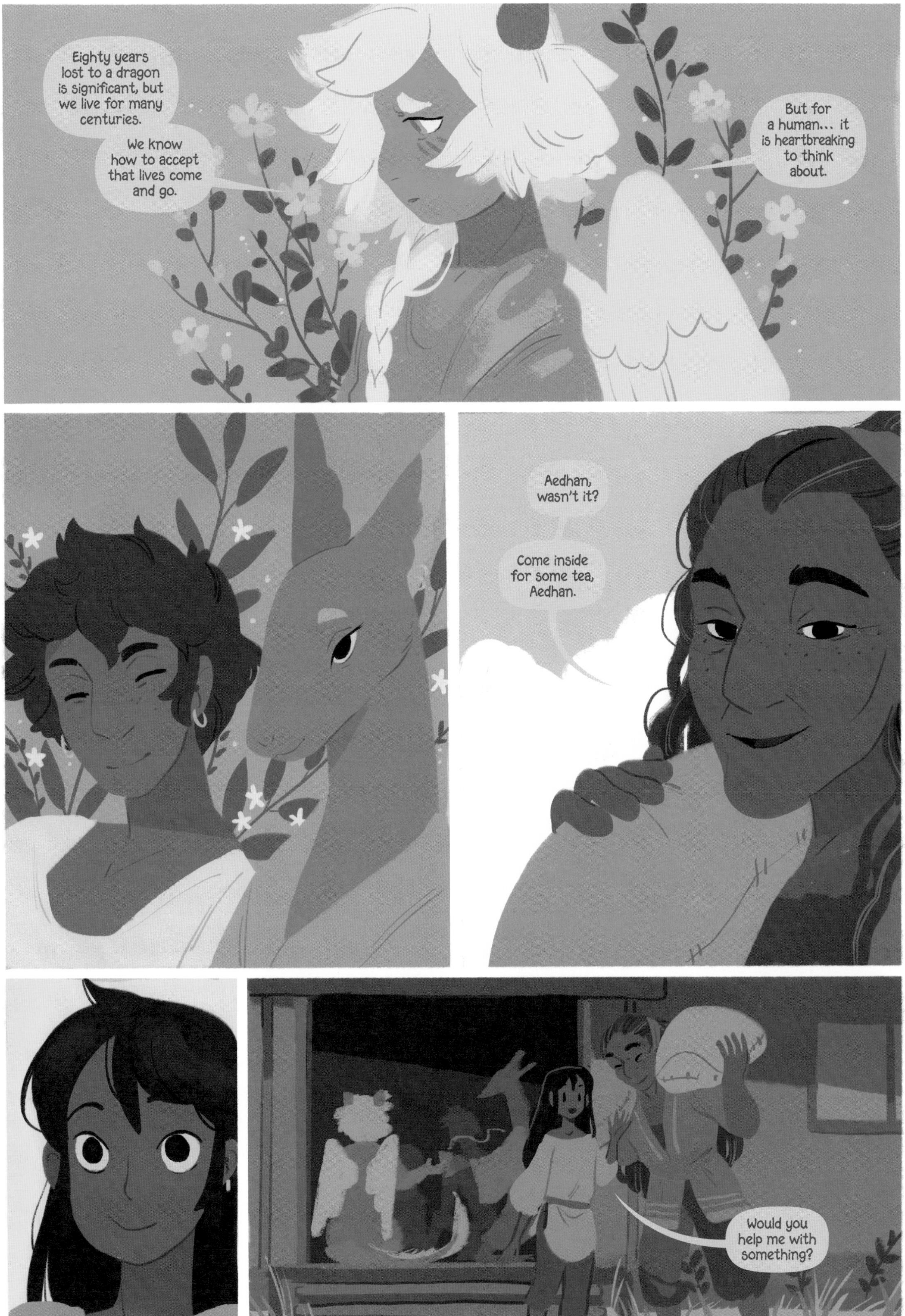
Eighty years lost to a dragon is significant, but we live for many centuries.
We know how to accept that lives come and go.
But for a human... it is heartbreaking to think about.
Aedhan, wasn't it?
Come inside for some tea, Aedhan.
Would you help me with something?

Chapter Three

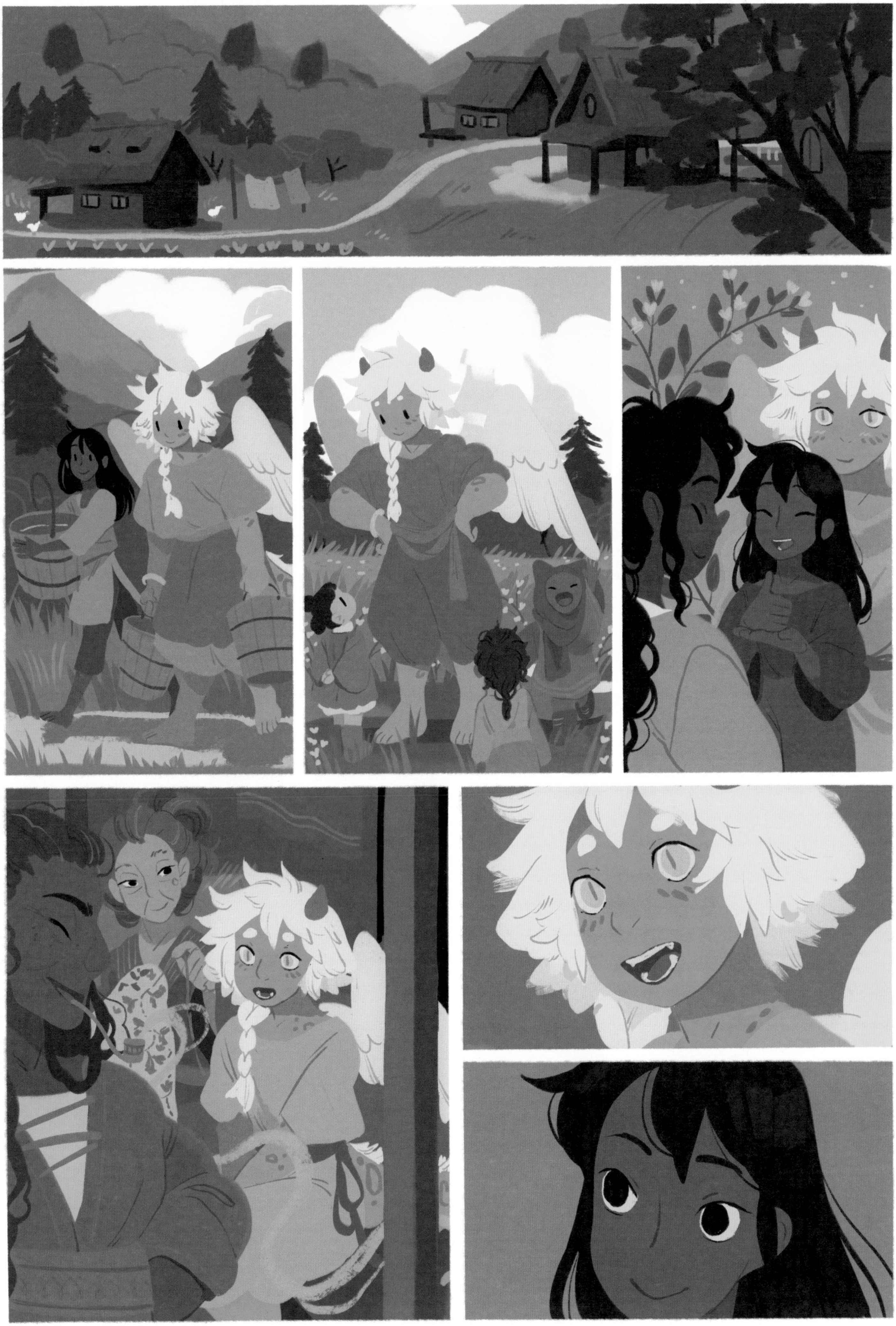

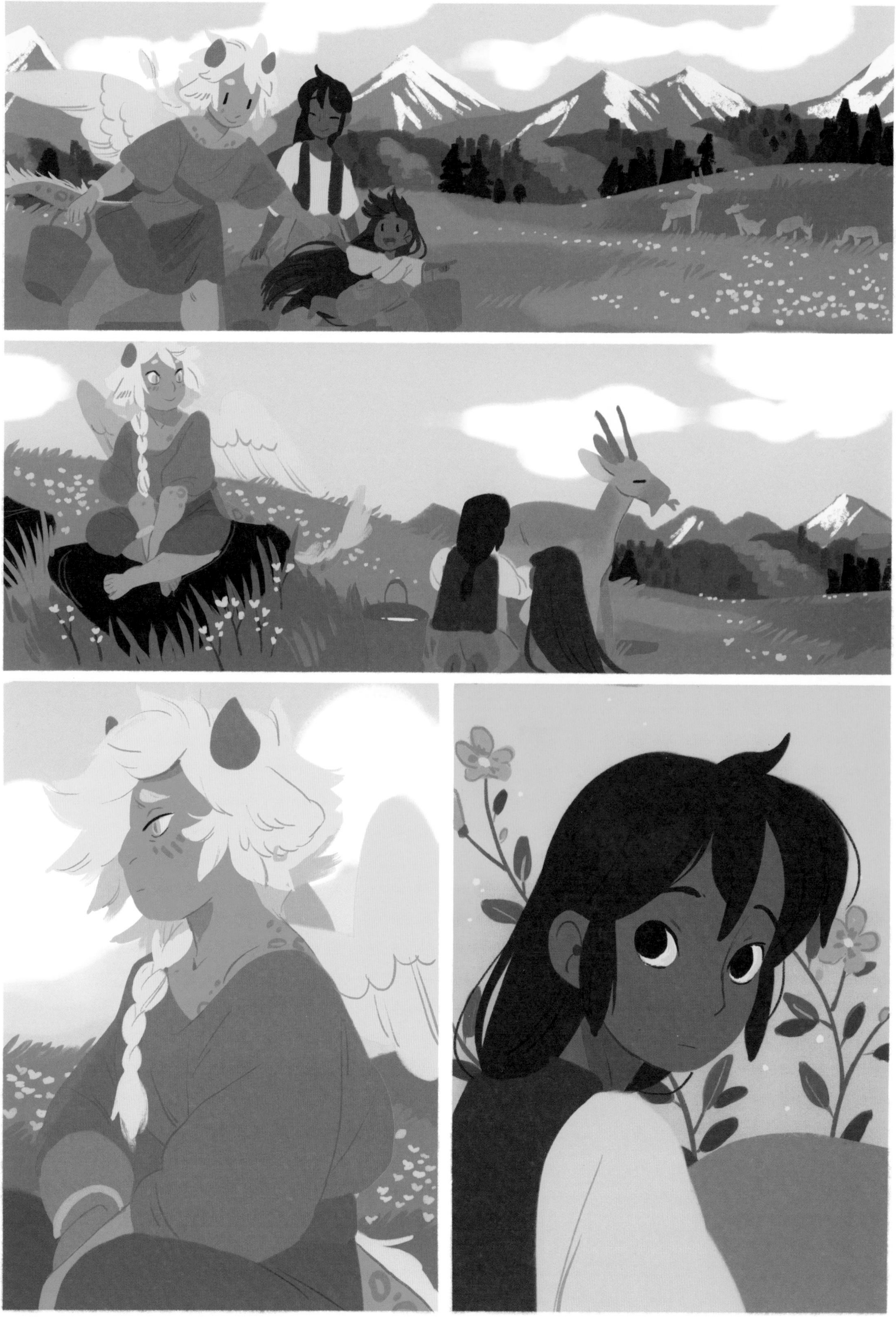

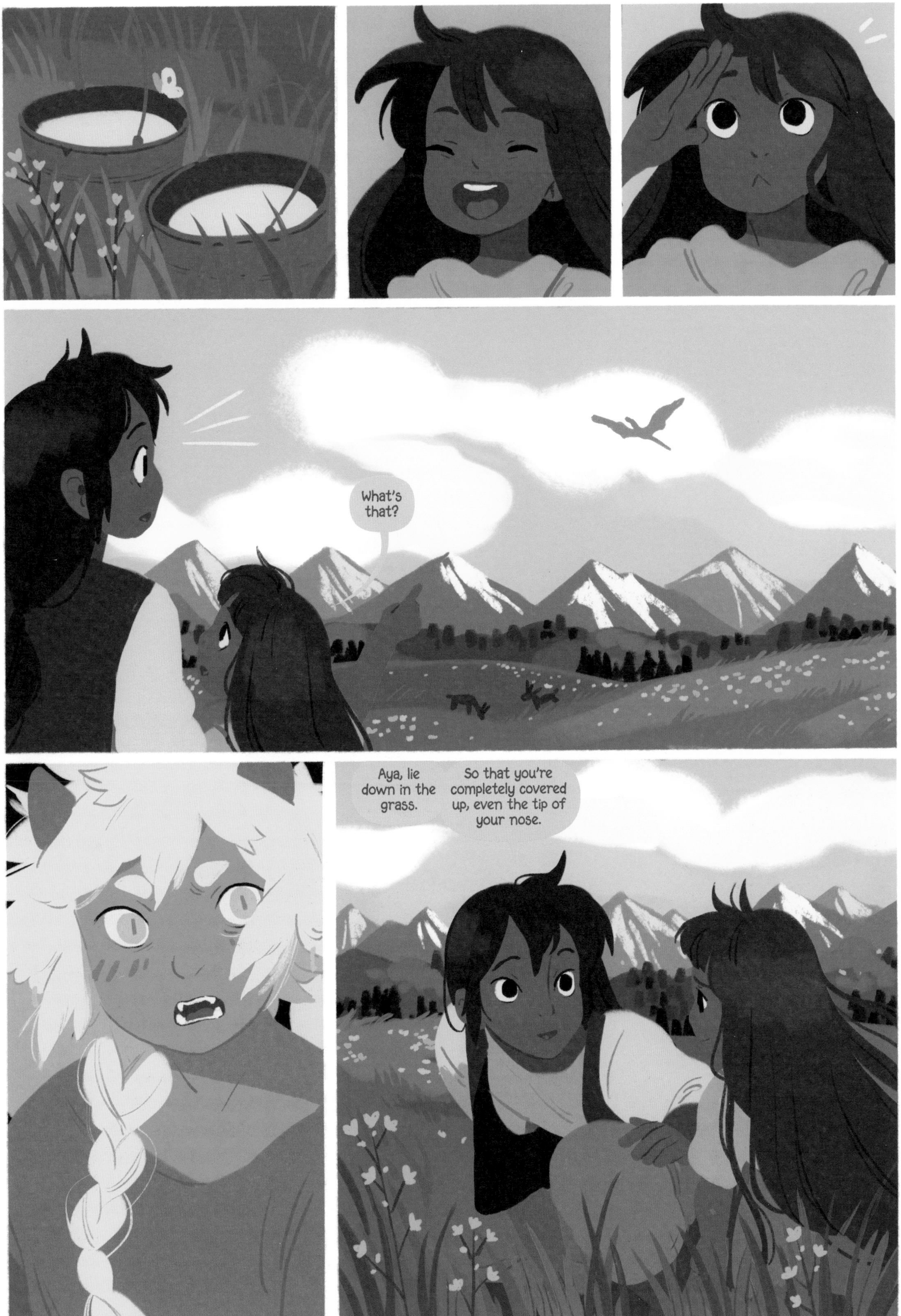
What's that?
Aya, lie down in the grass.
So that you're completely covered up, even the tip of your nose.

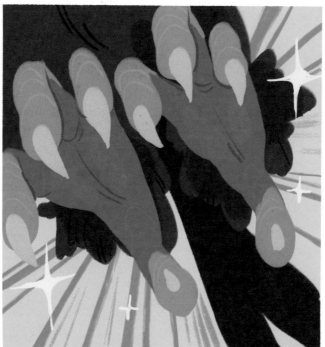

Rinn!! Aya!!
Hold on--

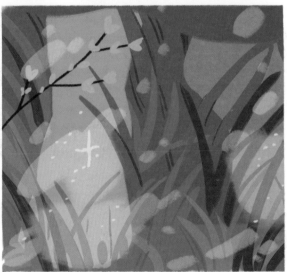

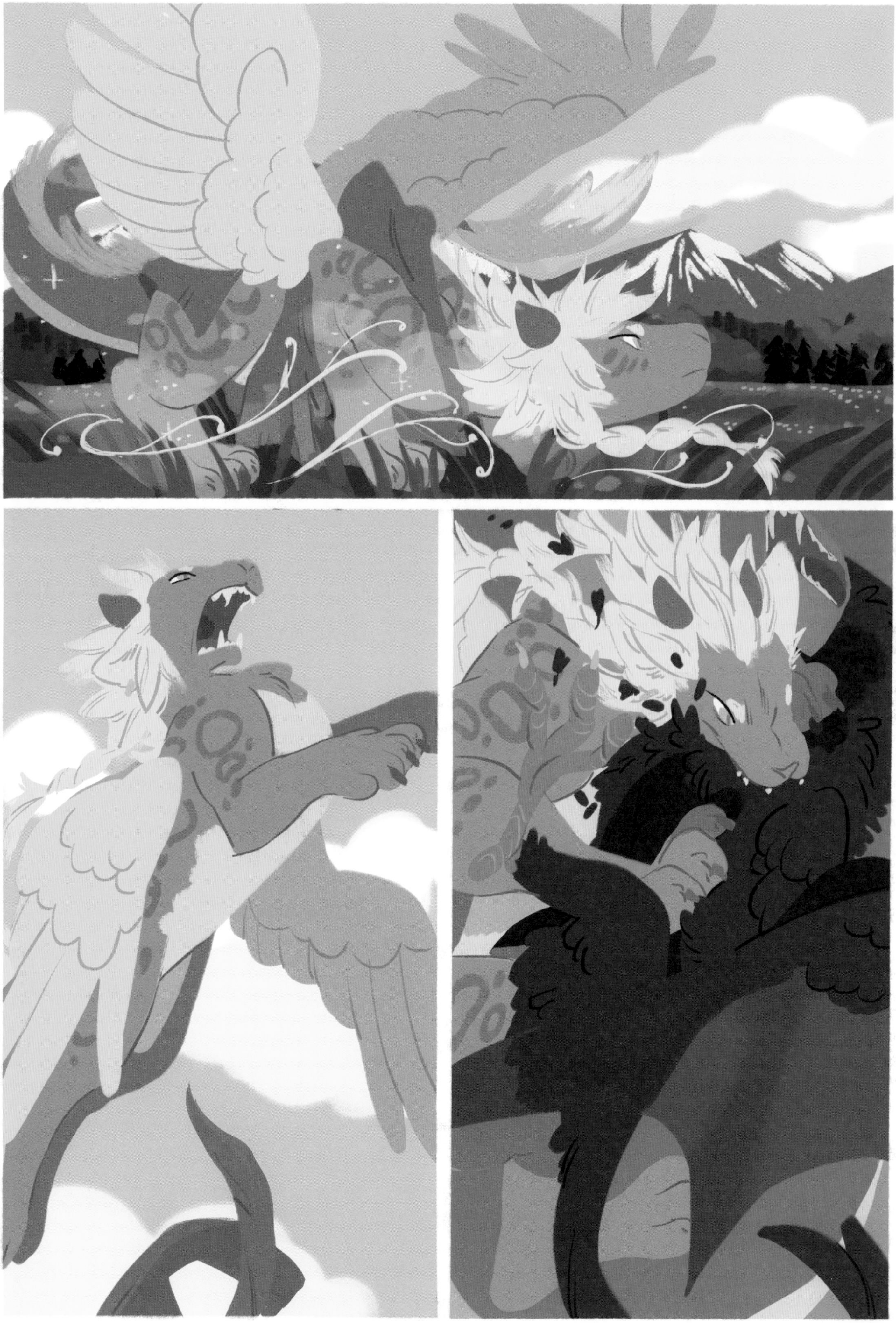

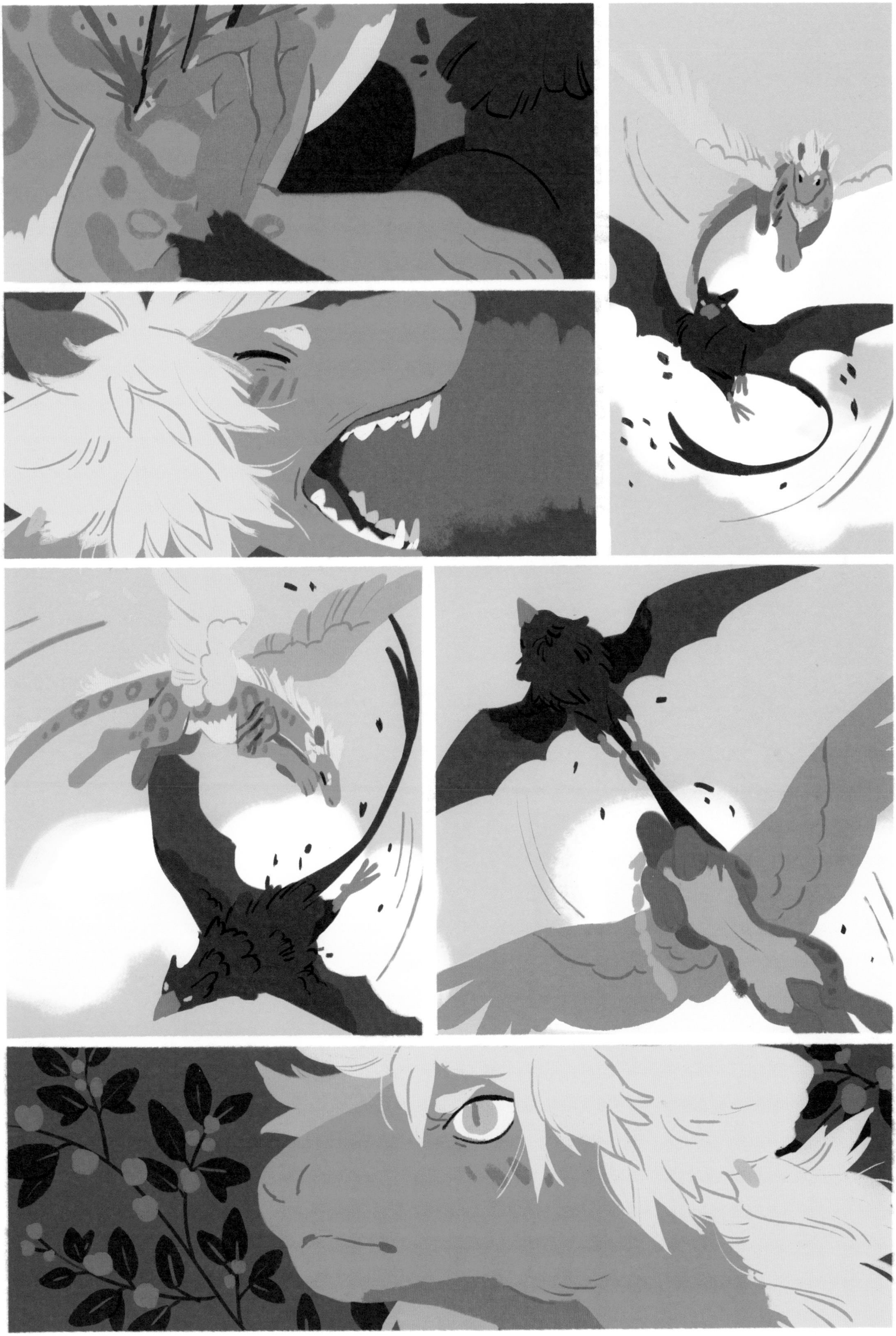

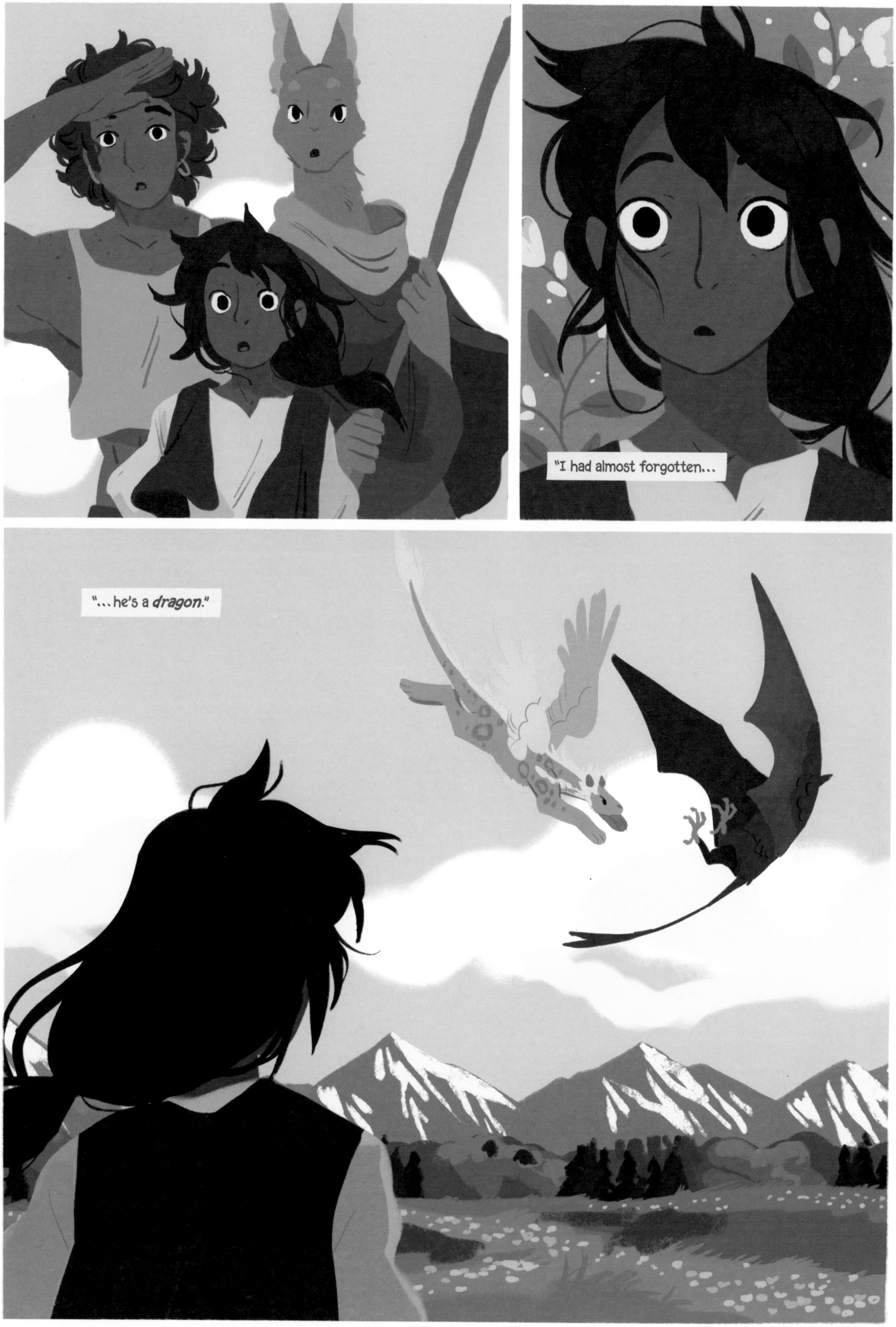
"I had almost forgotten...
"...he's a *dragon*."

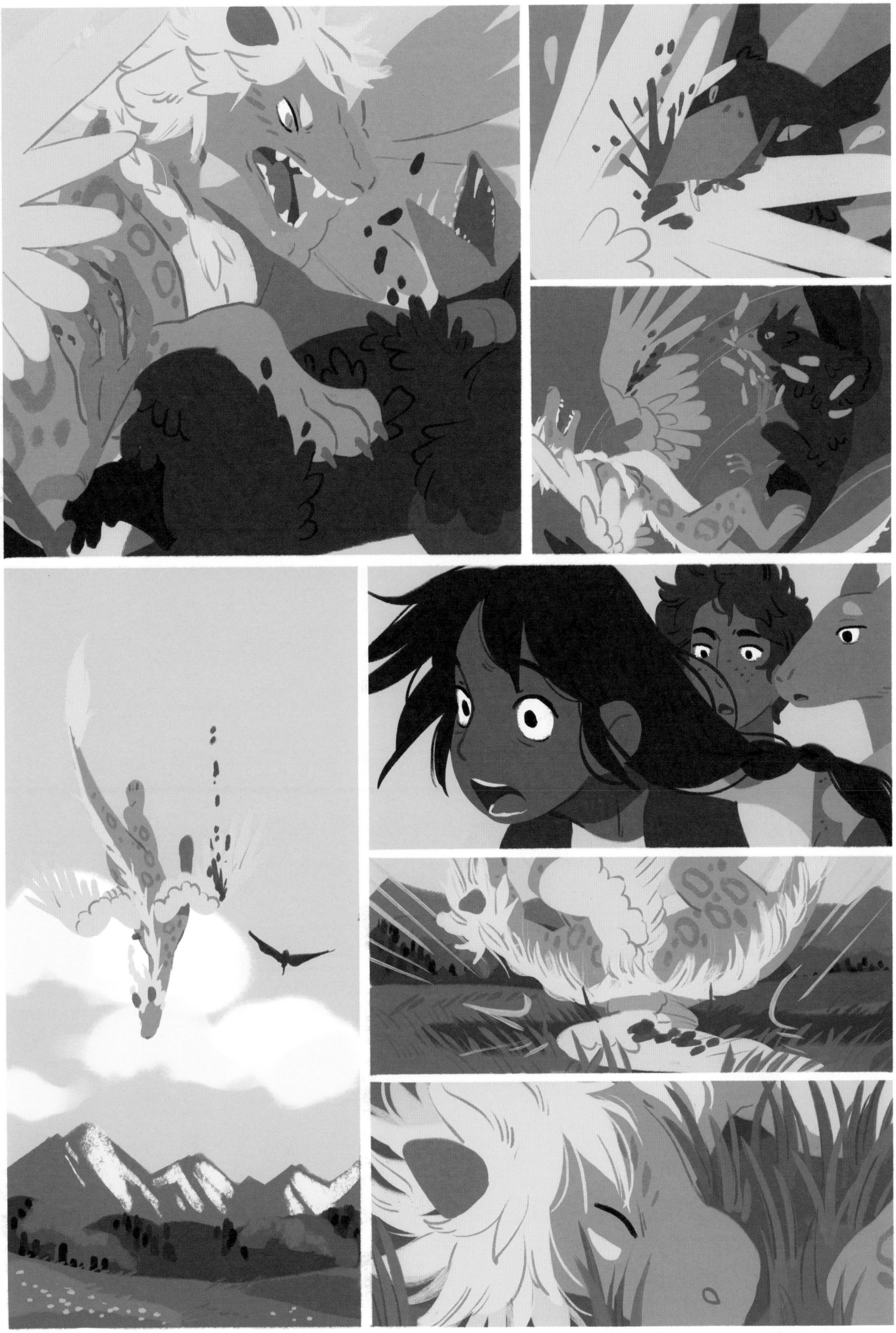

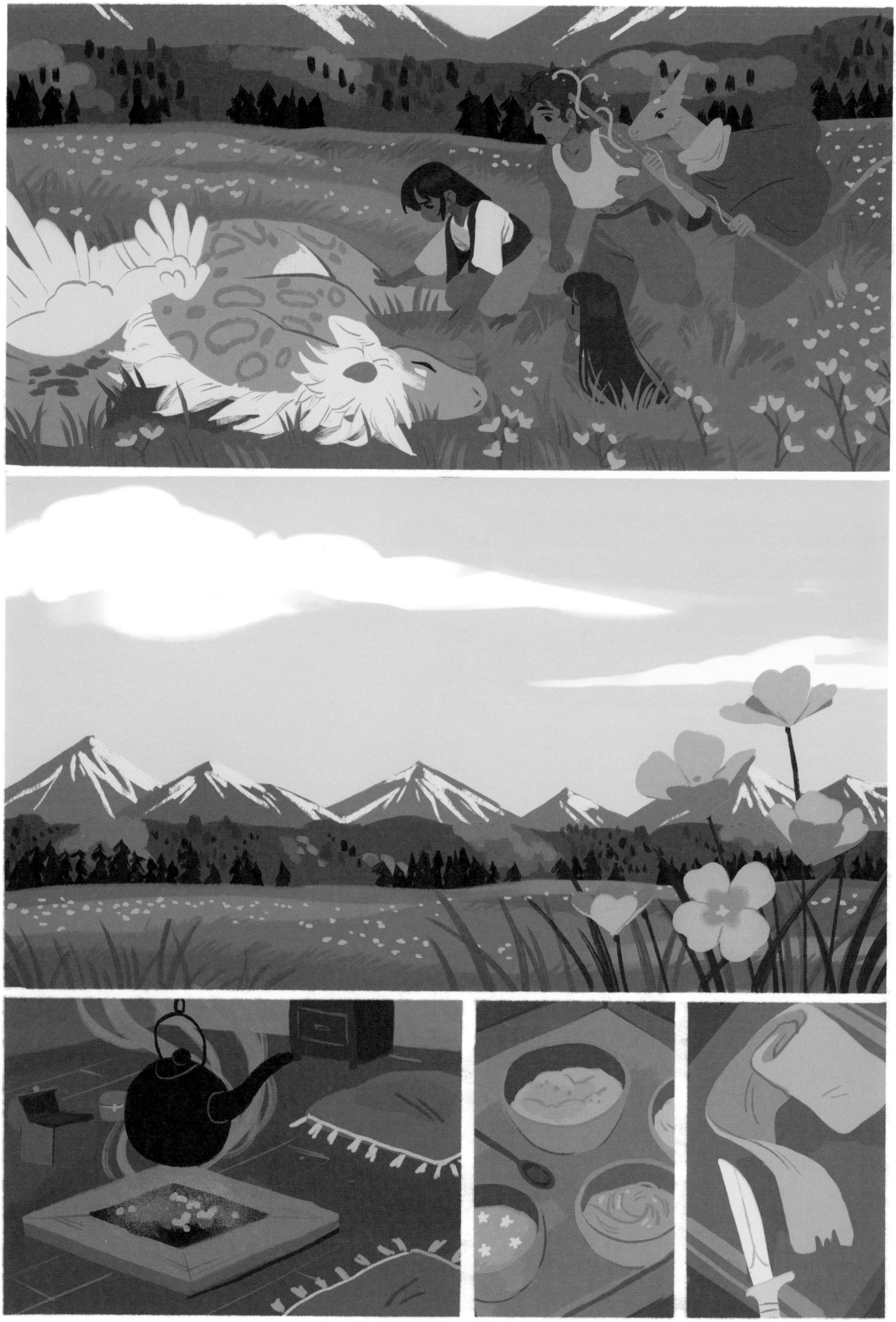

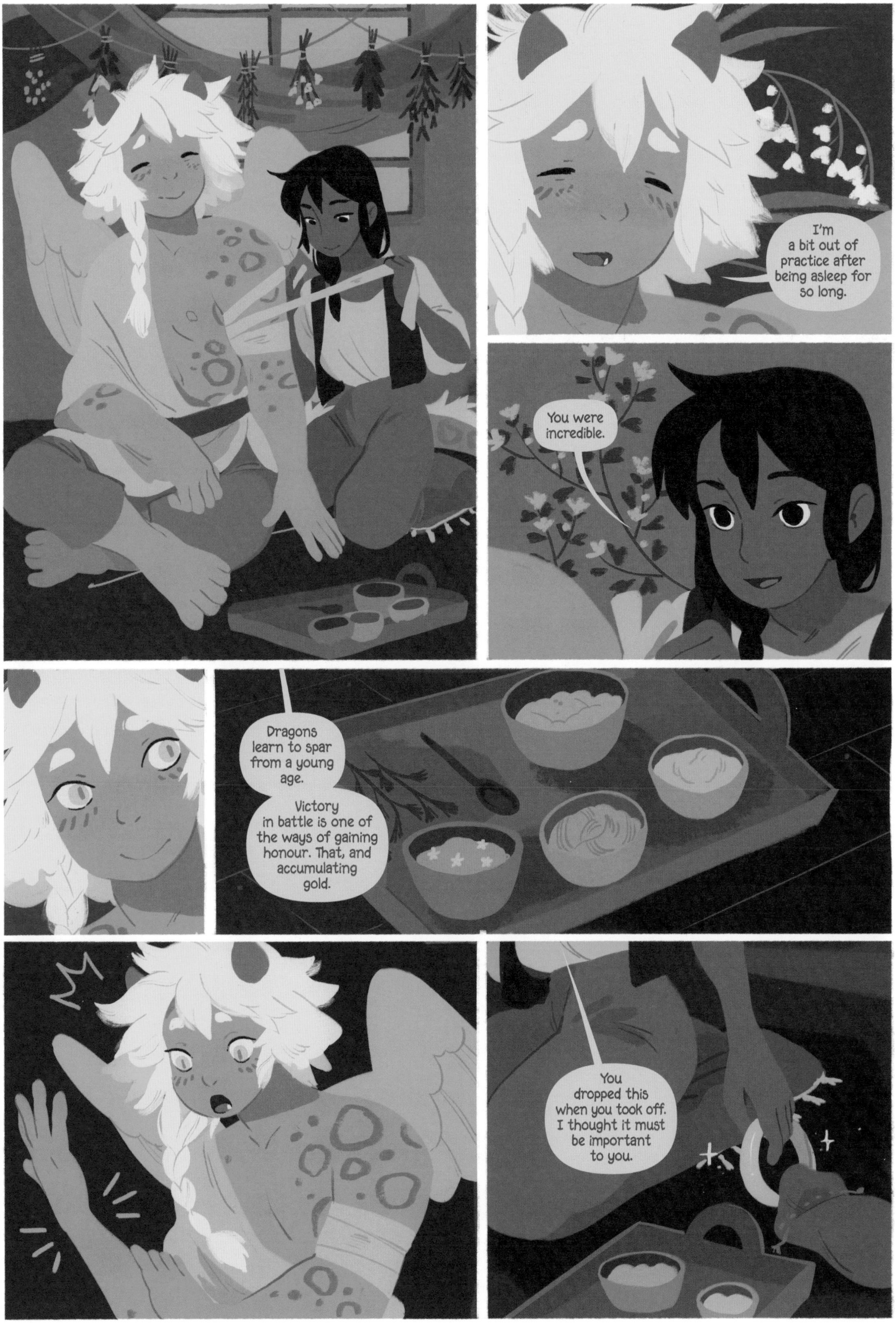
I'm a bit out of practice after being asleep for so long.
You were incredible.
Dragons learn to spar from a young age.
Victory in battle is one of the ways of gaining honour. That, and accumulating gold.
You dropped this when you took off. I thought it must be important to you.

It's beautiful.

Yes... and it's all I have.

I won't be gaining any respect from my clan through riches.

But you would for what you did today.

Perhaps....

I do not know if my clan even remembers where they sent me.

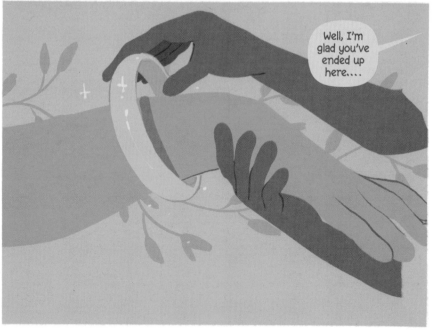

Well, I'm glad you've ended up here....

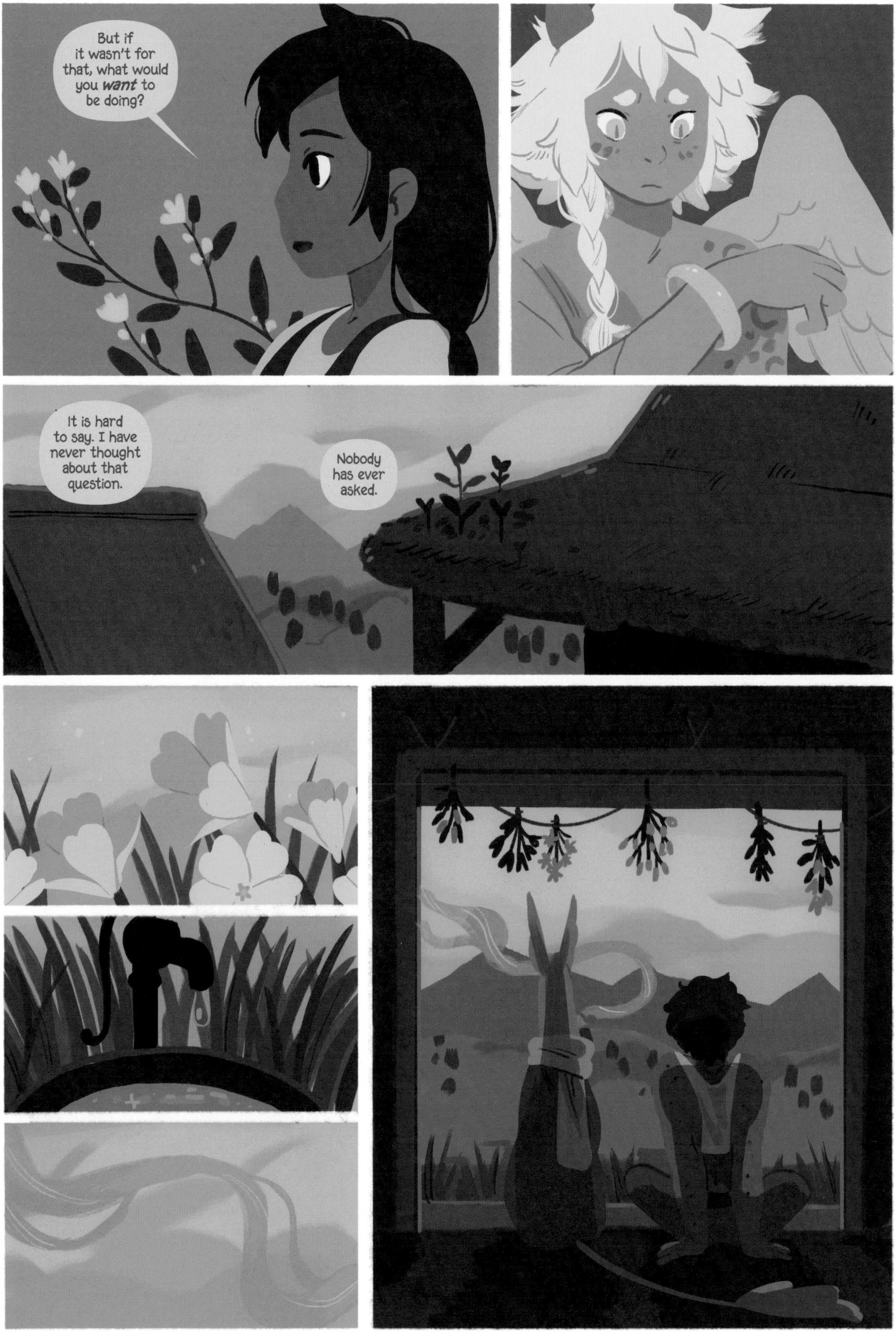
But if it wasn't for that, what would you *want* to be doing?
It is hard to say. I have never thought about that question.
Nobody has ever asked.

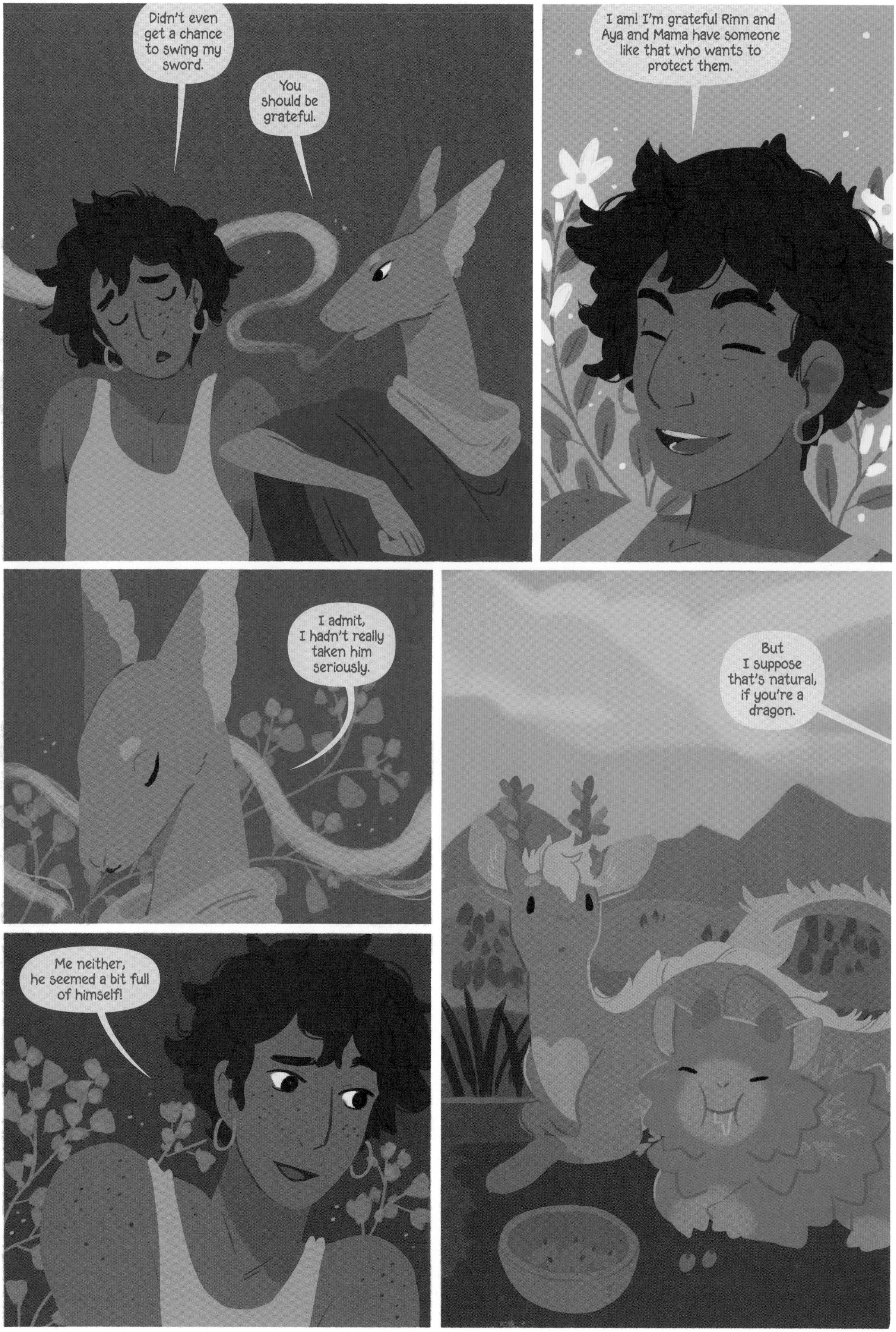
Didn't even get a chance to swing my sword.
You should be grateful.
I am! I'm grateful Rinn and Aya and Mama have someone like that who wants to protect them.
I admit, I hadn't really taken him seriously.
Me neither, he seemed a bit full of himself!
But I suppose that's natural, if you're a dragon.

Chapter Four

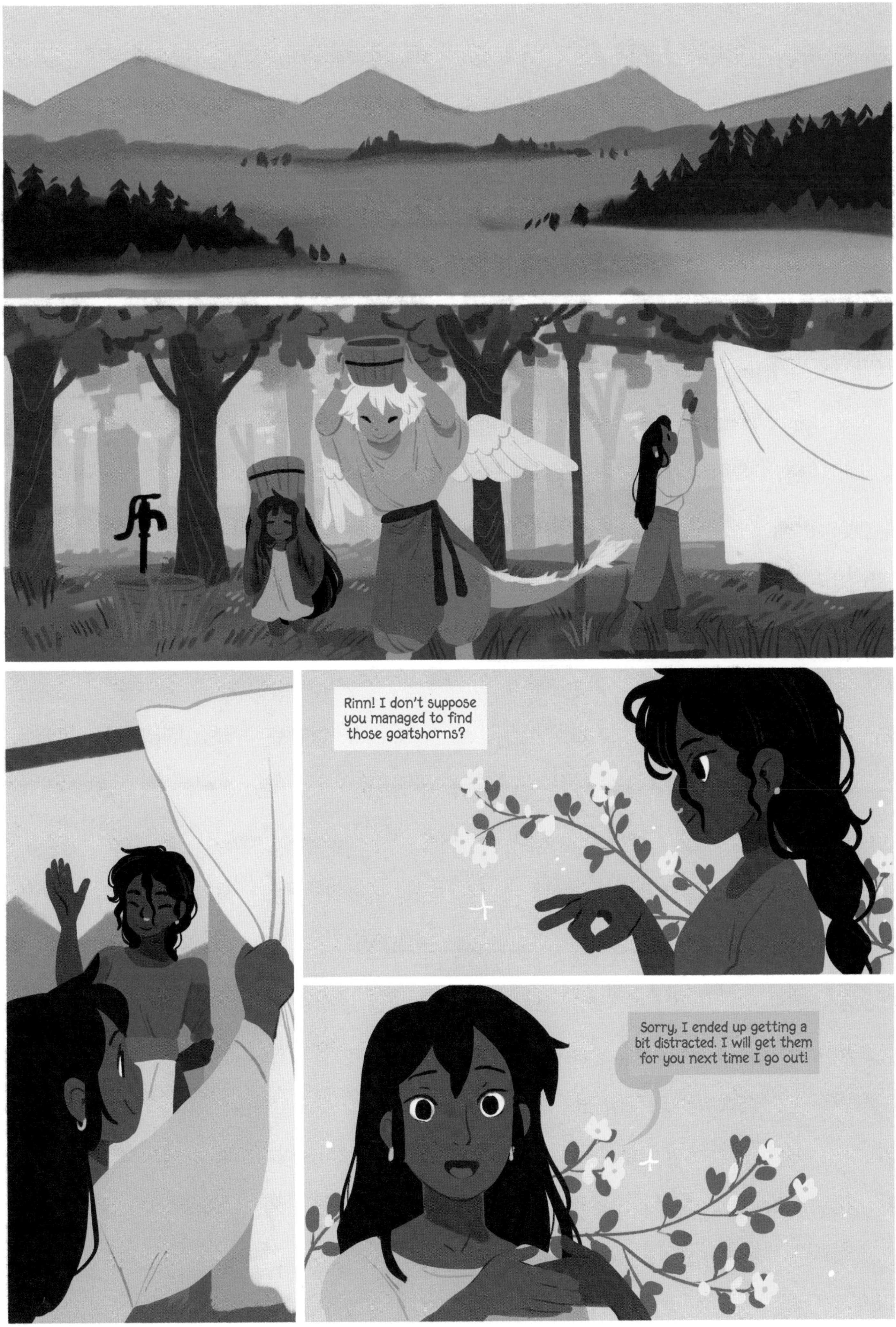
Rinn! I don't suppose you managed to find those goatshorns?
Sorry, I ended up getting a bit distracted. I will get them for you next time I go out!

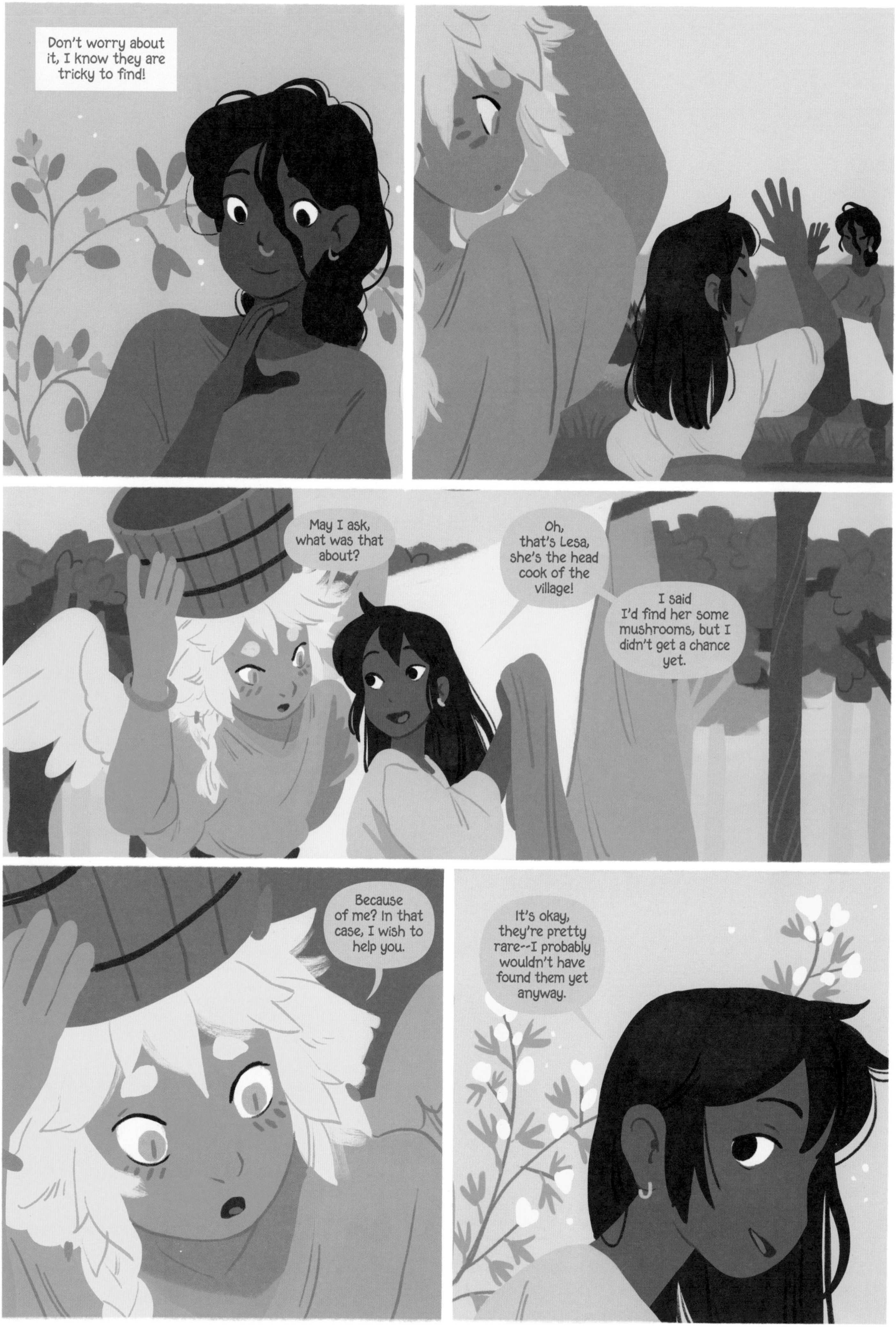
Don't worry about it, I know they are tricky to find!
May I ask, what was that about?
Oh, that's Lesa, she's the head cook of the village!
I said I'd find her some mushrooms, but I didn't get a chance yet.
Because of me? In that case, I wish to help you.
It's okay, they're pretty rare--I probably wouldn't have found them yet anyway.

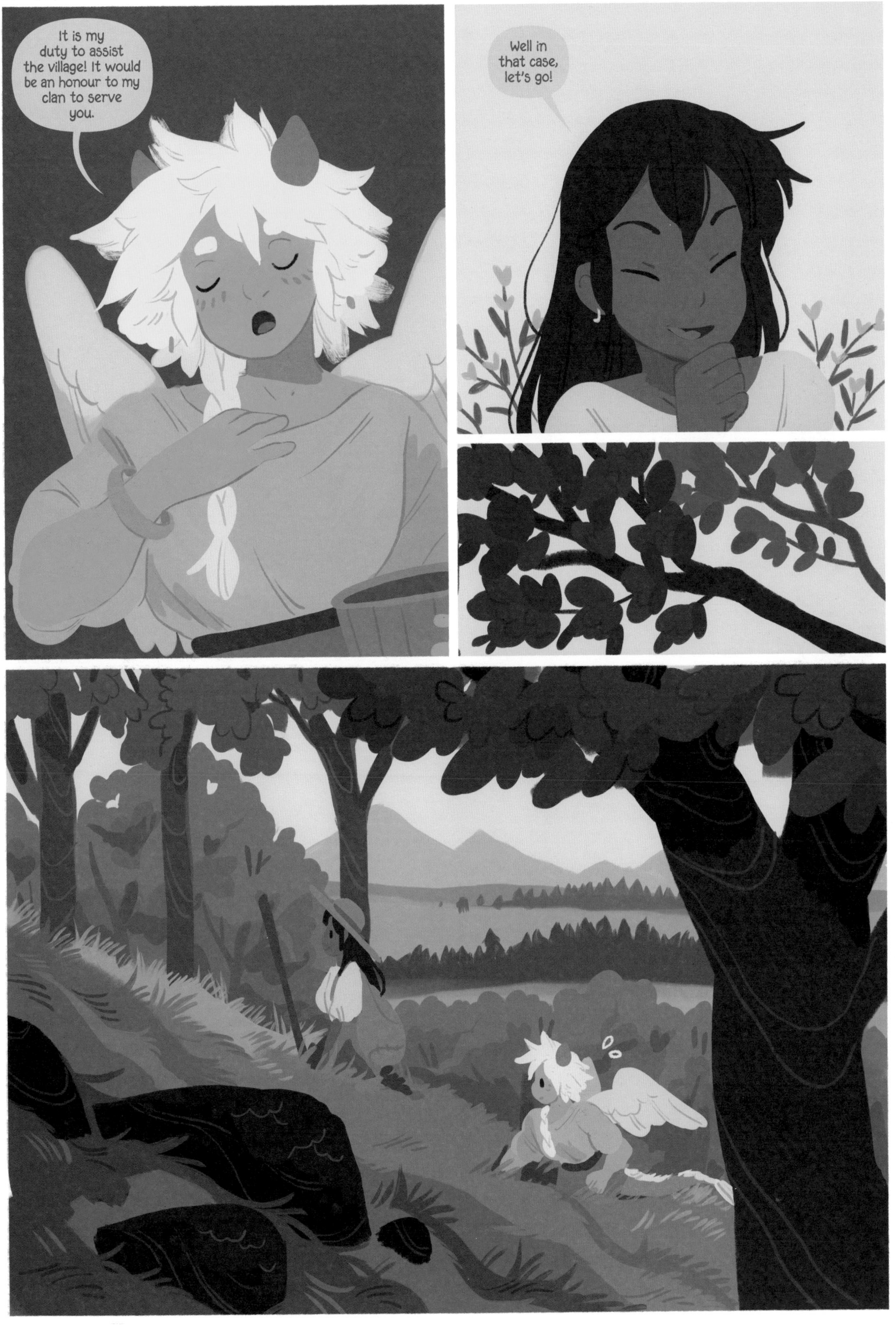

It is my duty to assist the village! It would be an honour to my clan to serve you.
Well in that case, let's go!

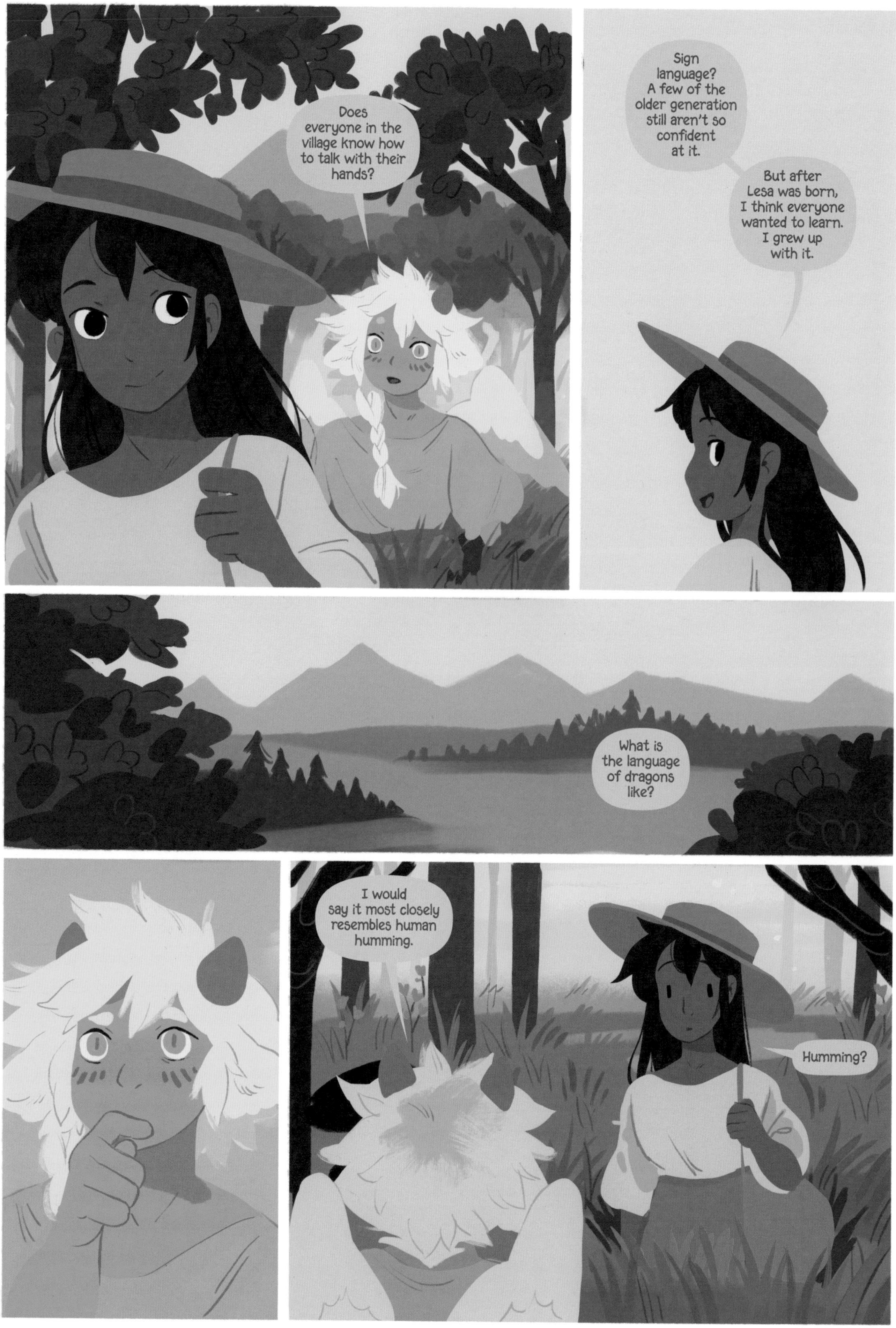
Does everyone in the village know how to talk with their hands?
Sign language? A few of the older generation still aren't so confident at it.
But after Lesa was born, I think everyone wanted to learn. I grew up with it.
What is the language of dragons like?
I would say it most closely resembles human humming.
Humming?

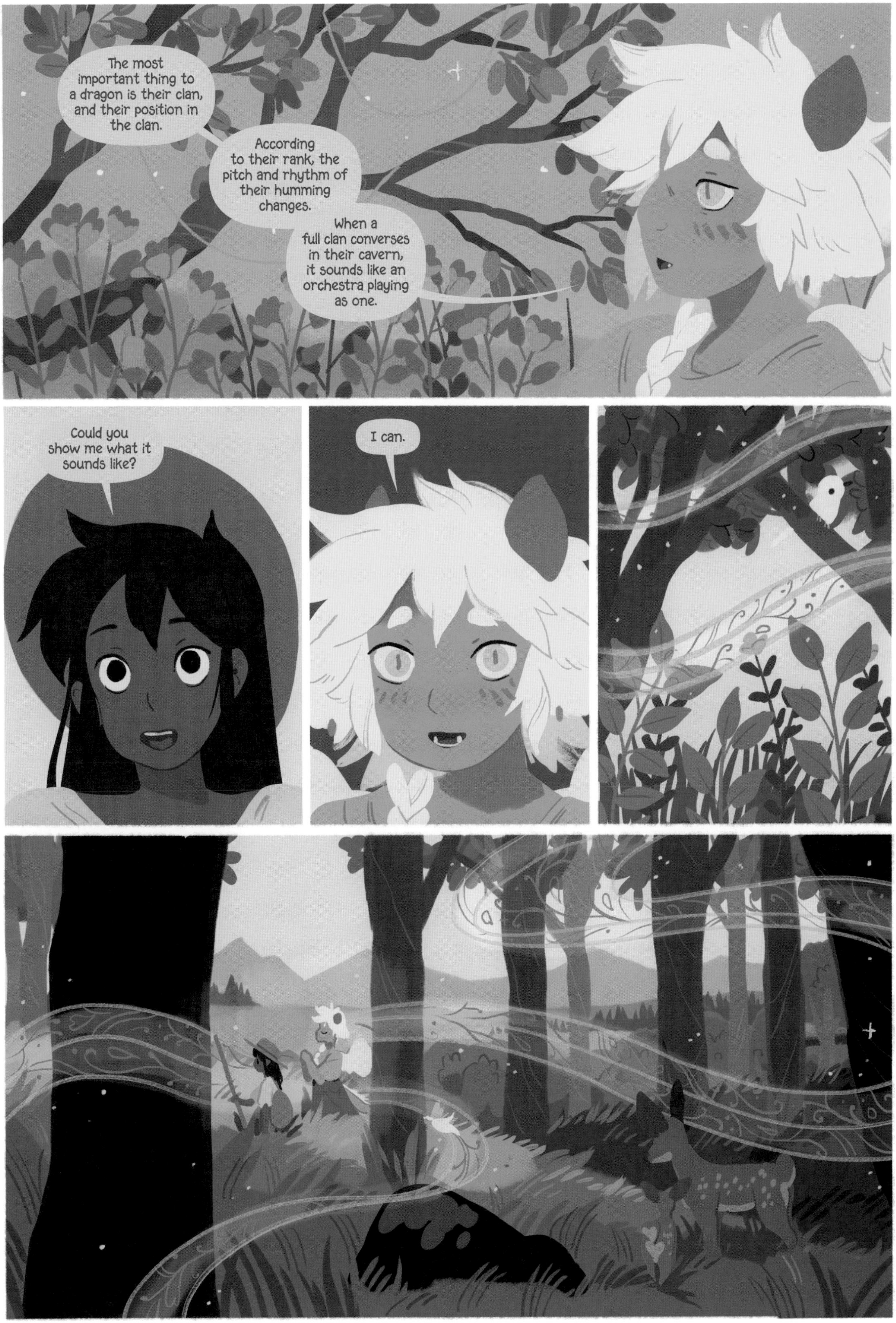
The most important thing to a dragon is their clan, and their position in the clan.
According to their rank, the pitch and rhythm of their humming changes.
When a full clan converses in their cavern, it sounds like an orchestra playing as one.
Could you show me what it sounds like?
I can.

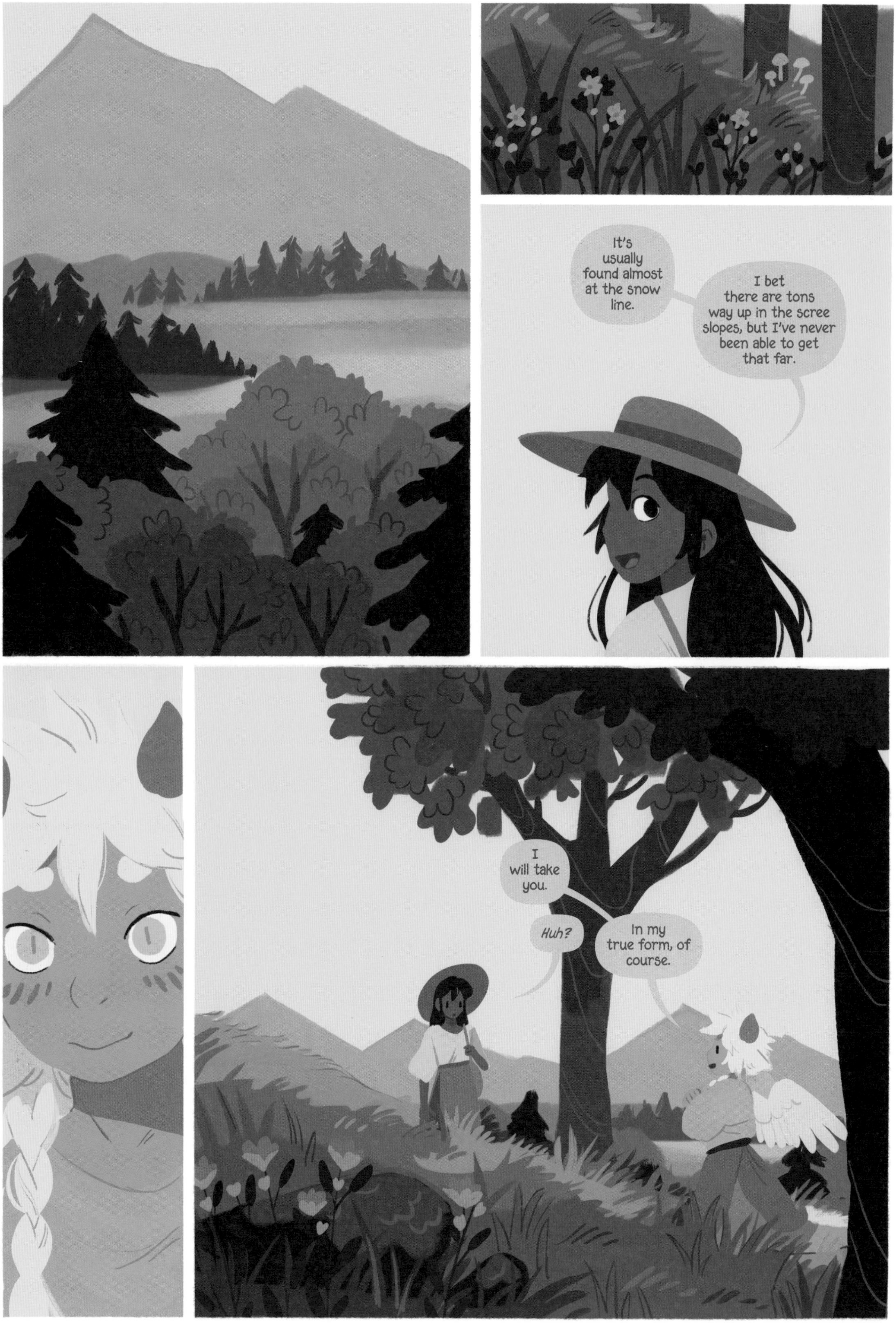
It's usually found almost at the snow line.
I bet there are tons way up in the scree slopes, but I've never been able to get that far.
I will take you.
Huh?
In my true form, of course.

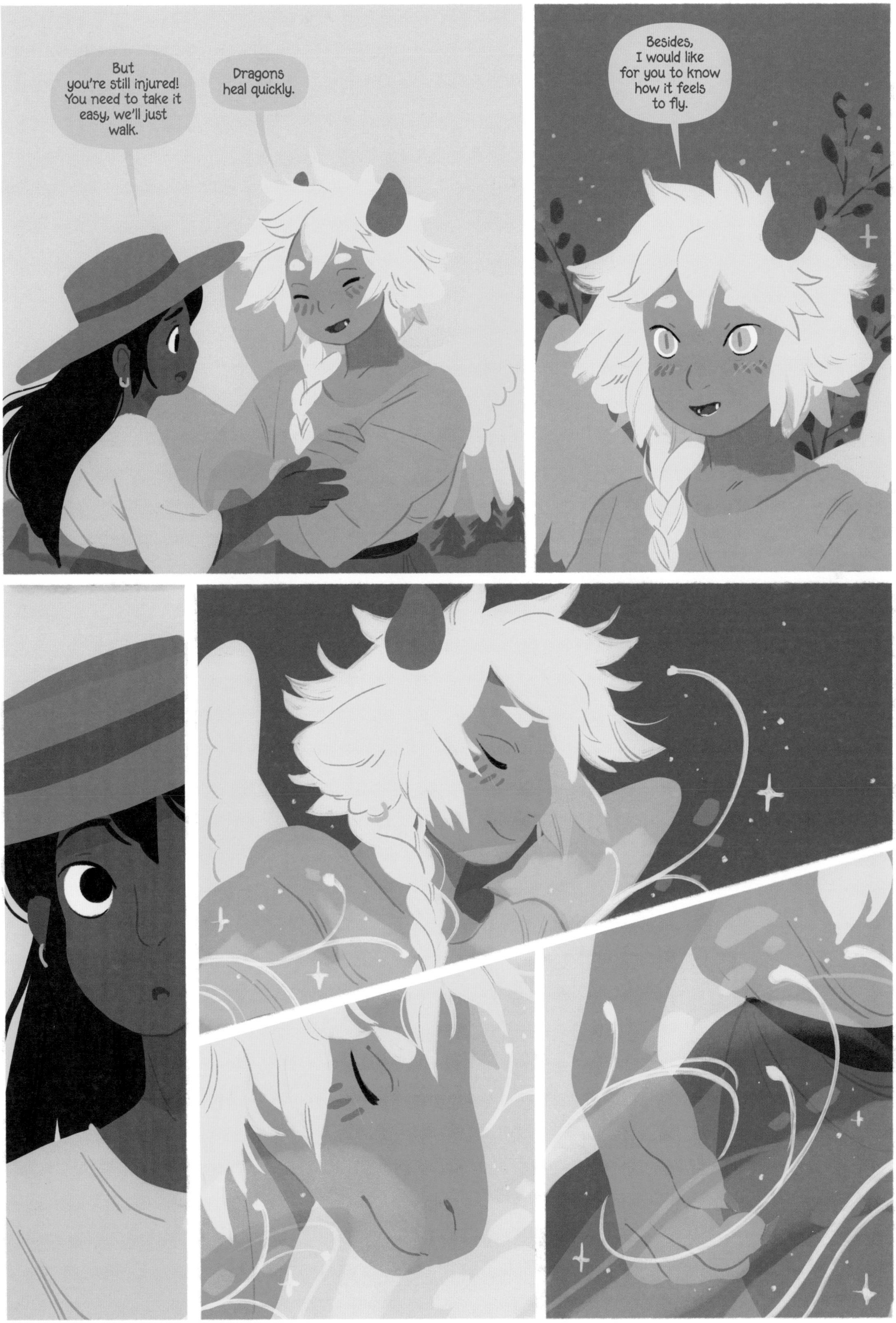
But you're still injured! You need to take it easy, we'll just walk.
Dragons heal quickly.
Besides, I would like for you to know how it feels to fly.

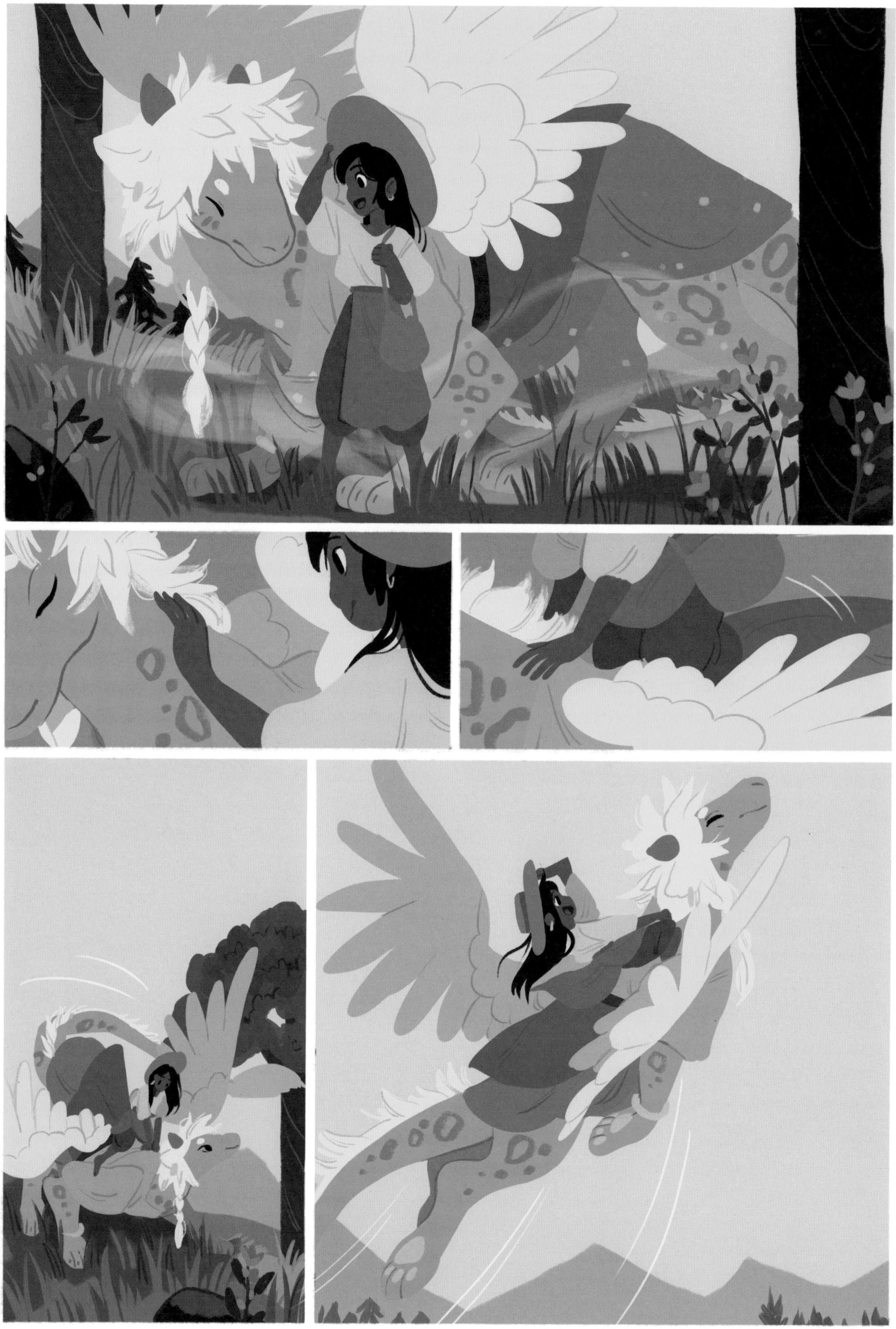

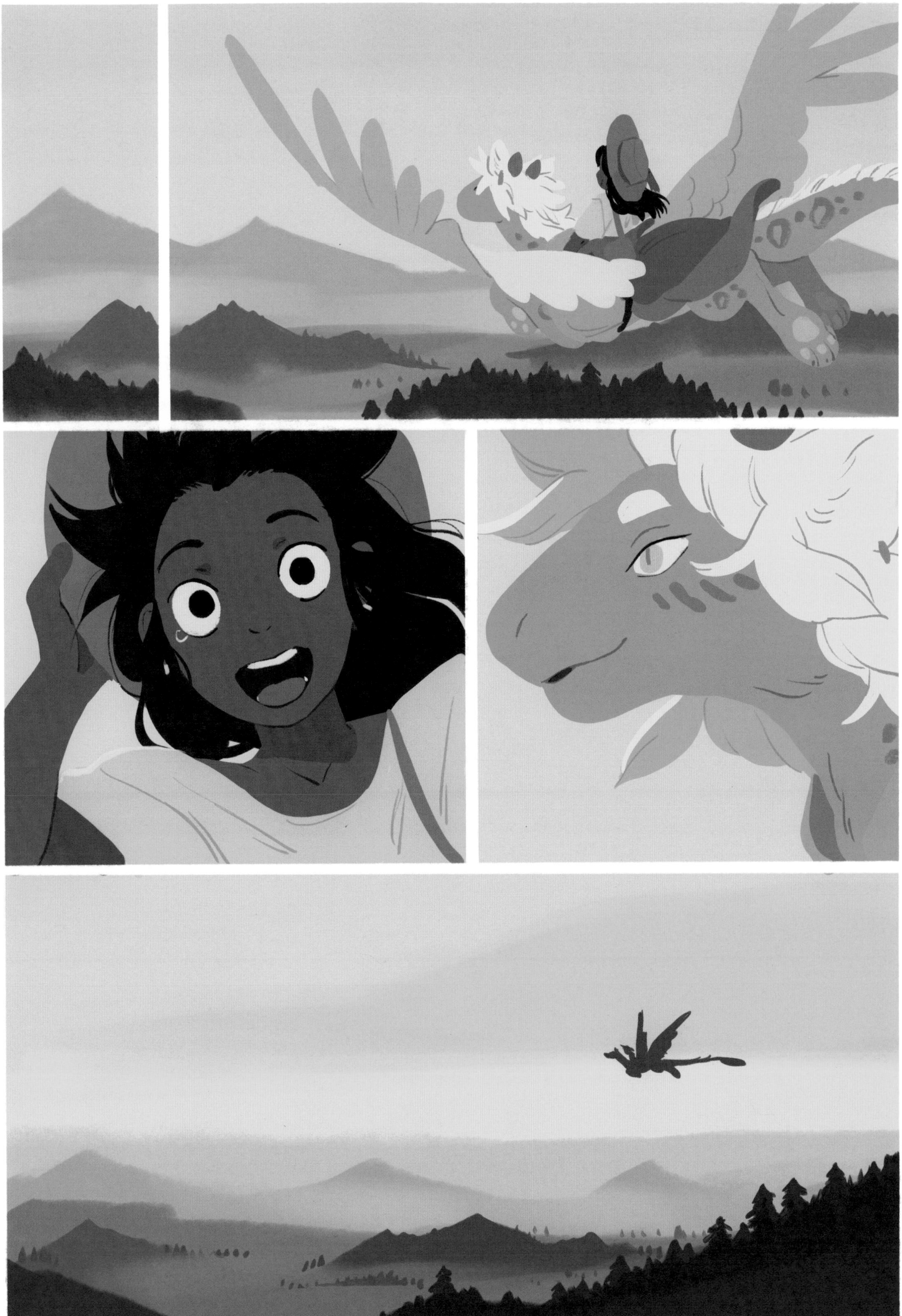

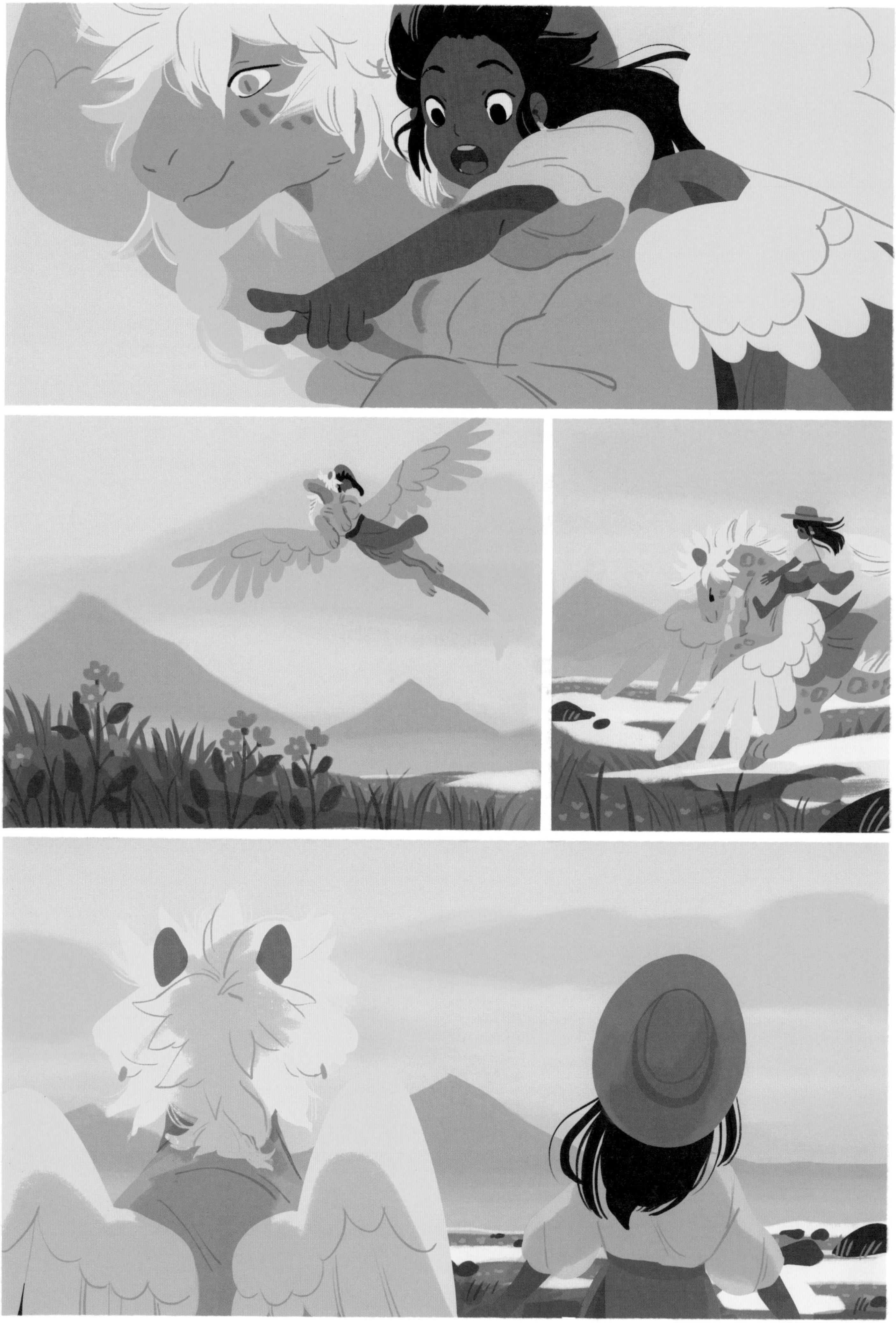

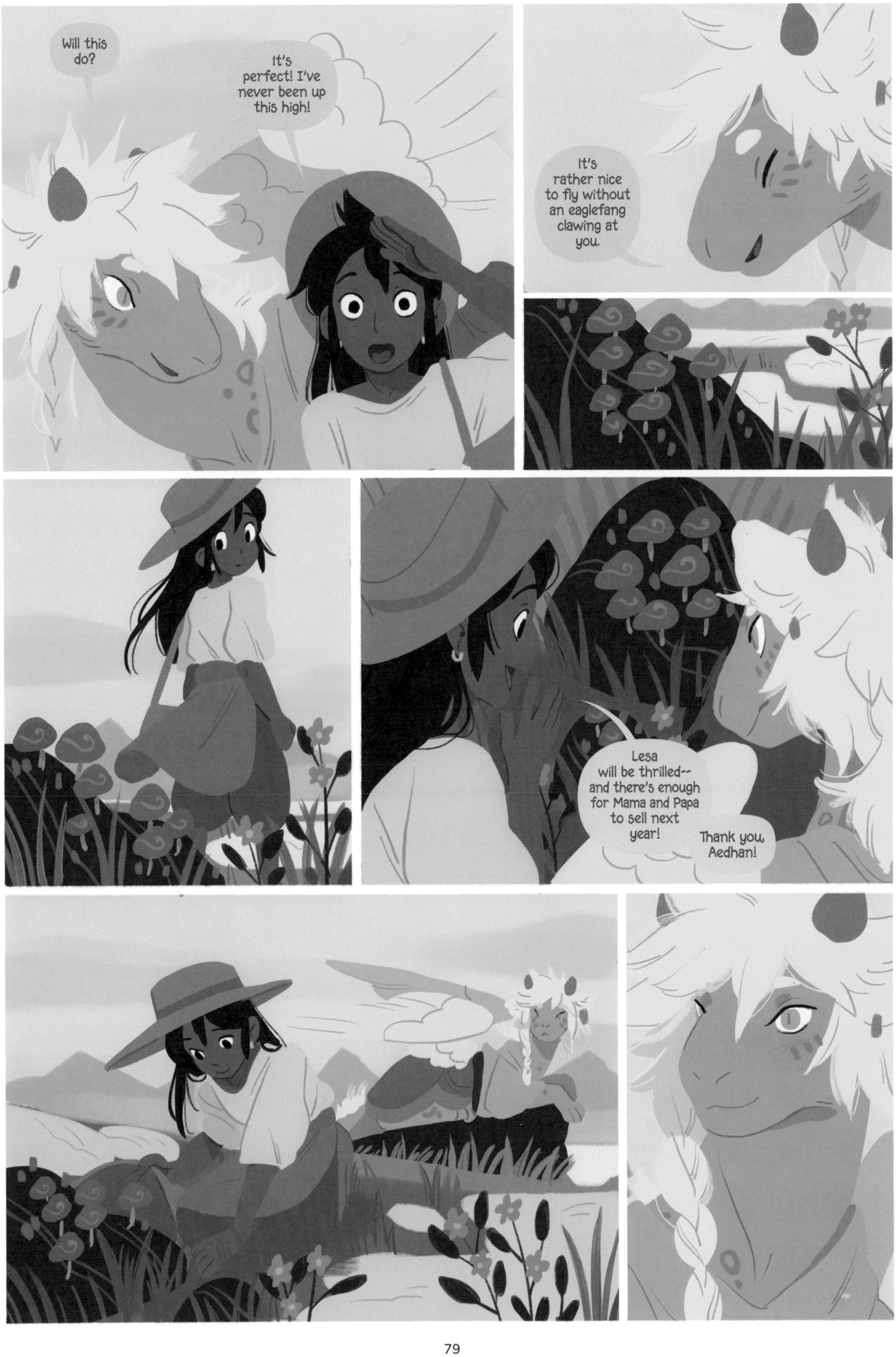
Will this do?
It's perfect! I've never been up this high!
It's rather nice to fly without an eaglefang clawing at you.
Lesa will be thrilled--and there's enough for Mama and Papa to sell next year!
Thank you, Aedhan!

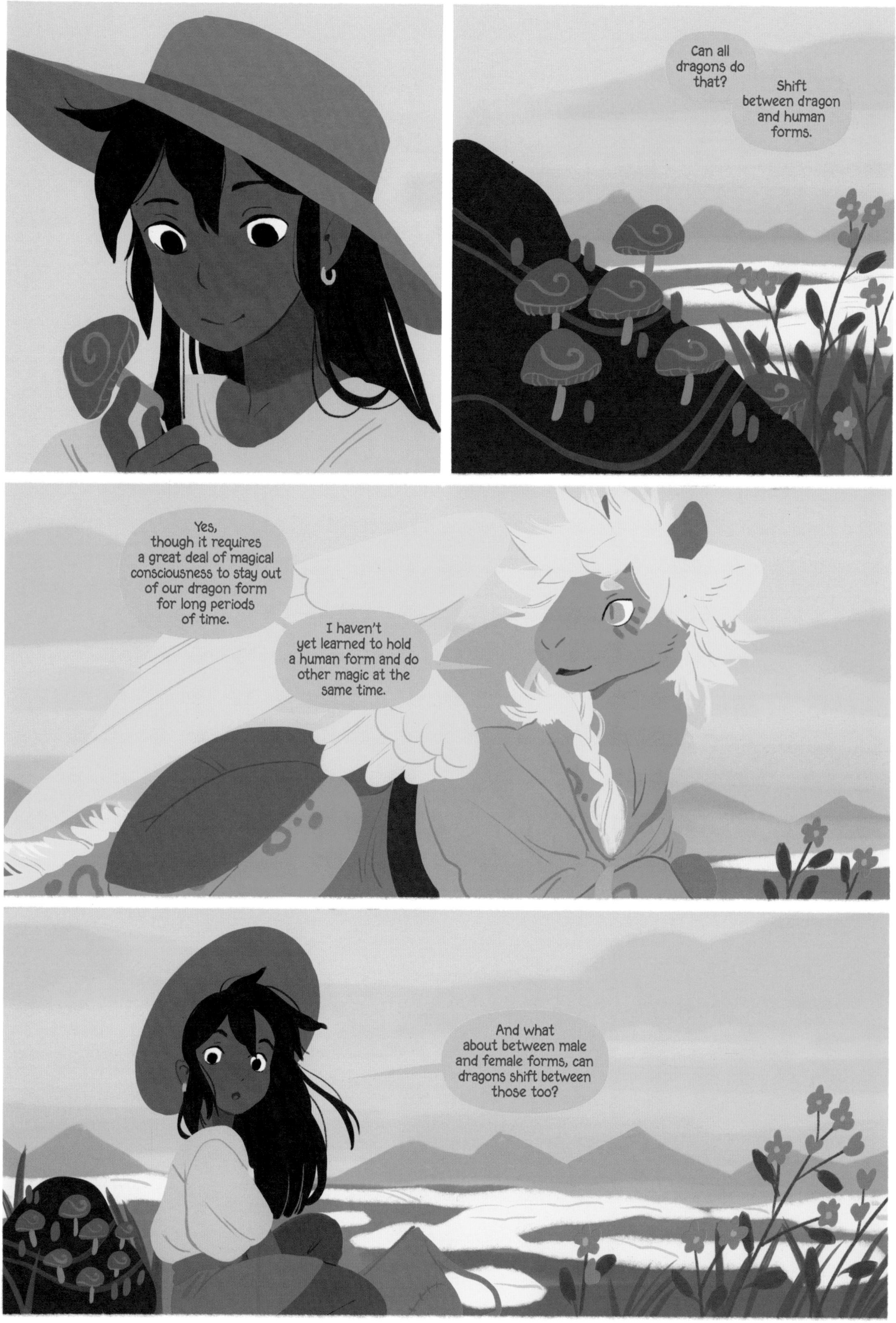
Can all dragons do that?
Shift between dragon and human forms.
Yes, though it requires a great deal of magical consciousness to stay out of our dragon form for long periods of time.
I haven't yet learned to hold a human form and do other magic at the same time.
And what about between male and female forms, can dragons shift between those too?

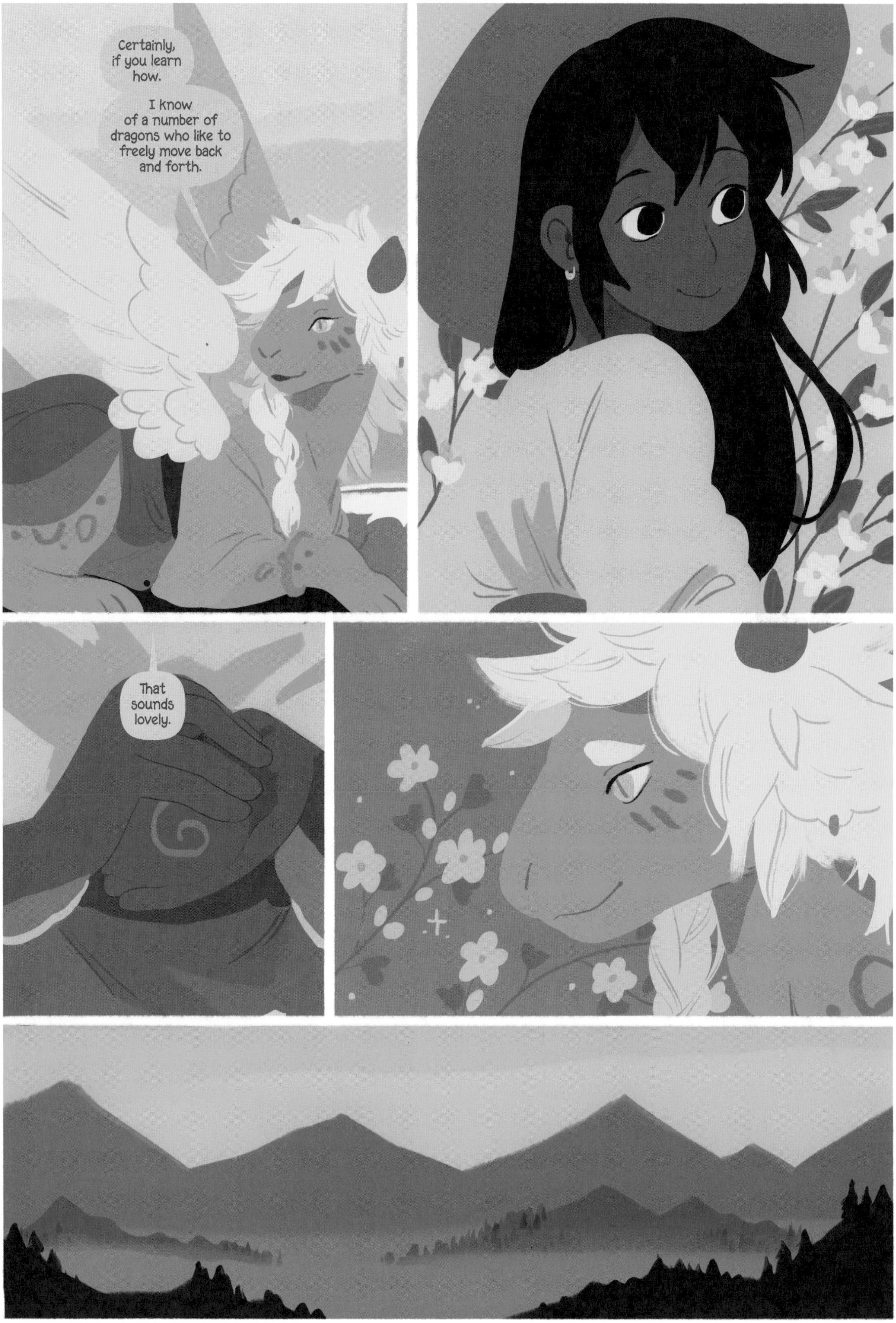
Certainly, if you learn how.
I know of a number of dragons who like to freely move back and forth.
That sounds lovely.

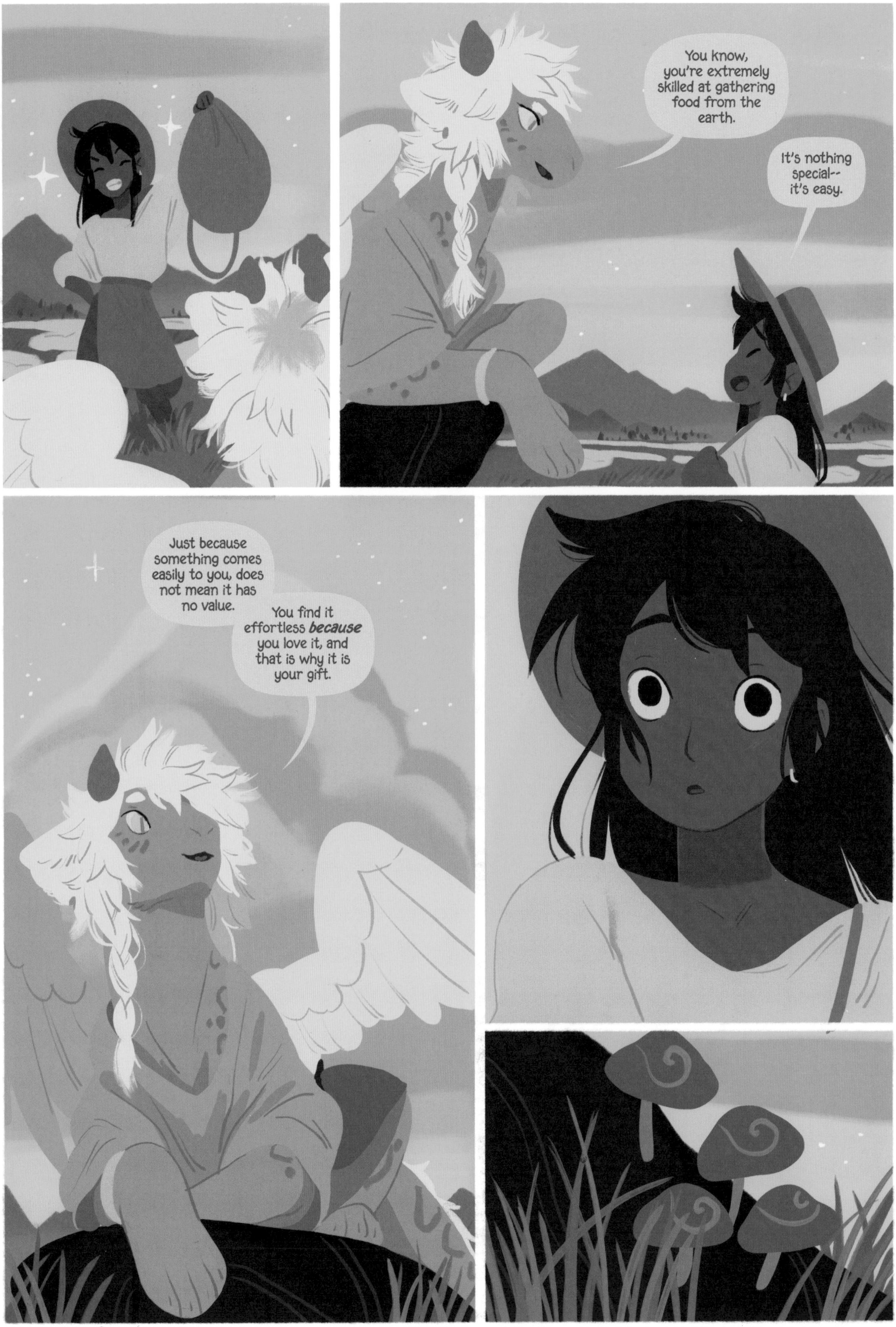

You know, you're extremely skilled at gathering food from the earth.
It's nothing special-- it's easy.
Just because something comes easily to you, does not mean it has no value.
You find it effortless ***because*** you love it, and that is why it is your gift.

Chapter Five

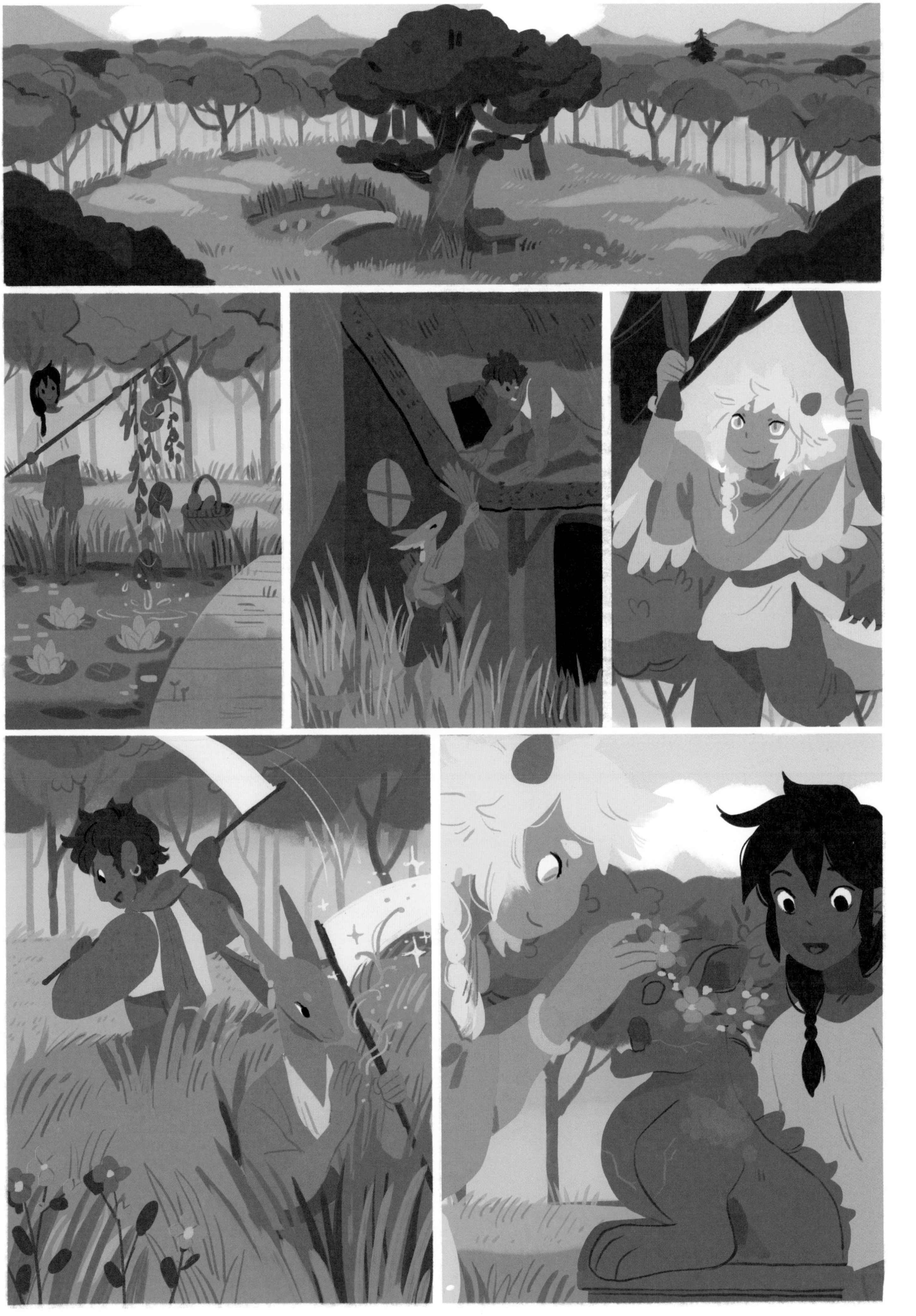

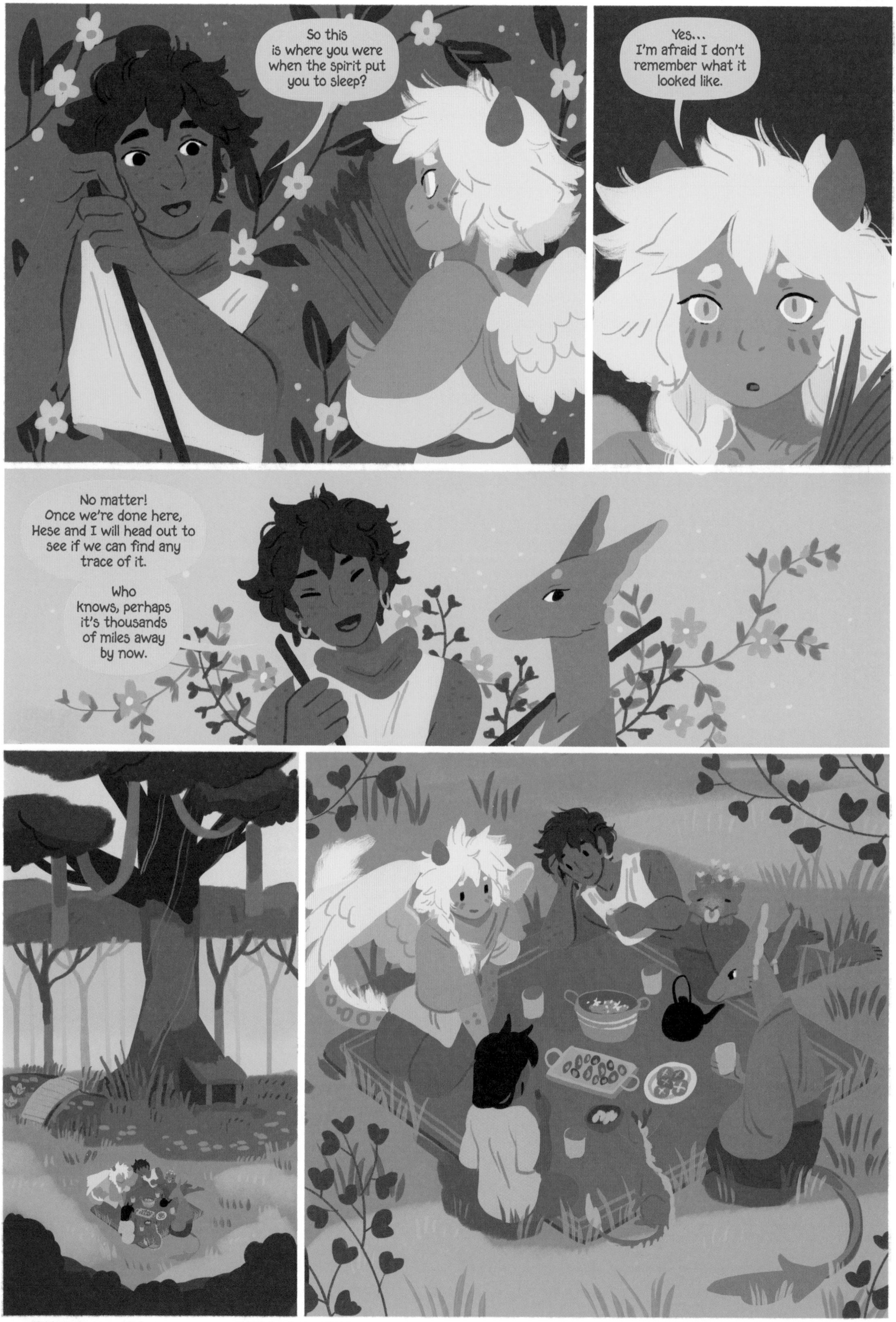
So this is where you were when the spirit put you to sleep?
Yes... I'm afraid I don't remember what it looked like.
No matter! Once we're done here, Hese and I will head out to see if we can find any trace of it.
Who knows, perhaps it's thousands of miles away by now.

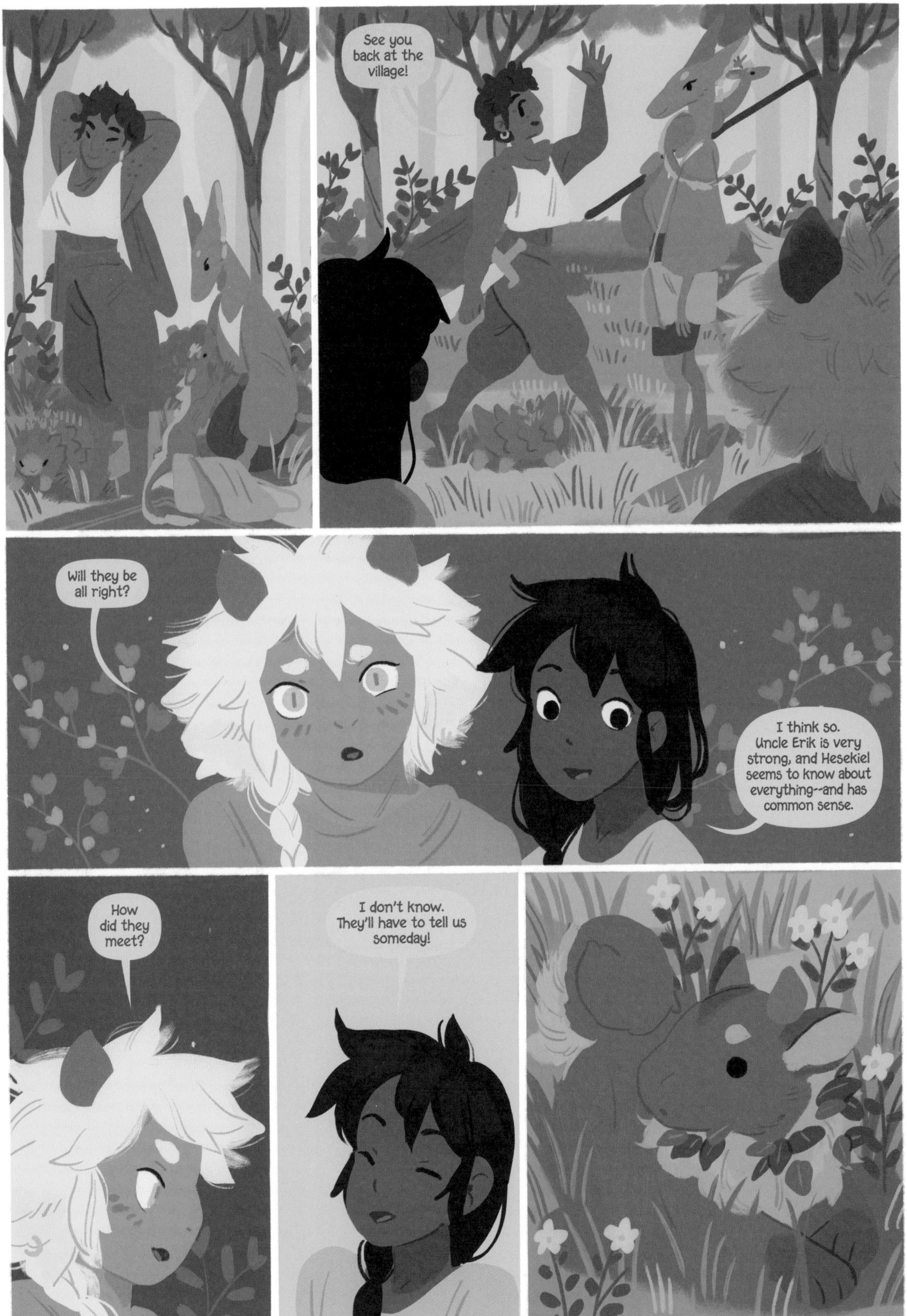
See you back at the village!
Will they be all right?
I think so. Uncle Erik is very strong, and Hesekiel seems to know about everything--and has common sense.
How did they meet?
I don't know. They'll have to tell us someday!

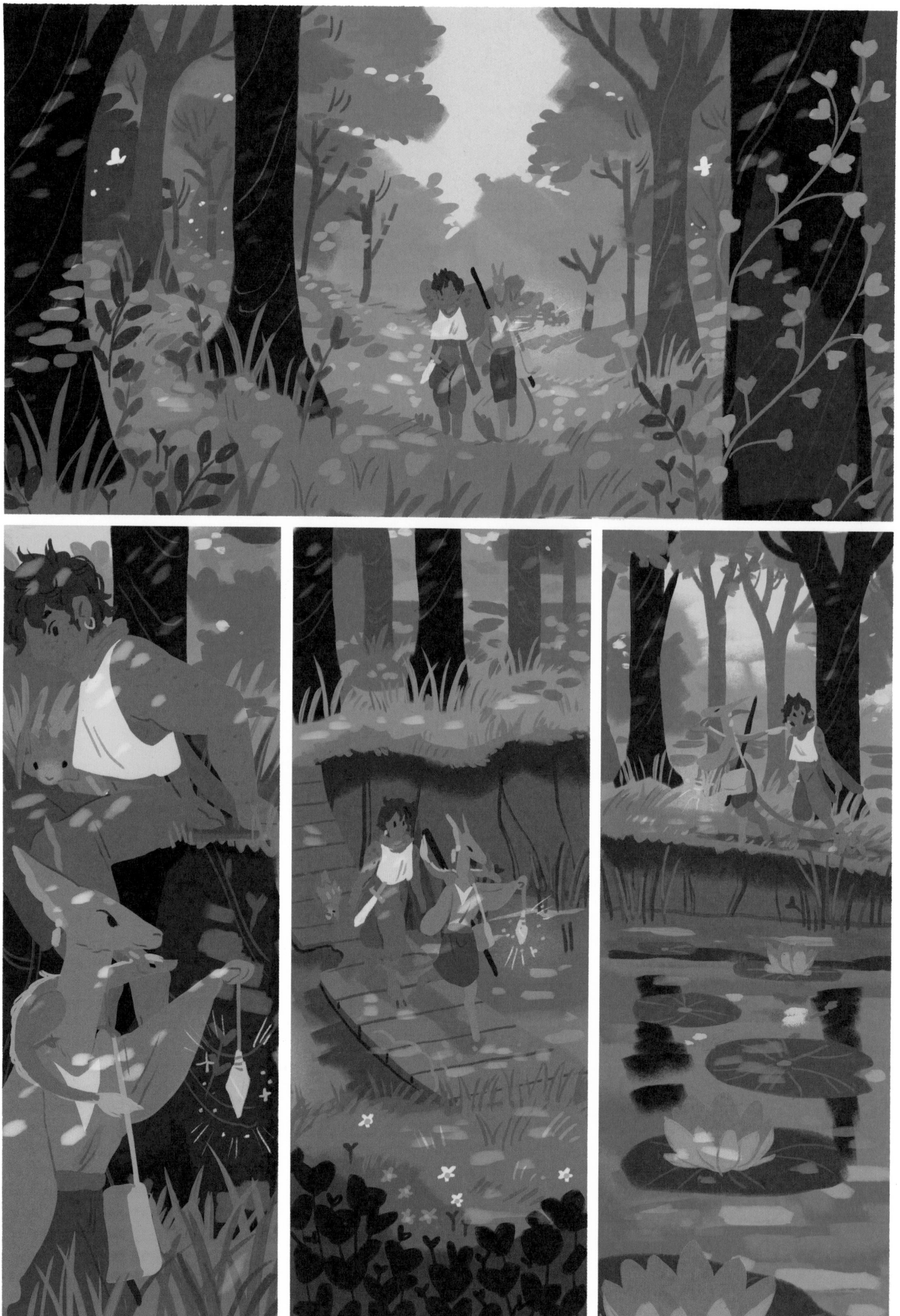

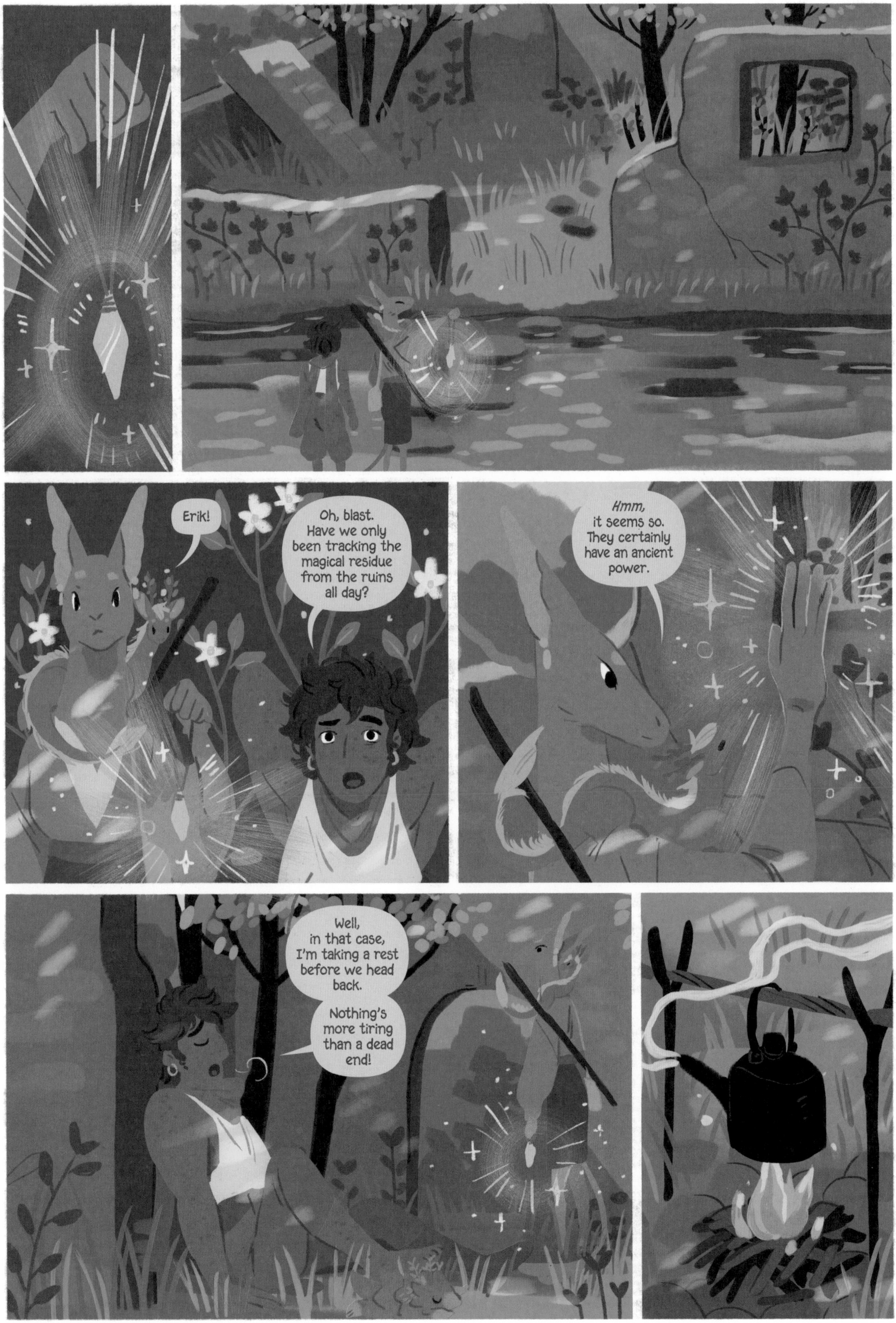
Erik!
Oh, blast. Have we only been tracking the magical residue from the ruins all day?
Hmm, it seems so. They certainly have an ancient power.
Well, in that case, I'm taking a rest before we head back.
Nothing's more tiring than a dead end!

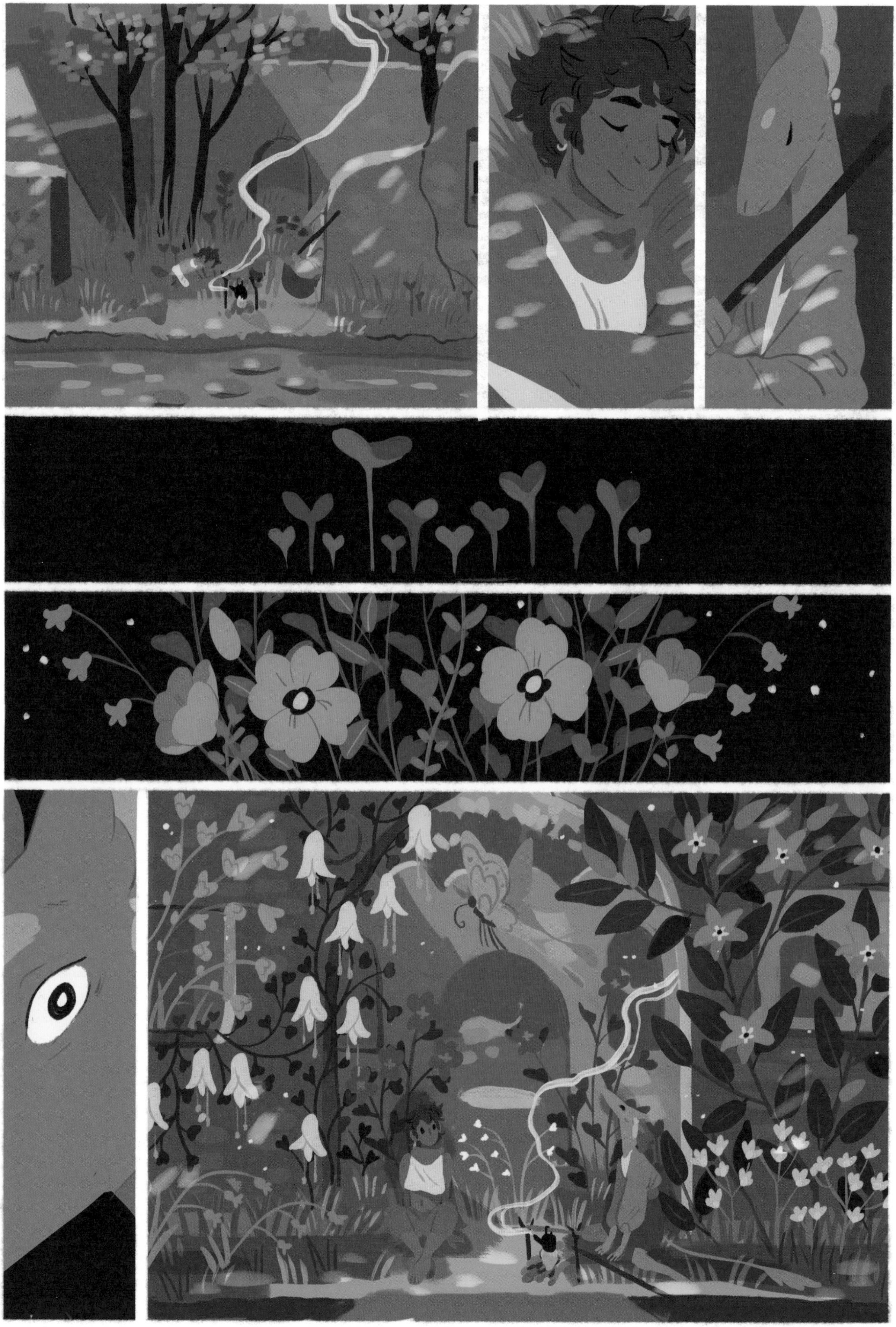

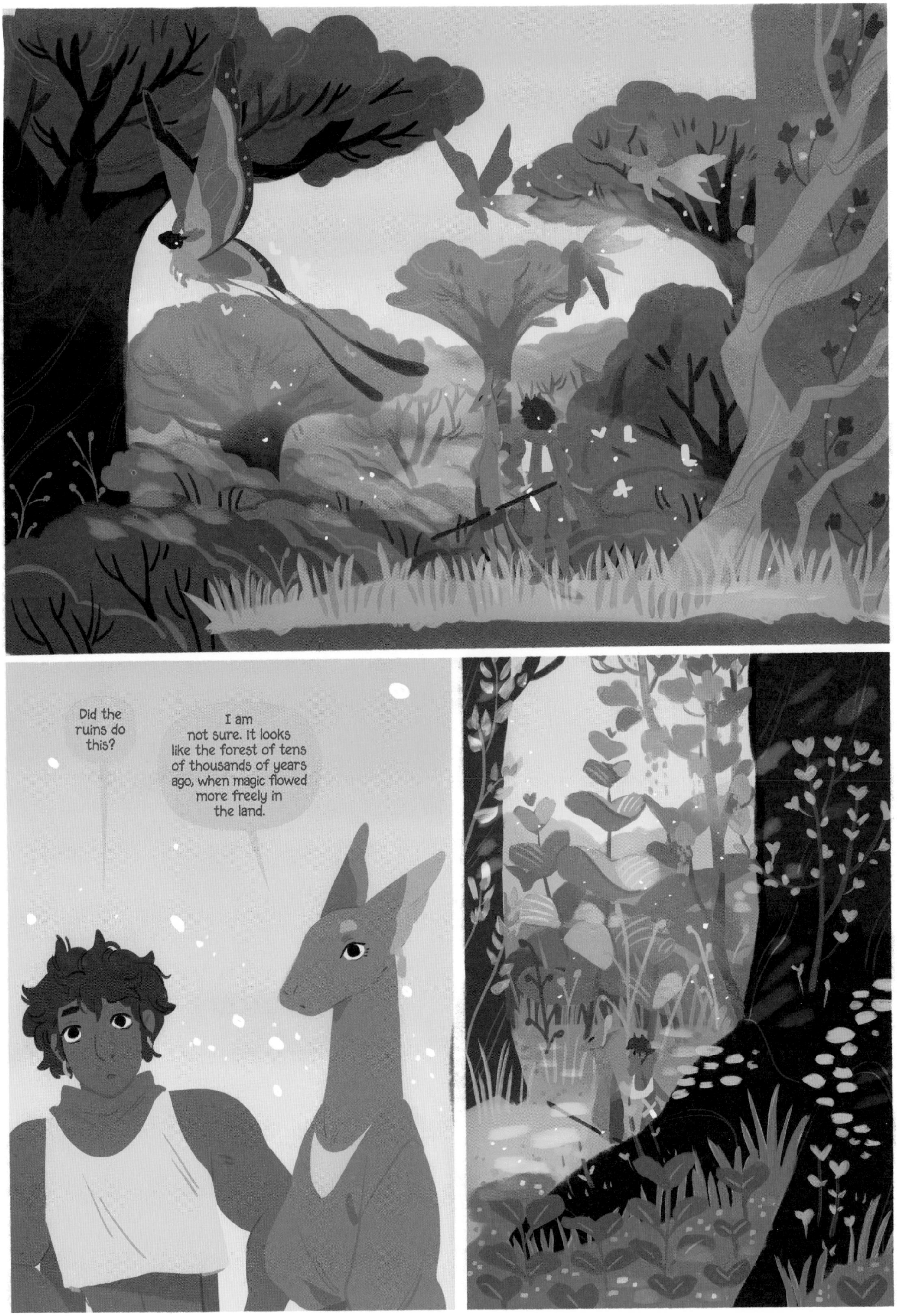
Did the ruins do this?
I am not sure. It looks like the forest of tens of thousands of years ago, when magic flowed more freely in the land.

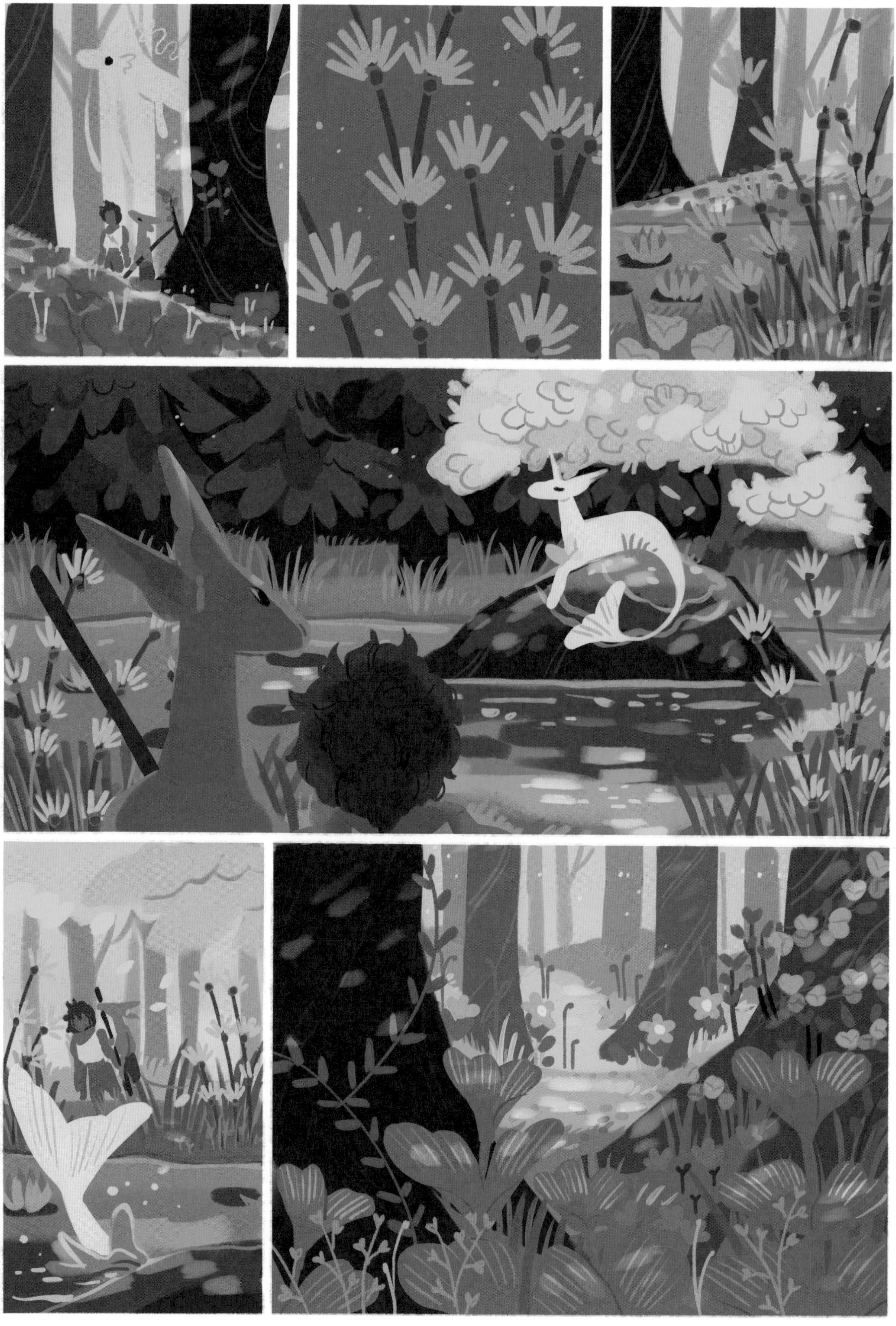

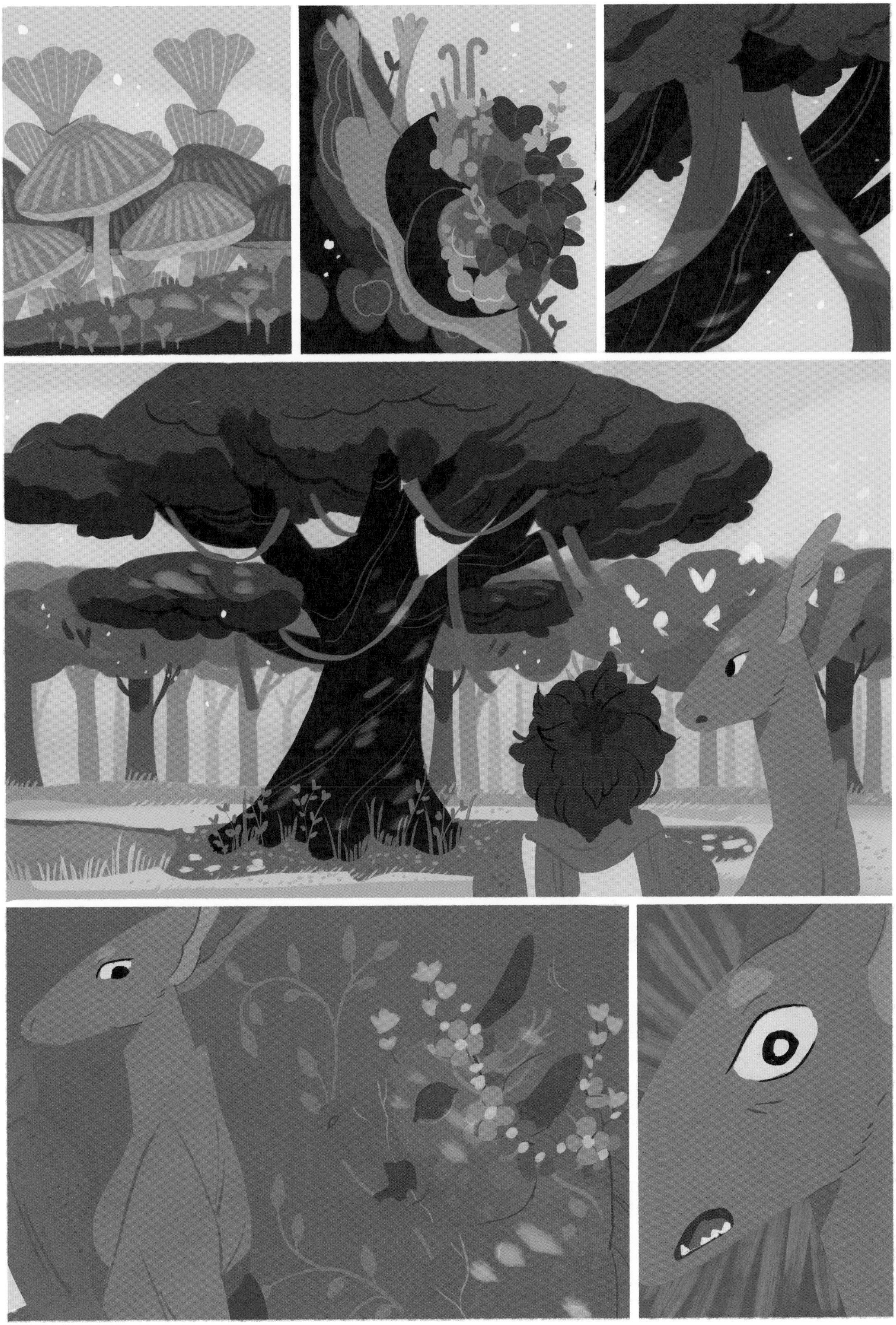

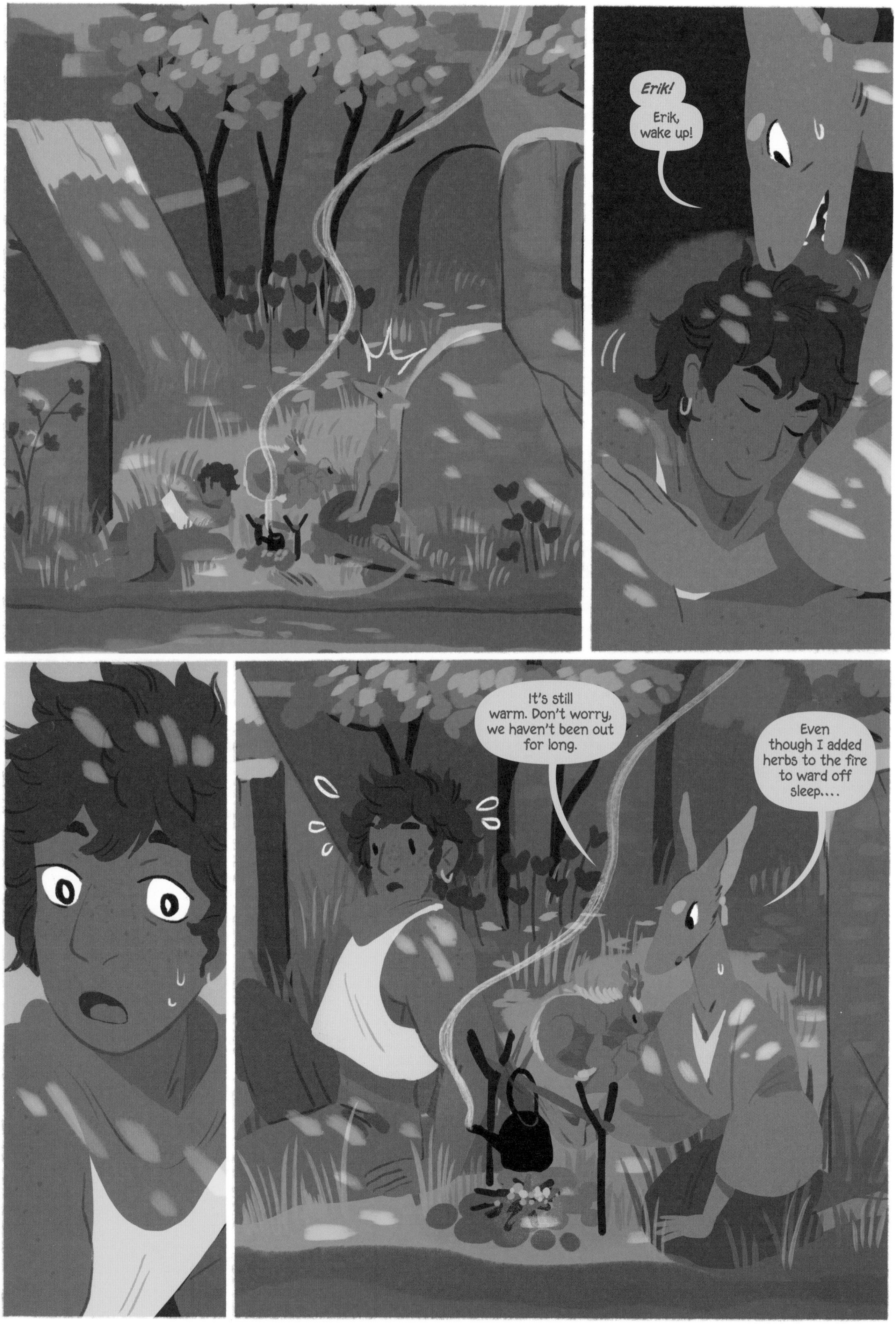
Erik!
Erik, wake up!
It's still warm. Don't worry, we haven't been out for long.
Even though I added herbs to the fire to ward off sleep....

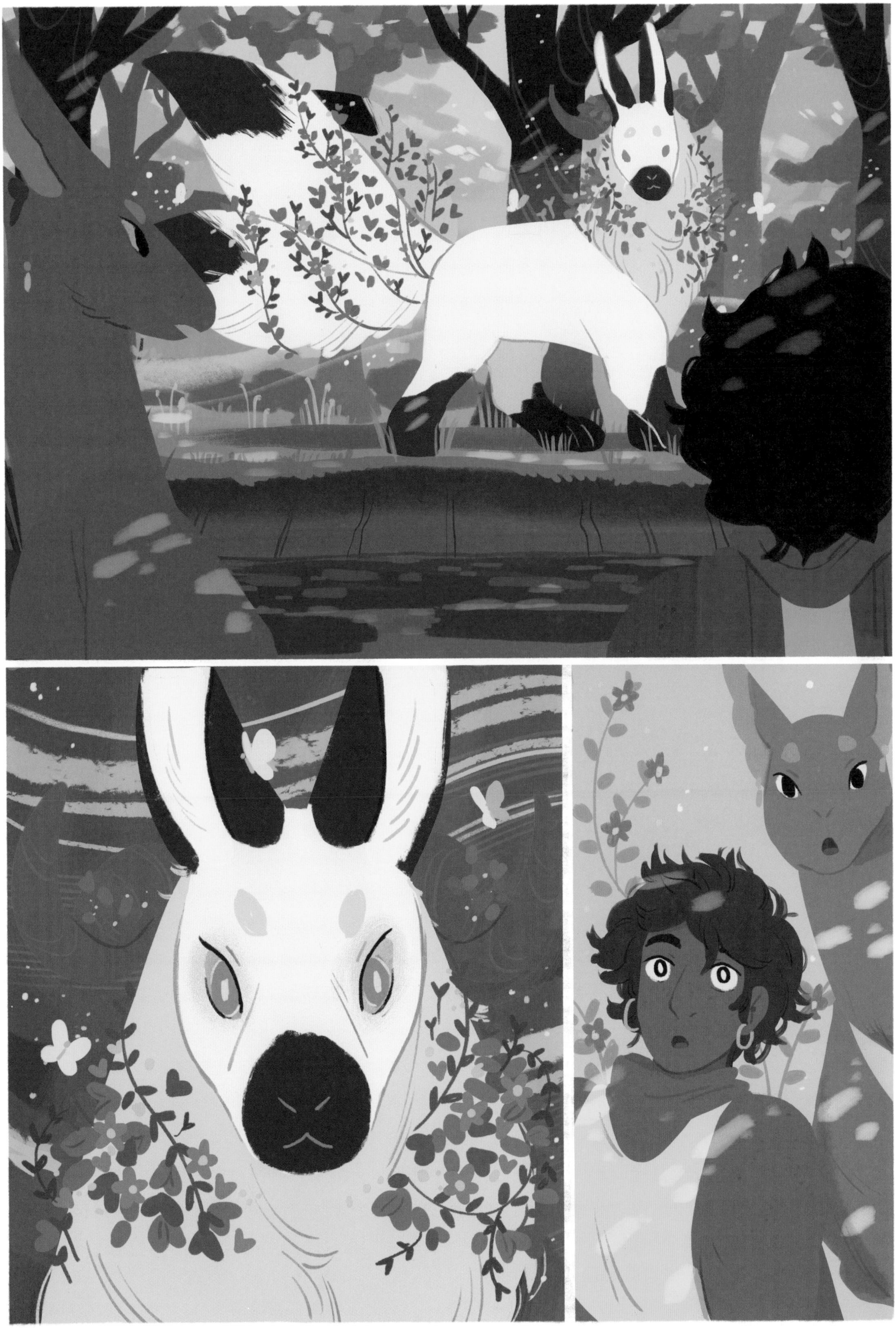

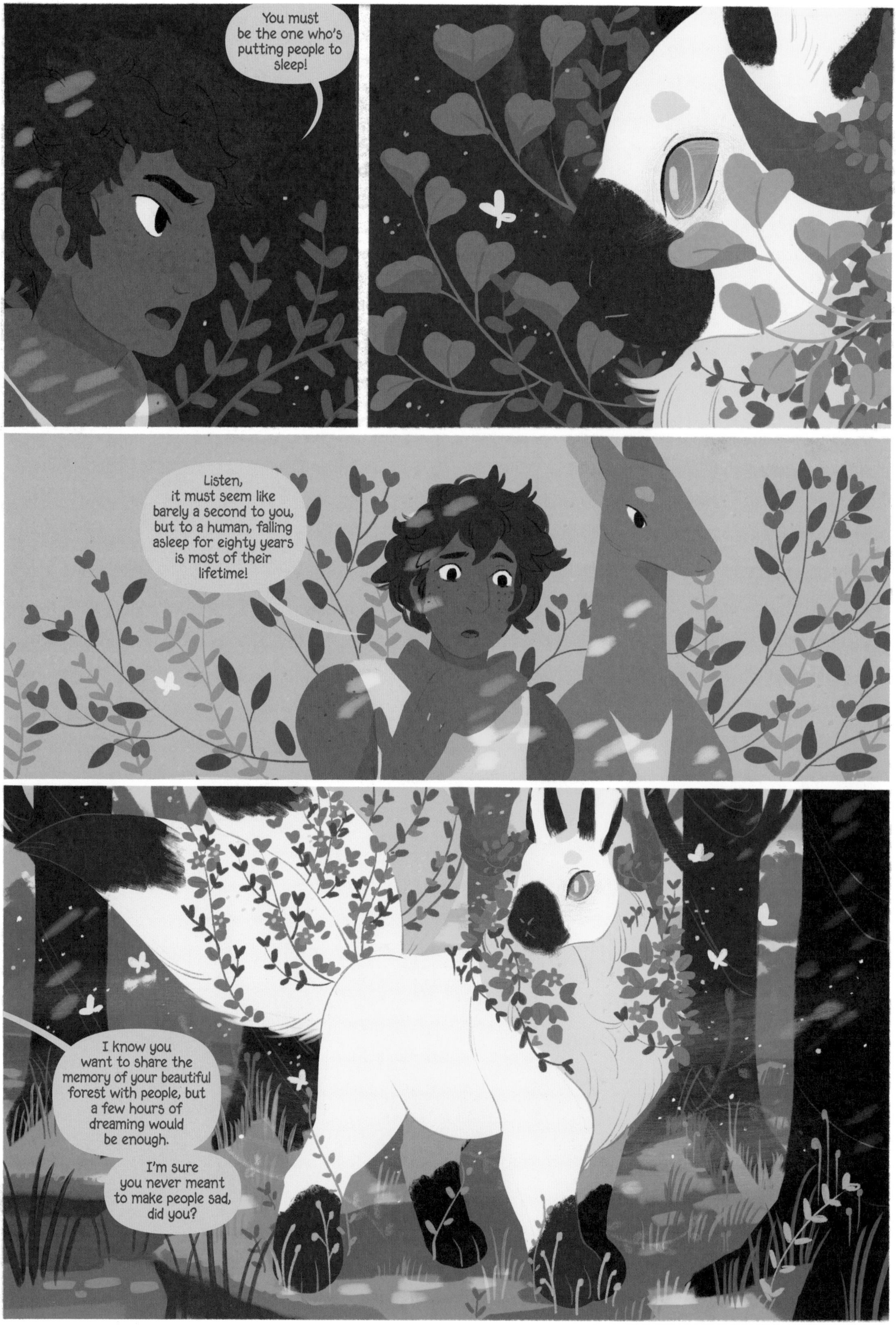
You must be the one who's putting people to sleep!
Listen, it must seem like barely a second to you, but to a human, falling asleep for eighty years is most of their lifetime!
I know you want to share the memory of your beautiful forest with people, but a few hours of dreaming would be enough.
I'm sure you never meant to make people sad, did you?

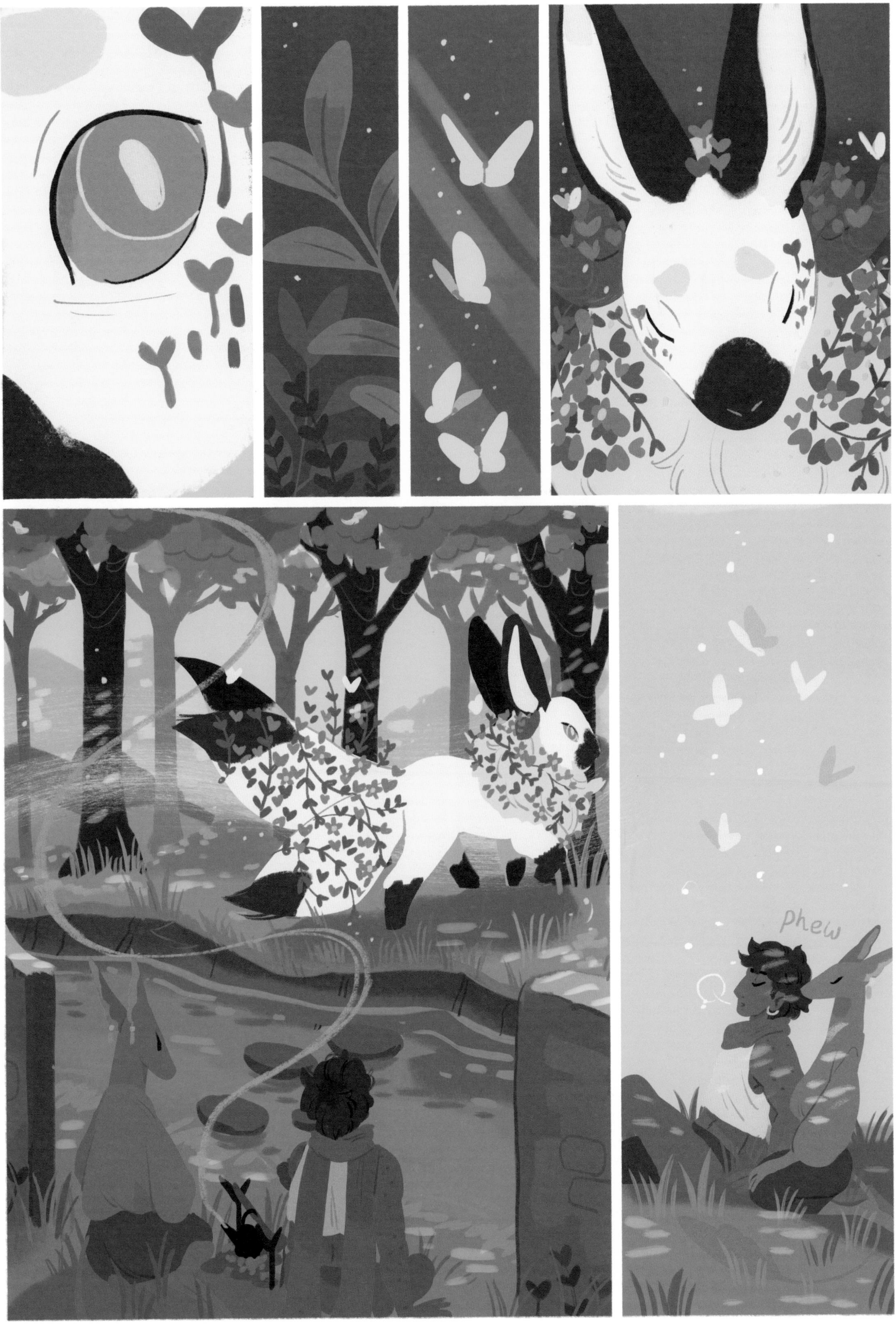
phew

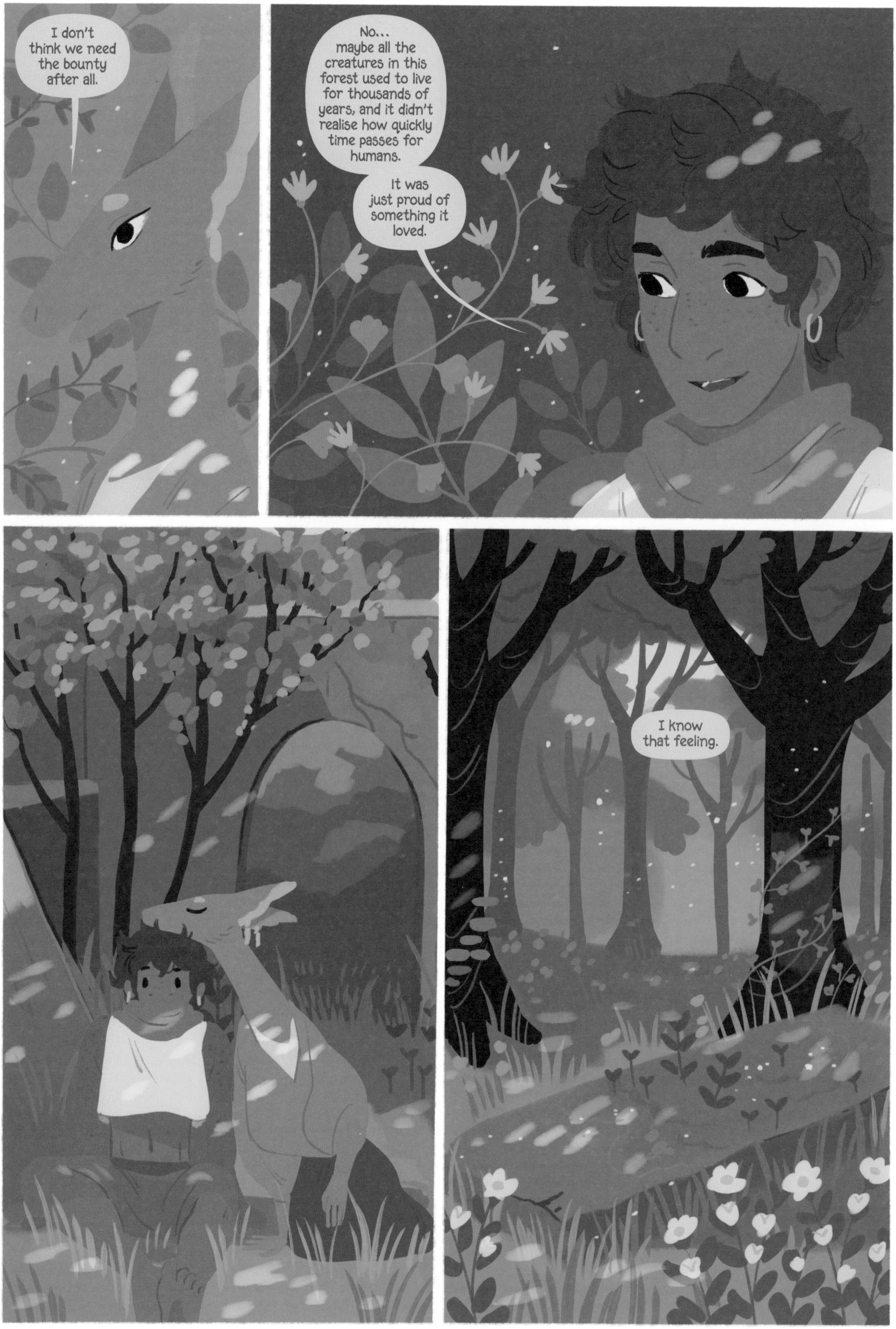
I don't think we need the bounty after all.
No... maybe all the creatures in this forest used to live for thousands of years, and it didn't realise how quickly time passes for humans.
It was just proud of something it loved.
I know that feeling.

Chapter Six

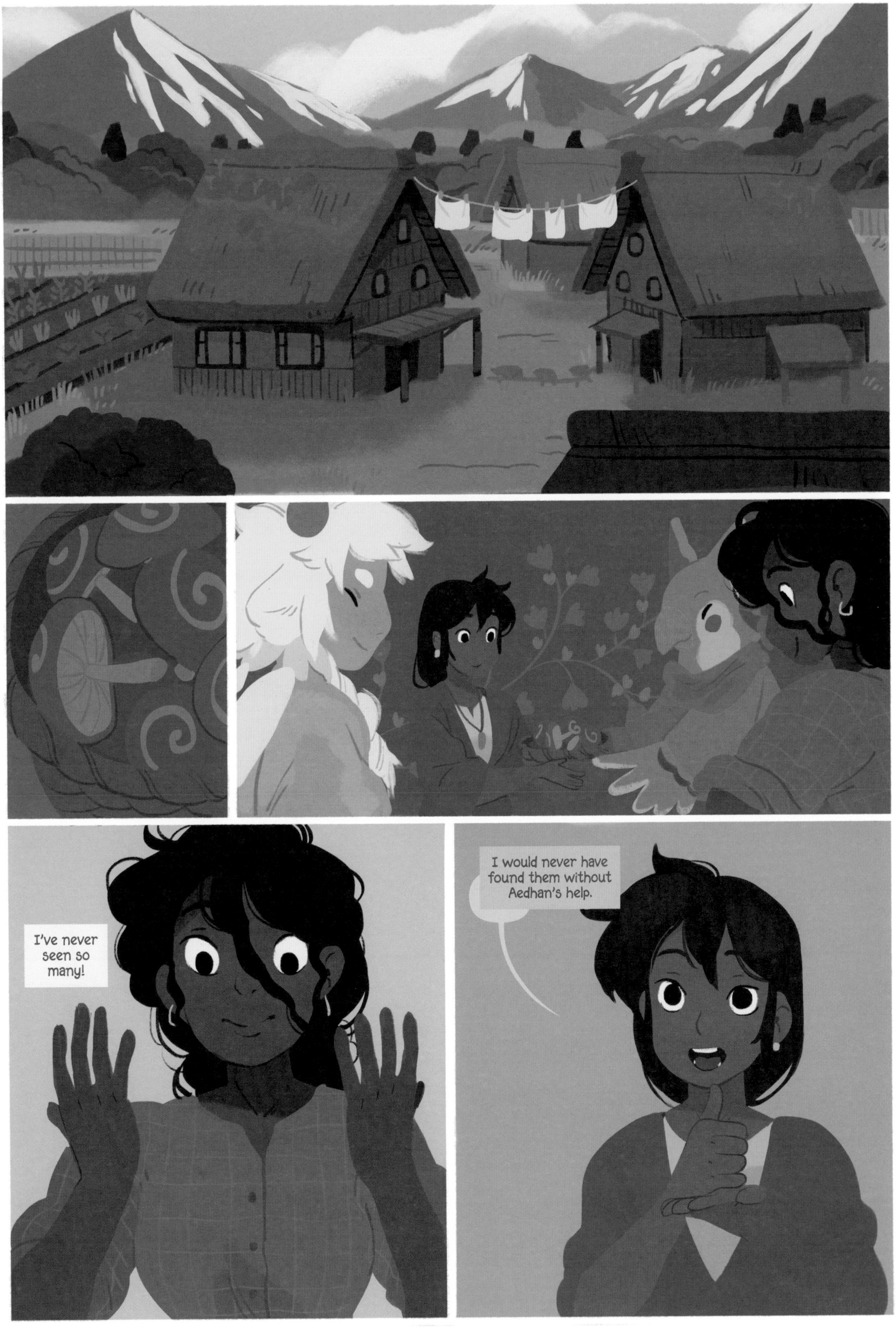
I've never seen so many!
I would never have found them without Aedhan's help.

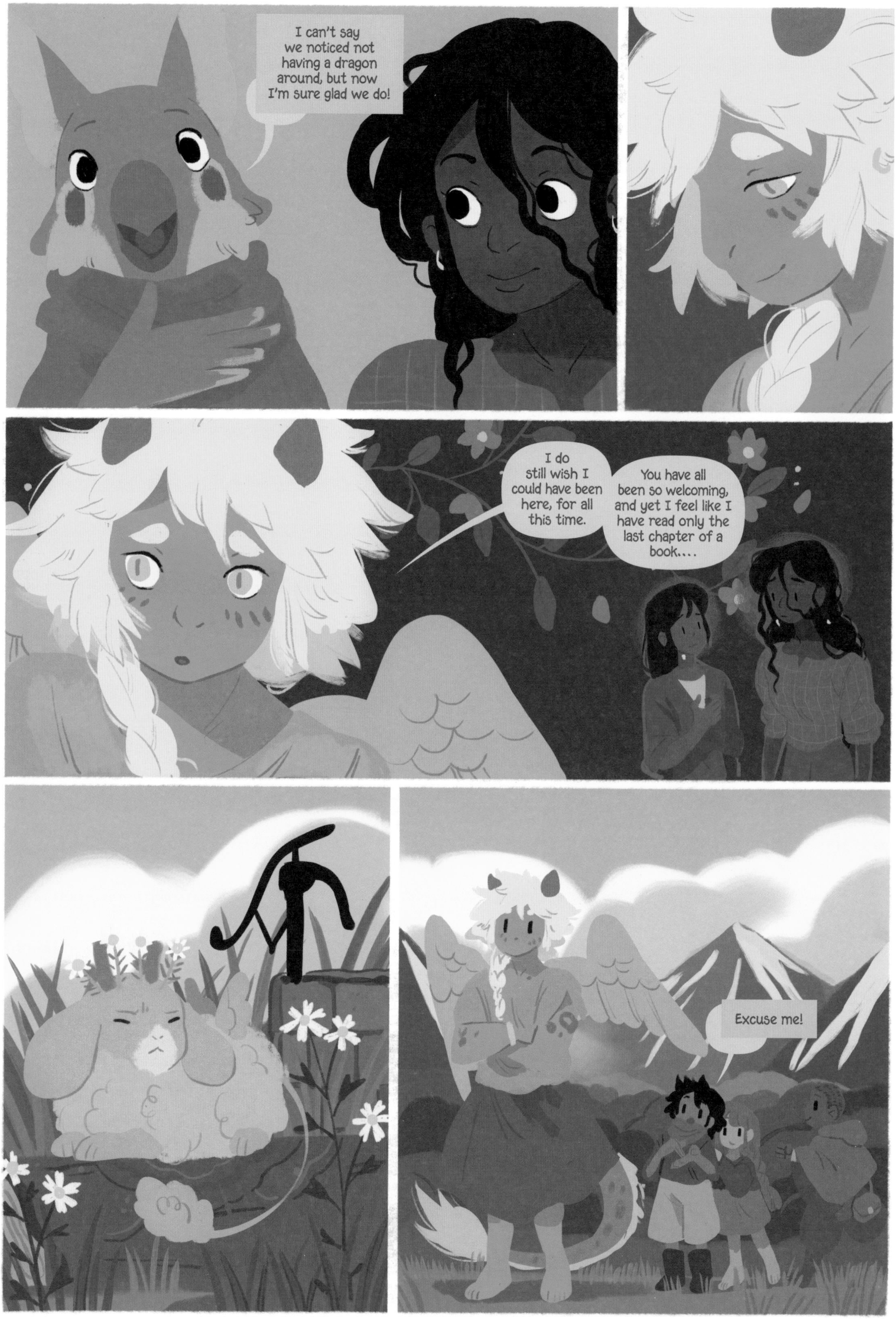
I can't say we noticed not having a dragon around, but now I'm sure glad we do!
I do still wish I could have been here, for all this time.
You have all been so welcoming, and yet I feel like I have read only the last chapter of a book....
Excuse me!

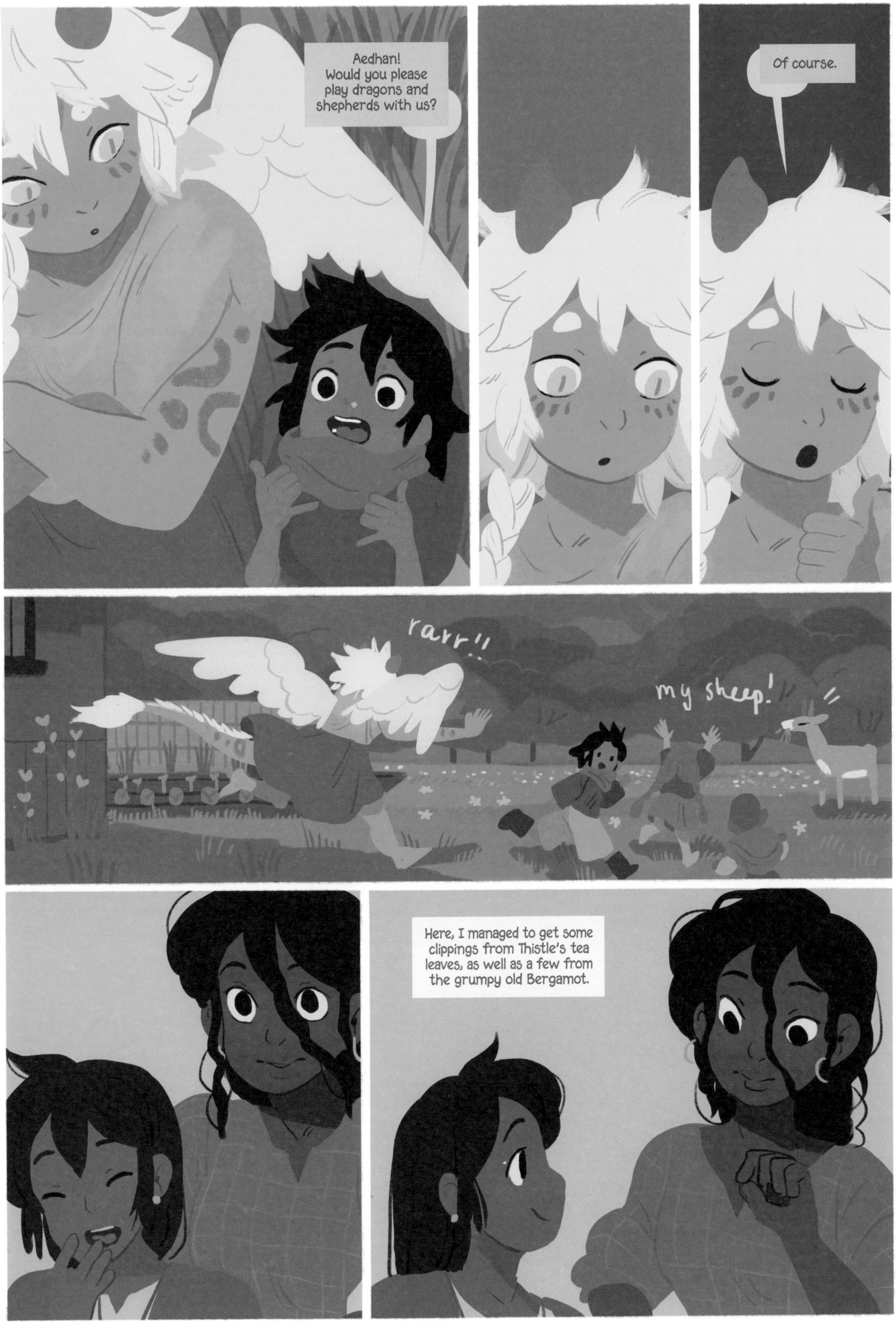
Aedhan! Would you please play dragons and shepherds with us?
Of course.
rarr!!
my sheep!
Here, I managed to get some clippings from Thistle's tea leaves, as well as a few from the grumpy old Bergamot.

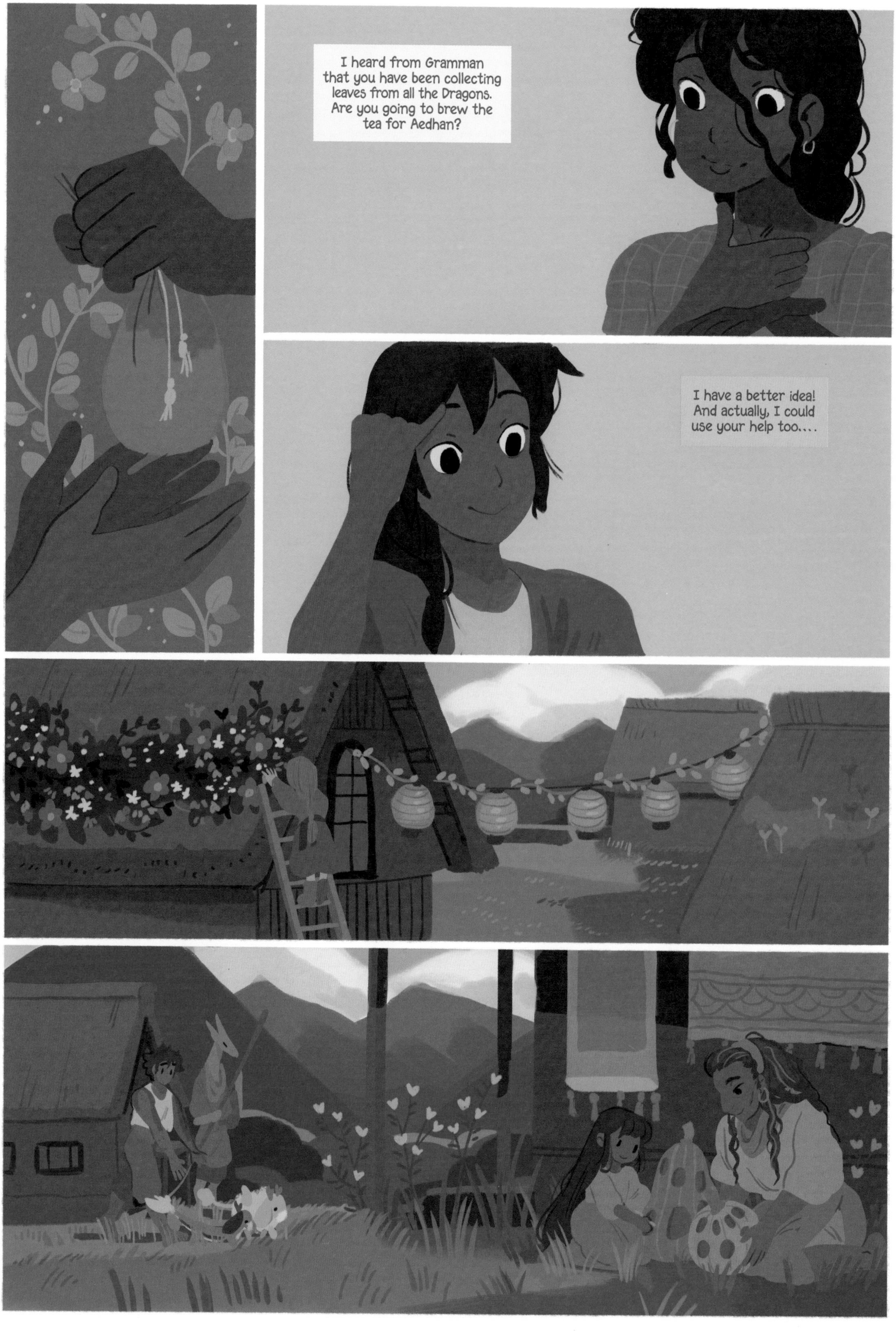
I heard from Gramman that you have been collecting leaves from all the Dragons. Are you going to brew the tea for Aedhan?
I have a better idea! And actually, I could use your help too....

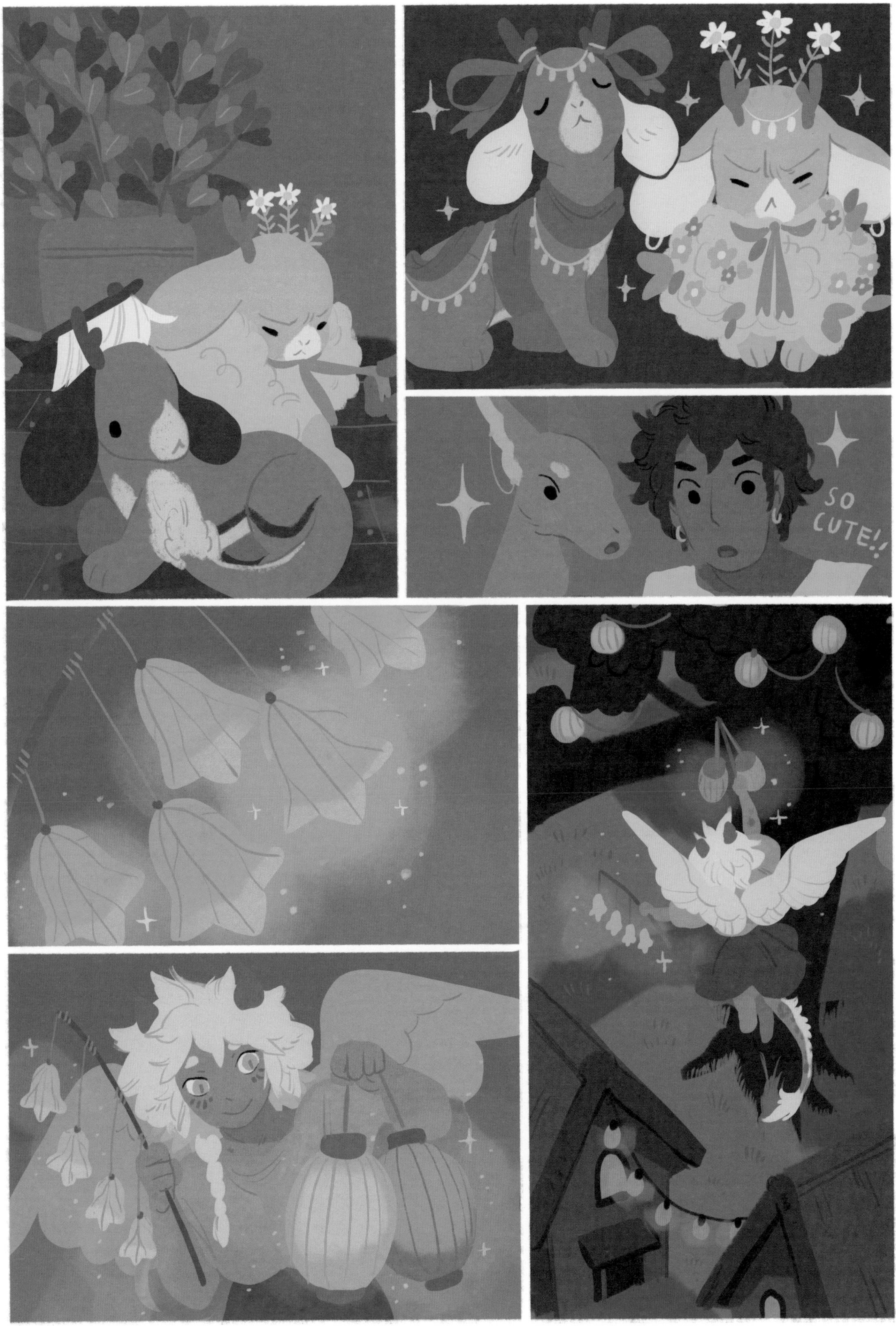
SO CUTE!!

D'you want any help in here?

No, thank you, your wings will be more useful outside!

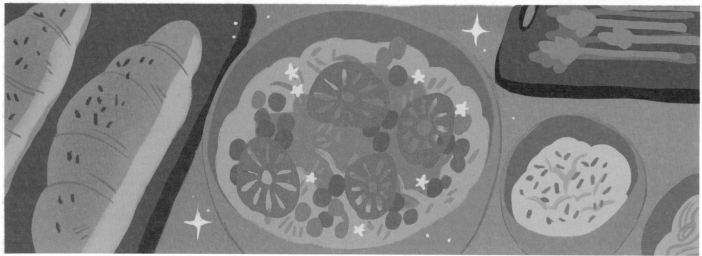

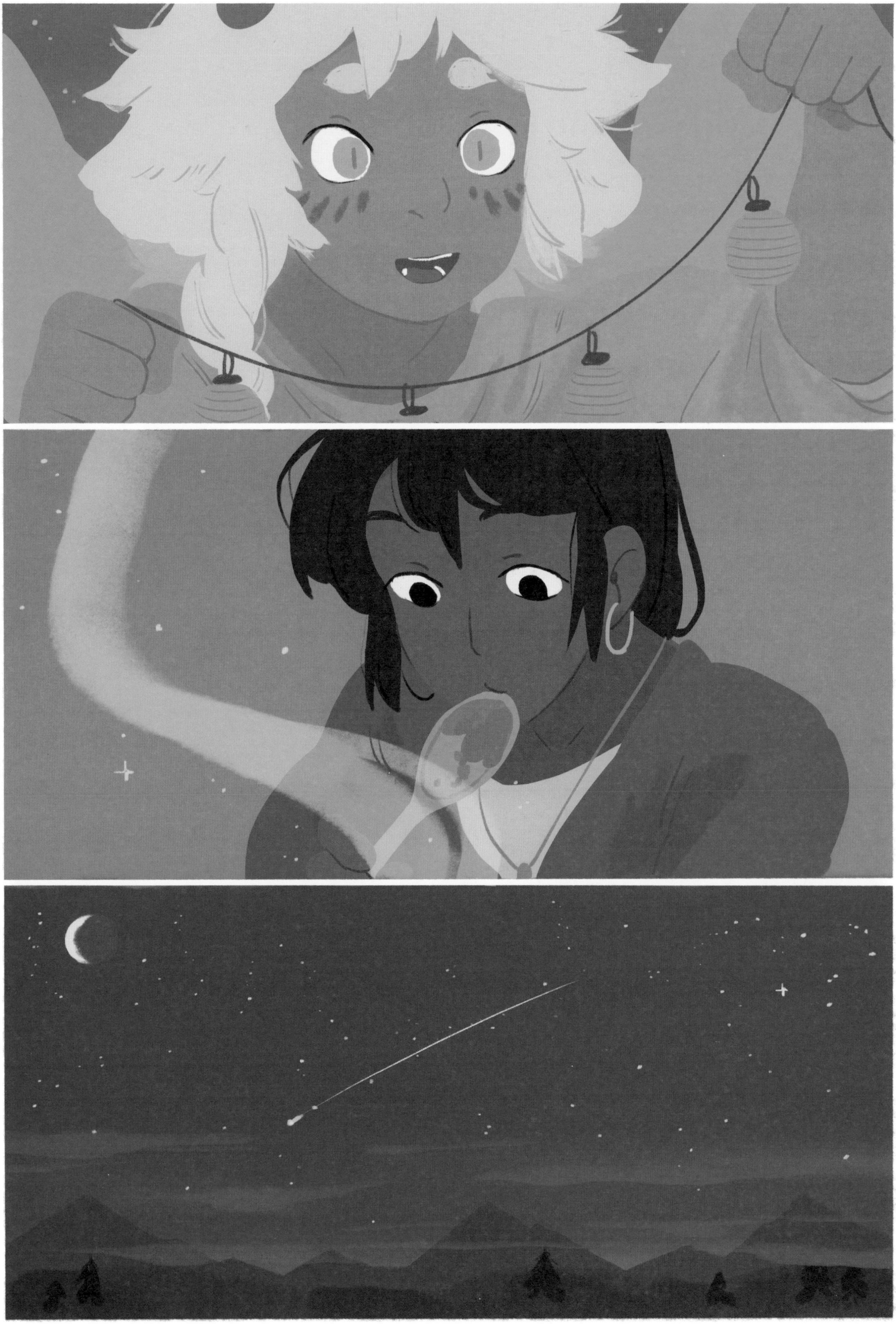

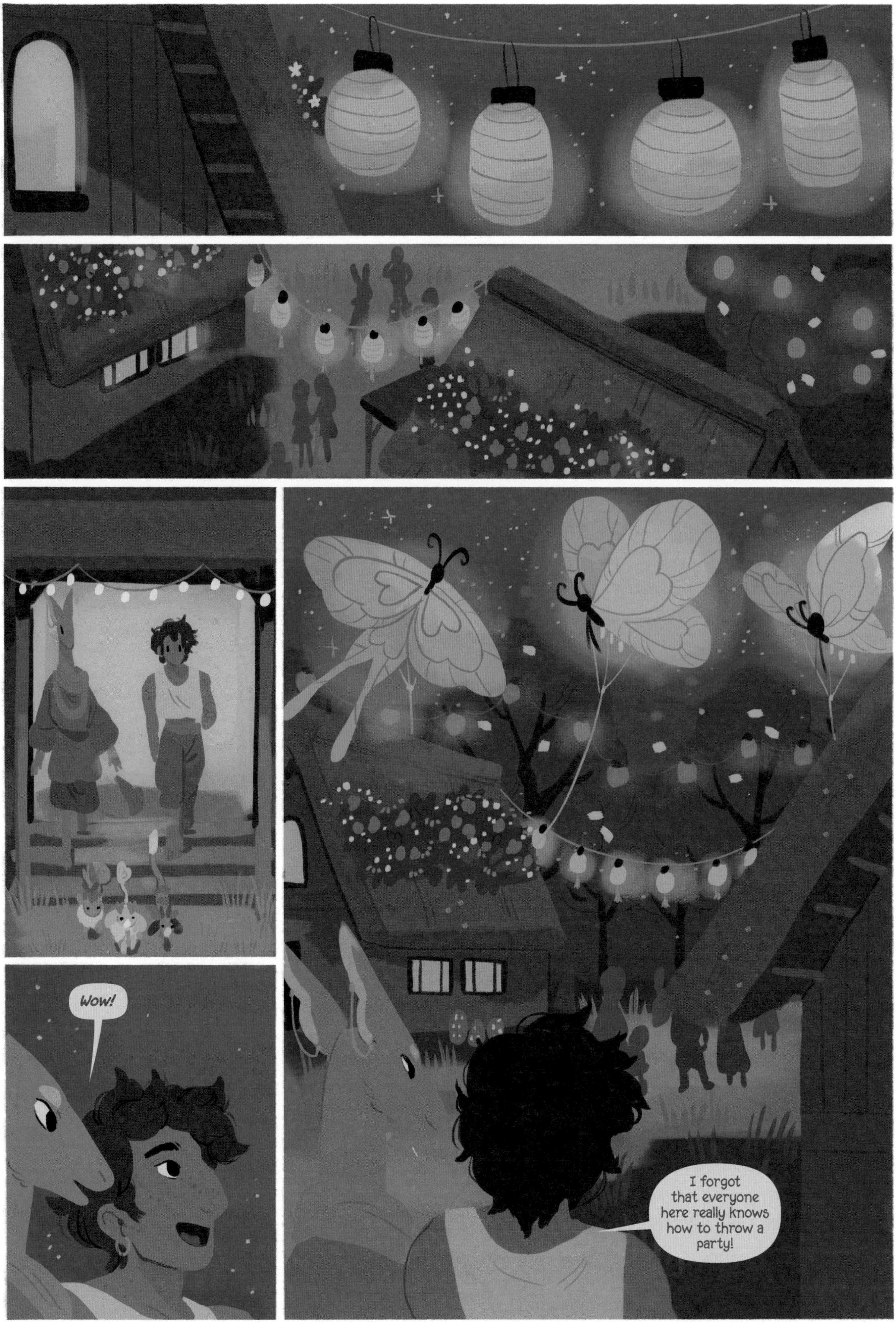
Wow!
I forgot that everyone here really knows how to throw a party!

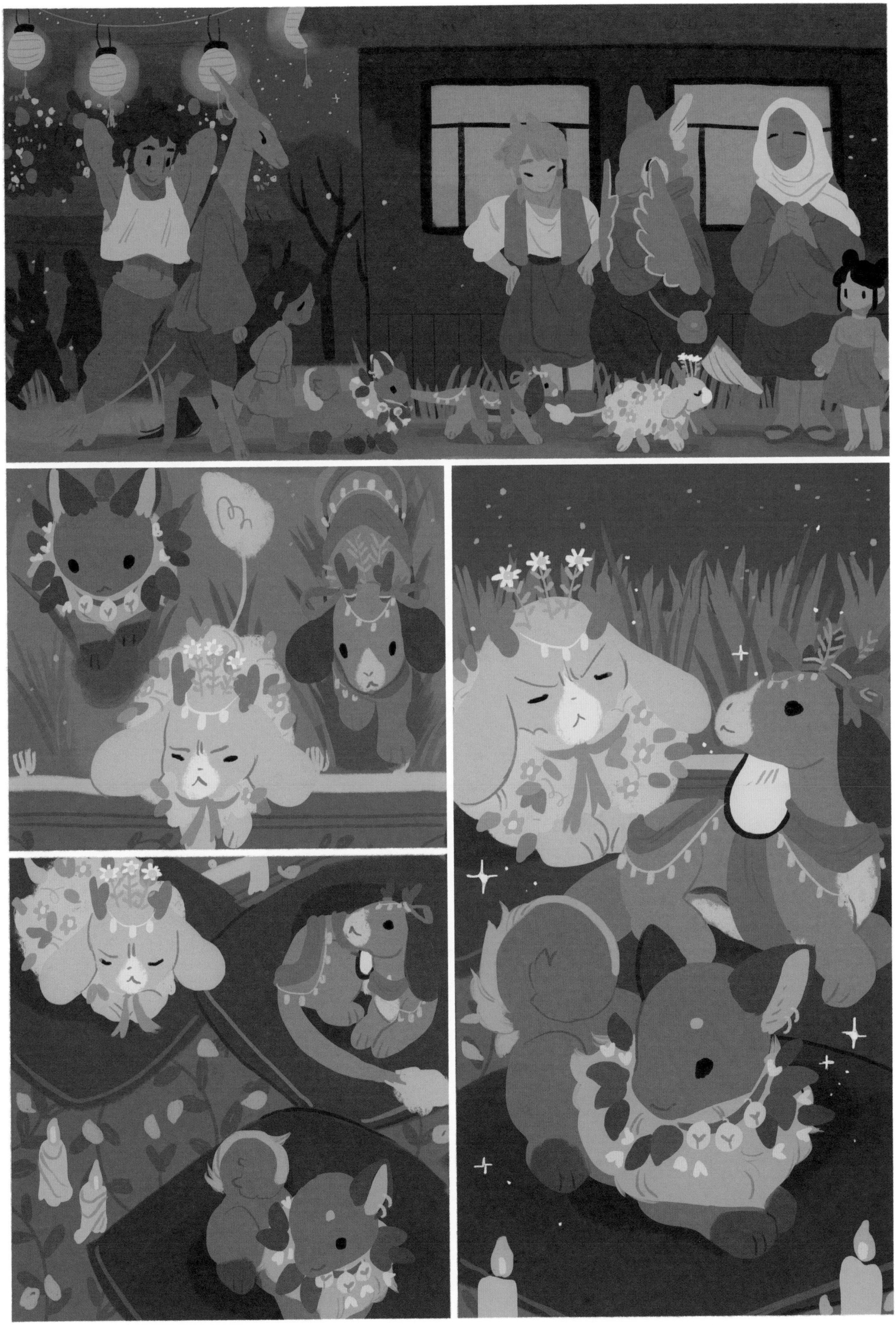

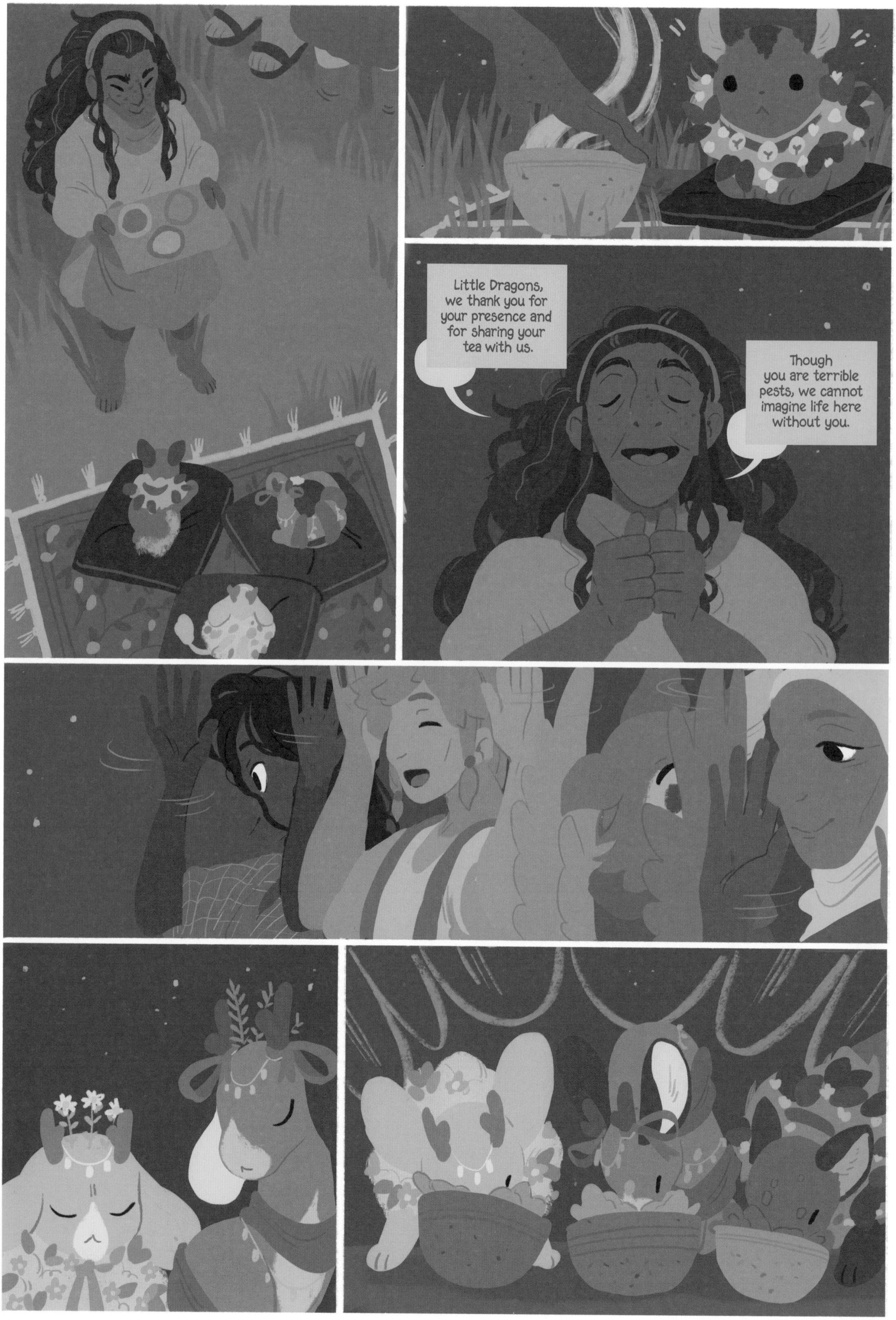
Little Dragons, we thank you for your presence and for sharing your tea with us.
Though you are terrible pests, we cannot imagine life here without you.

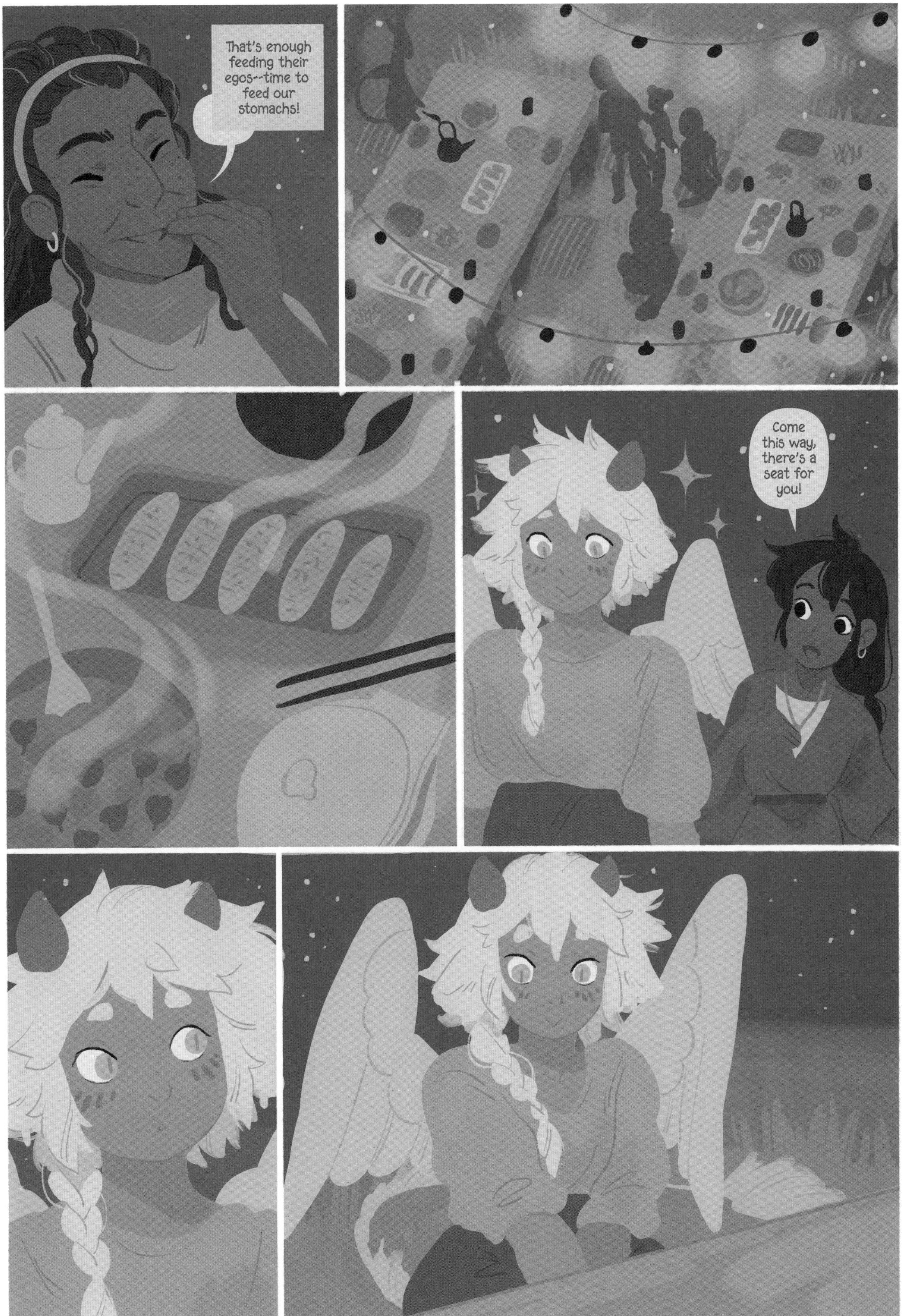
That's enough feeding their egos--time to feed our stomachs!
Come this way, there's a seat for you!

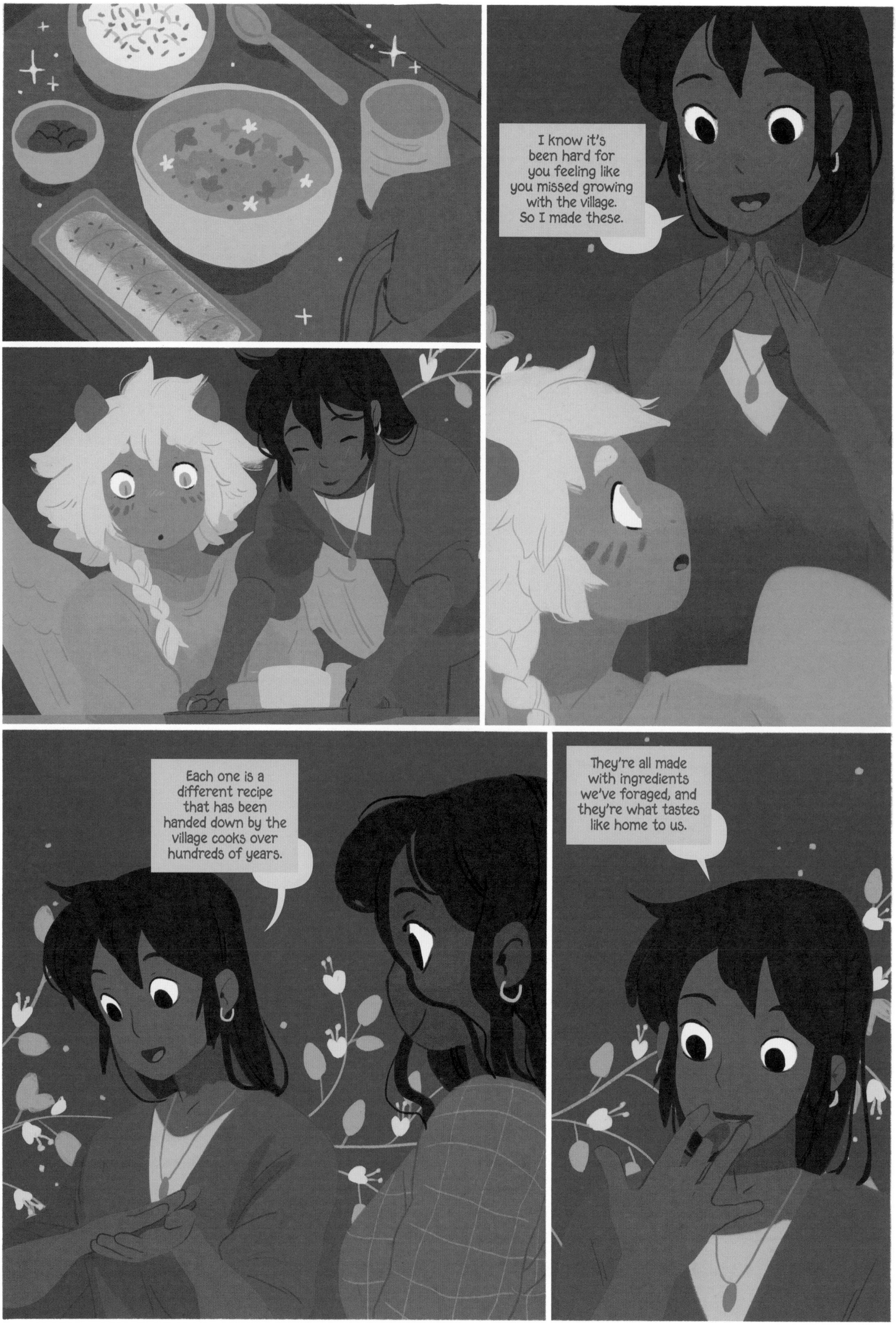
I know it's been hard for you feeling like you missed growing with the village. So I made these.
Each one is a different recipe that has been handed down by the village cooks over hundreds of years.
They're all made with ingredients we've foraged, and they're what tastes like home to us.

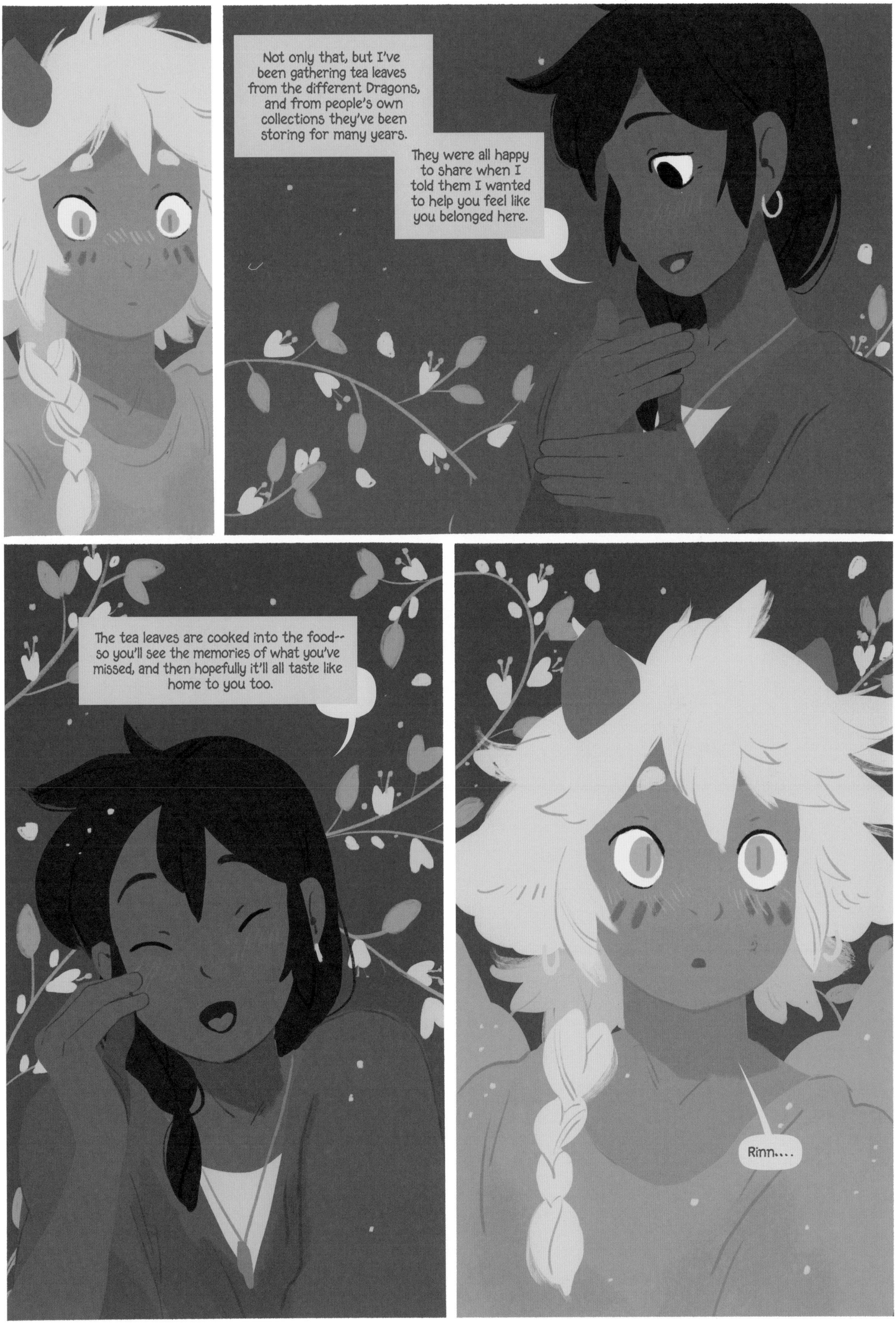
Not only that, but I've been gathering tea leaves from the different Dragons, and from people's own collections they've been storing for many years.
They were all happy to share when I told them I wanted to help you feel like you belonged here.
The tea leaves are cooked into the food--so you'll see the memories of what you've missed, and then hopefully it'll all taste like home to you too.
Rinn....

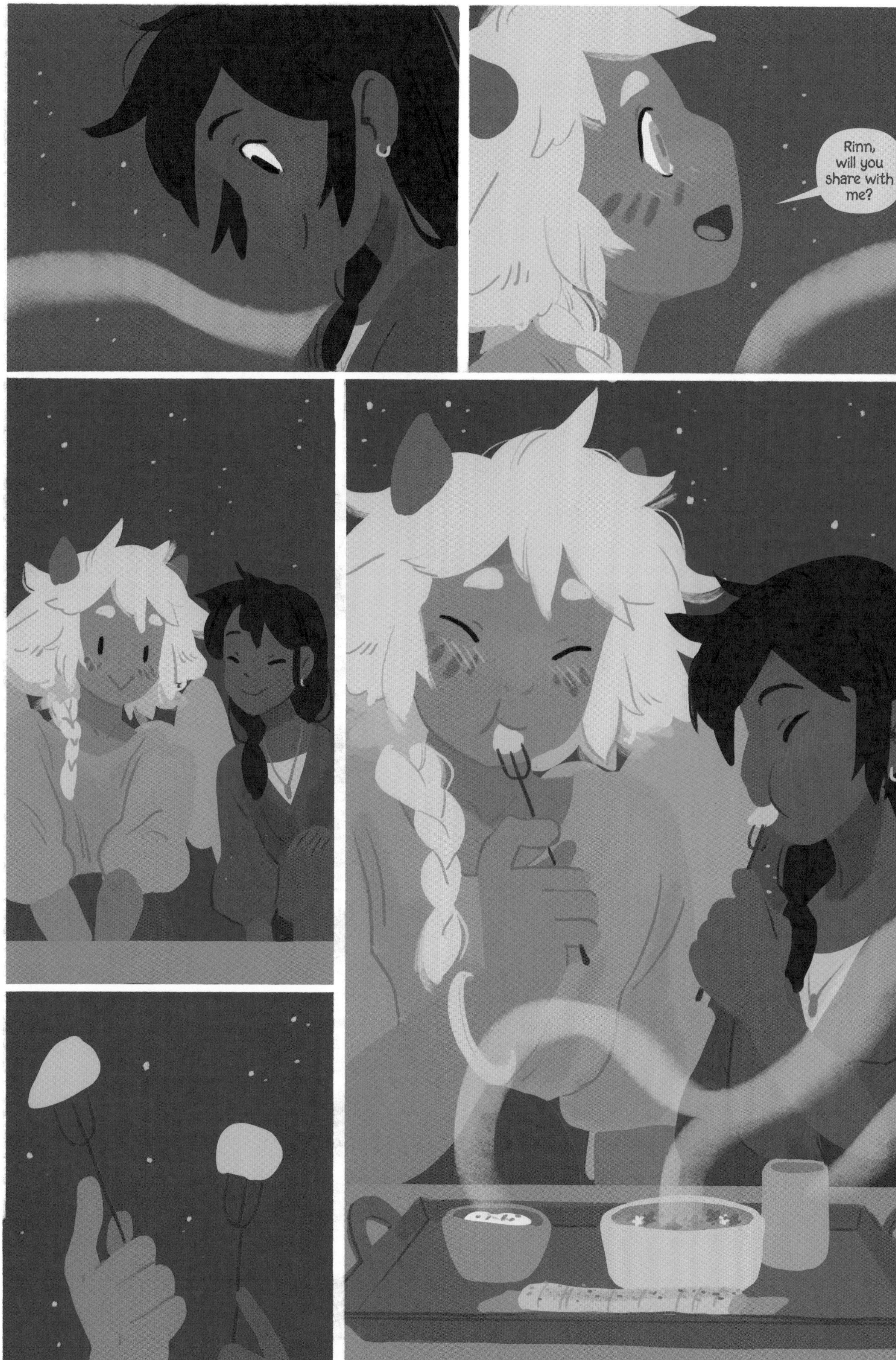
Rinn, will you share with me?

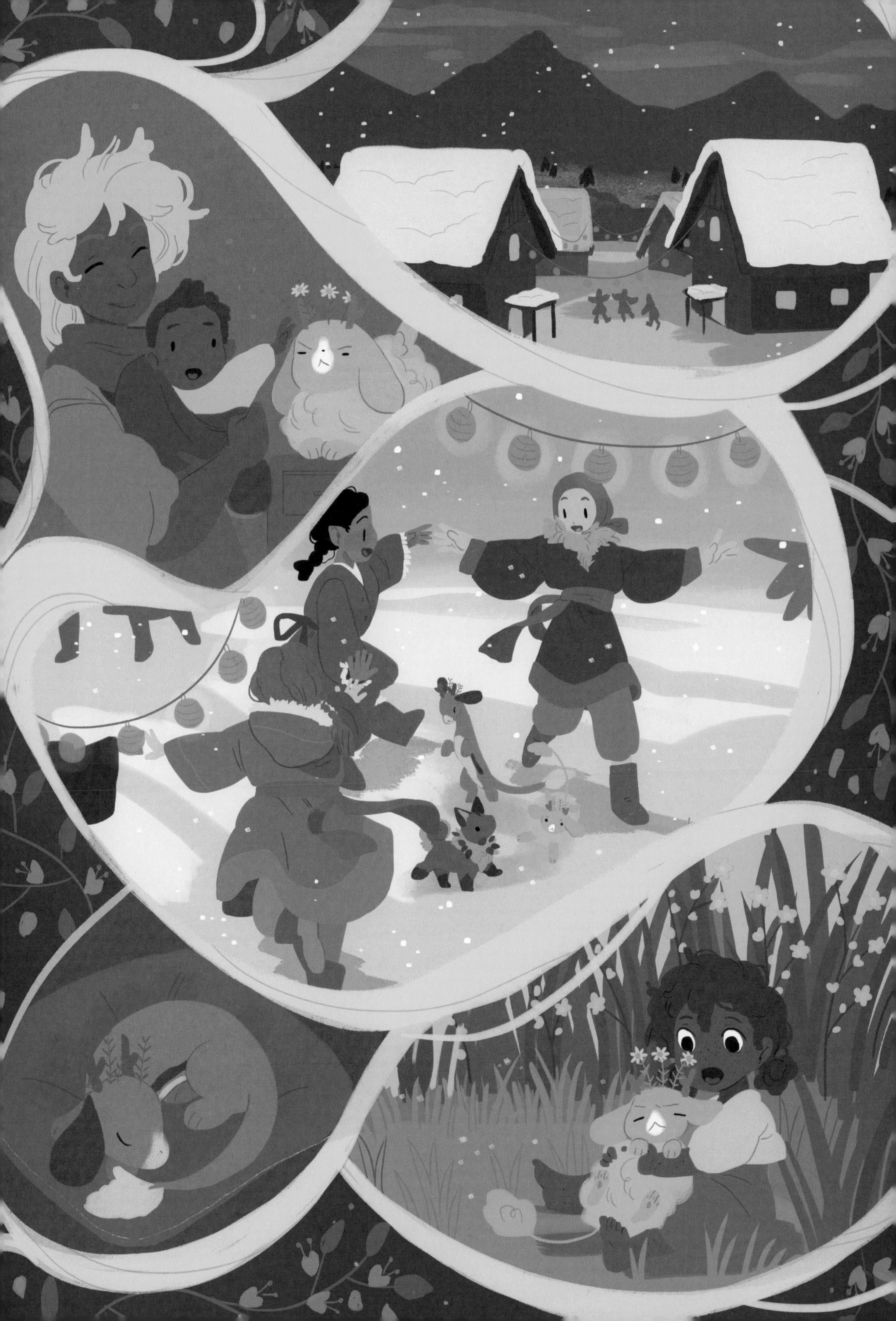

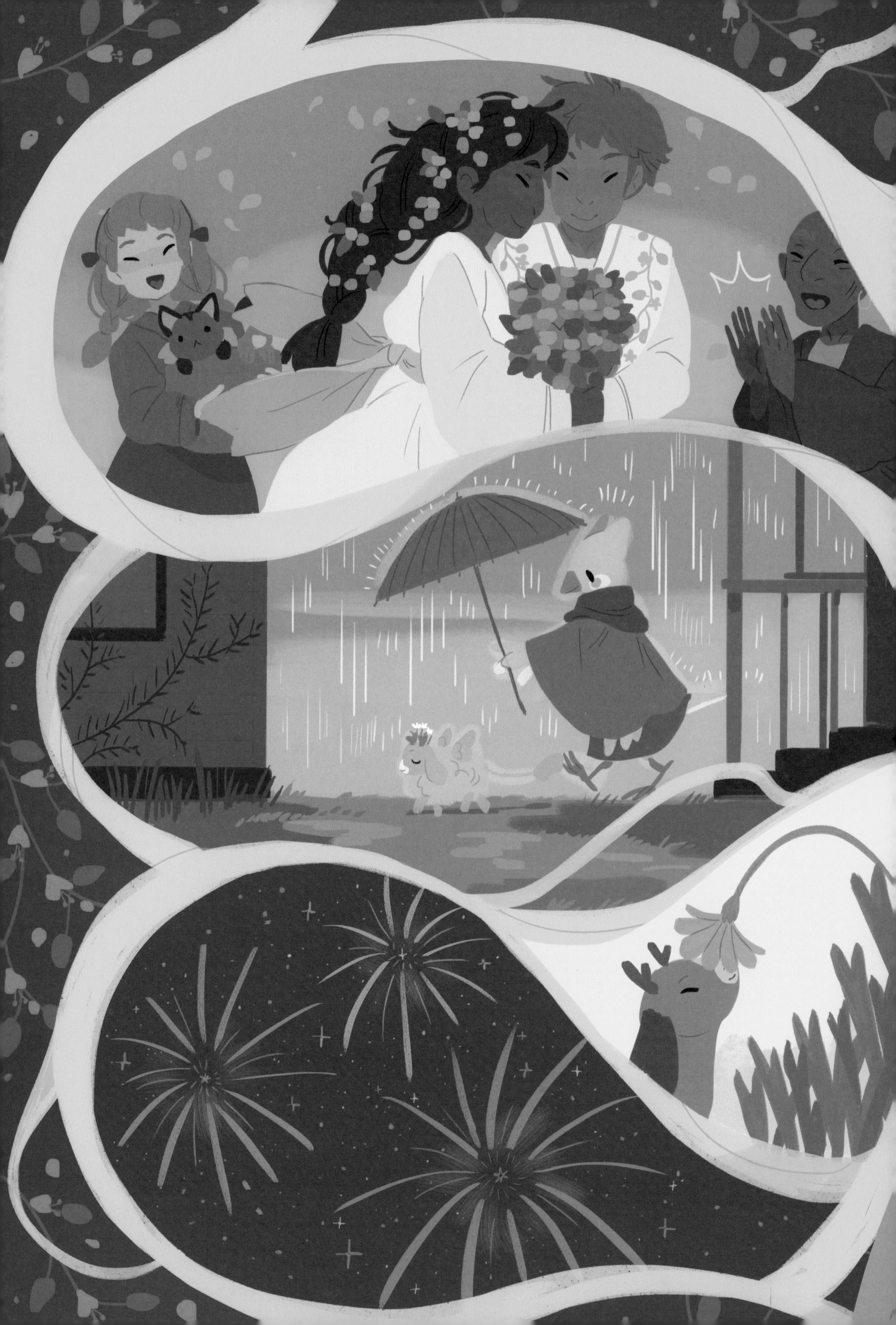

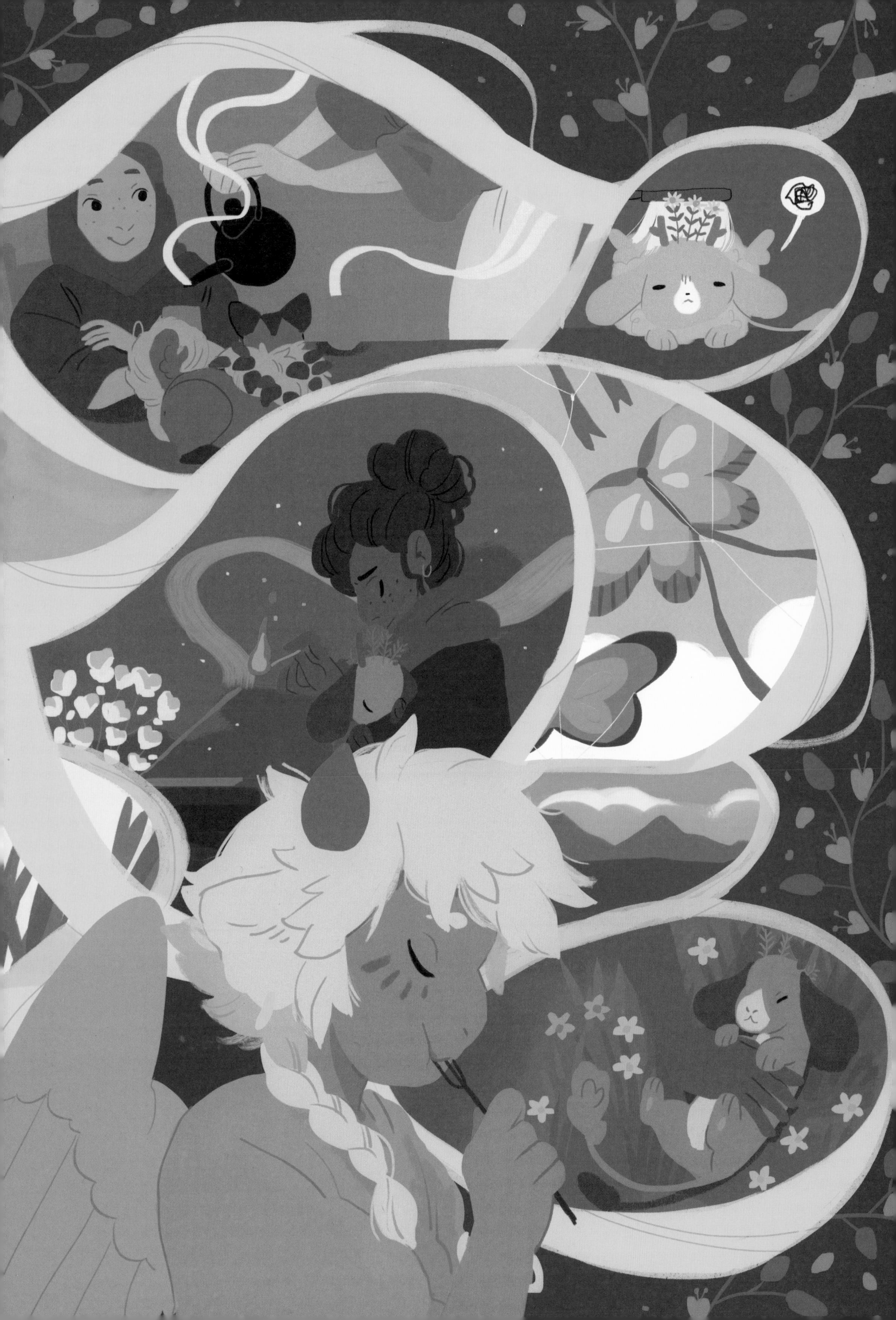

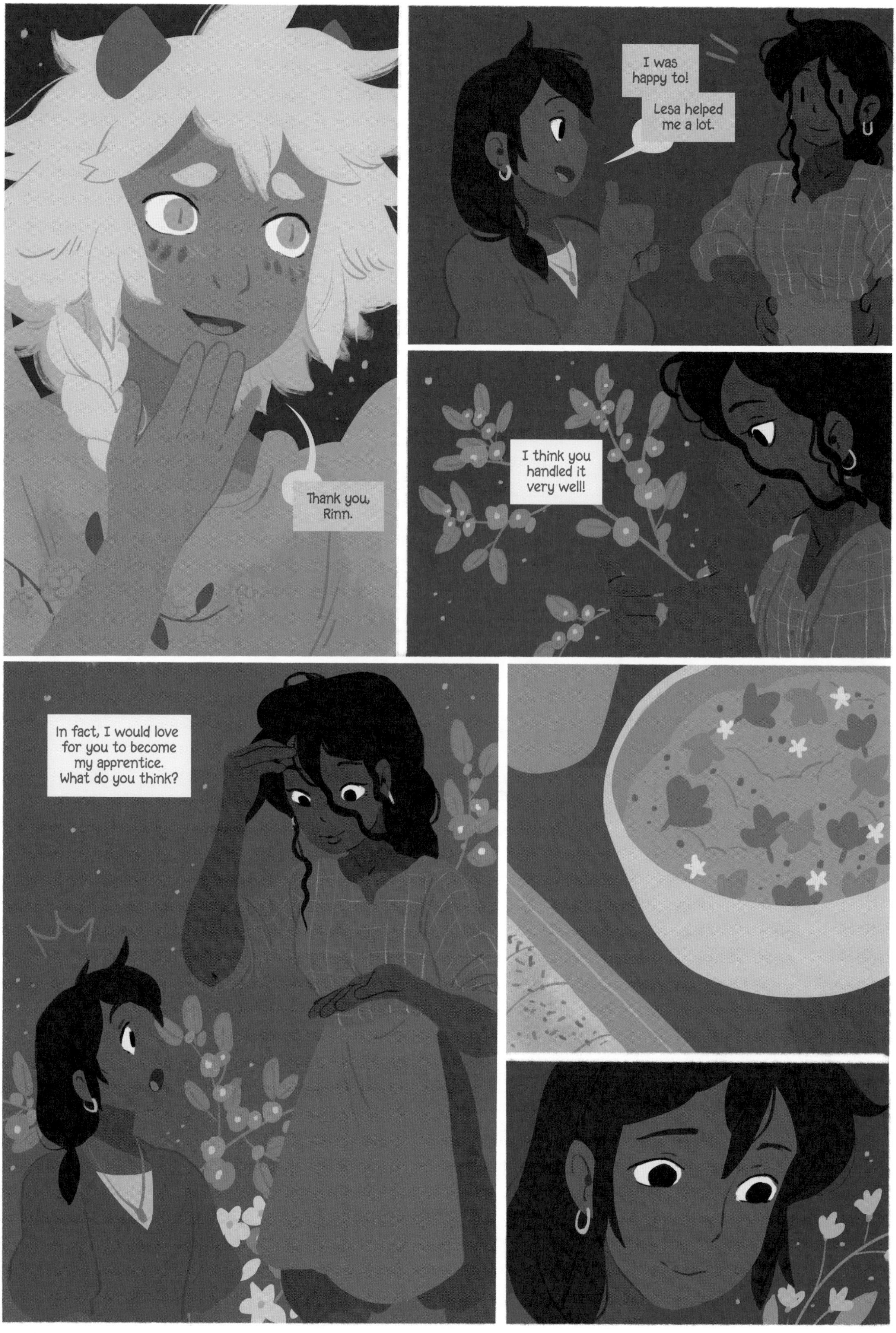
Thank you, Rinn.
I was happy to!
Lesa helped me a lot.
I think you handled it very well!
In fact, I would love for you to become my apprentice. What do you think?

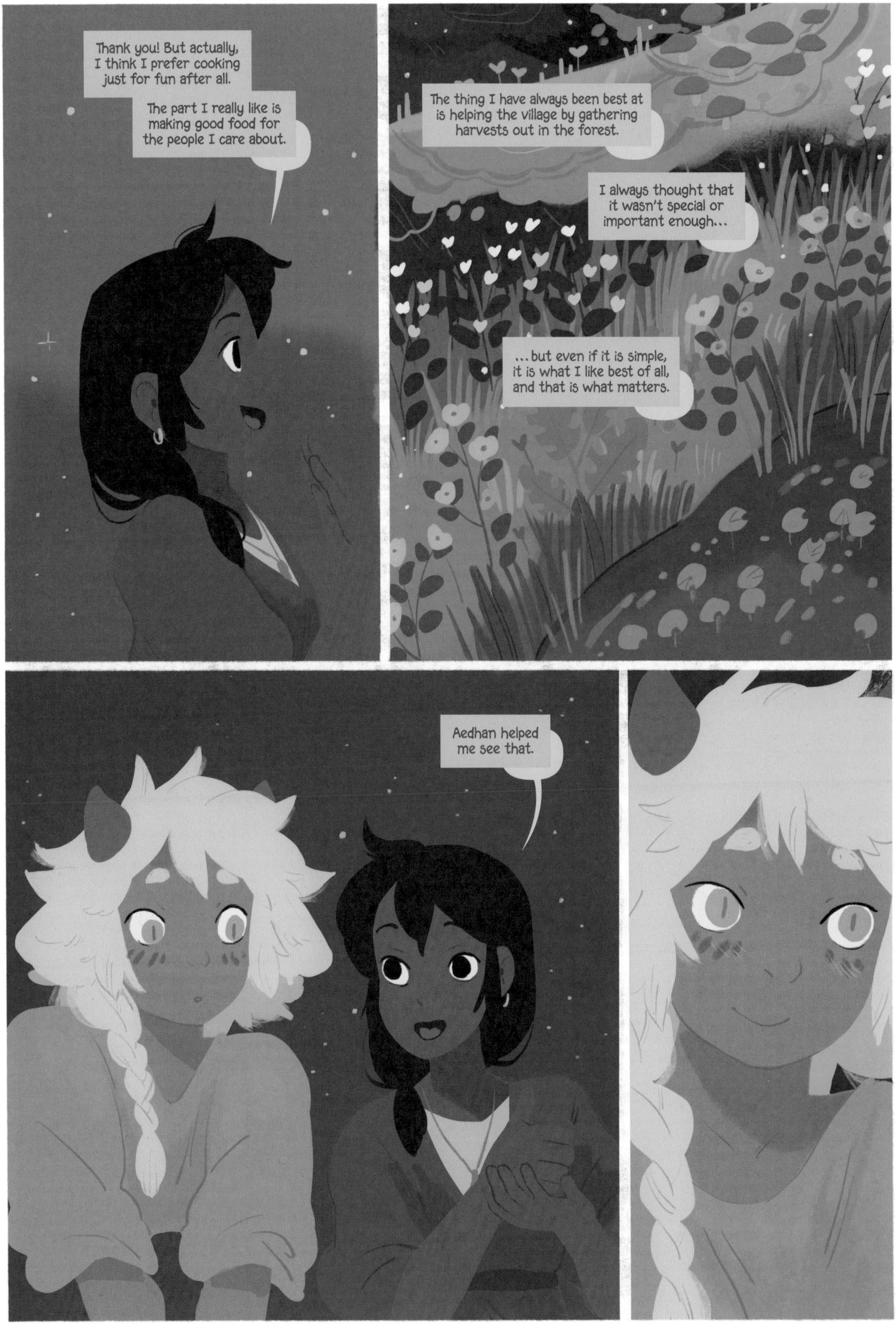
Thank you! But actually, I think I prefer cooking just for fun after all.
The part I really like is making good food for the people I care about.
The thing I have always been best at is helping the village by gathering harvests out in the forest.
I always thought that it wasn't special or important enough...
...but even if it is simple, it is what I like best of all, and that is what matters.
Aedhan helped me see that.

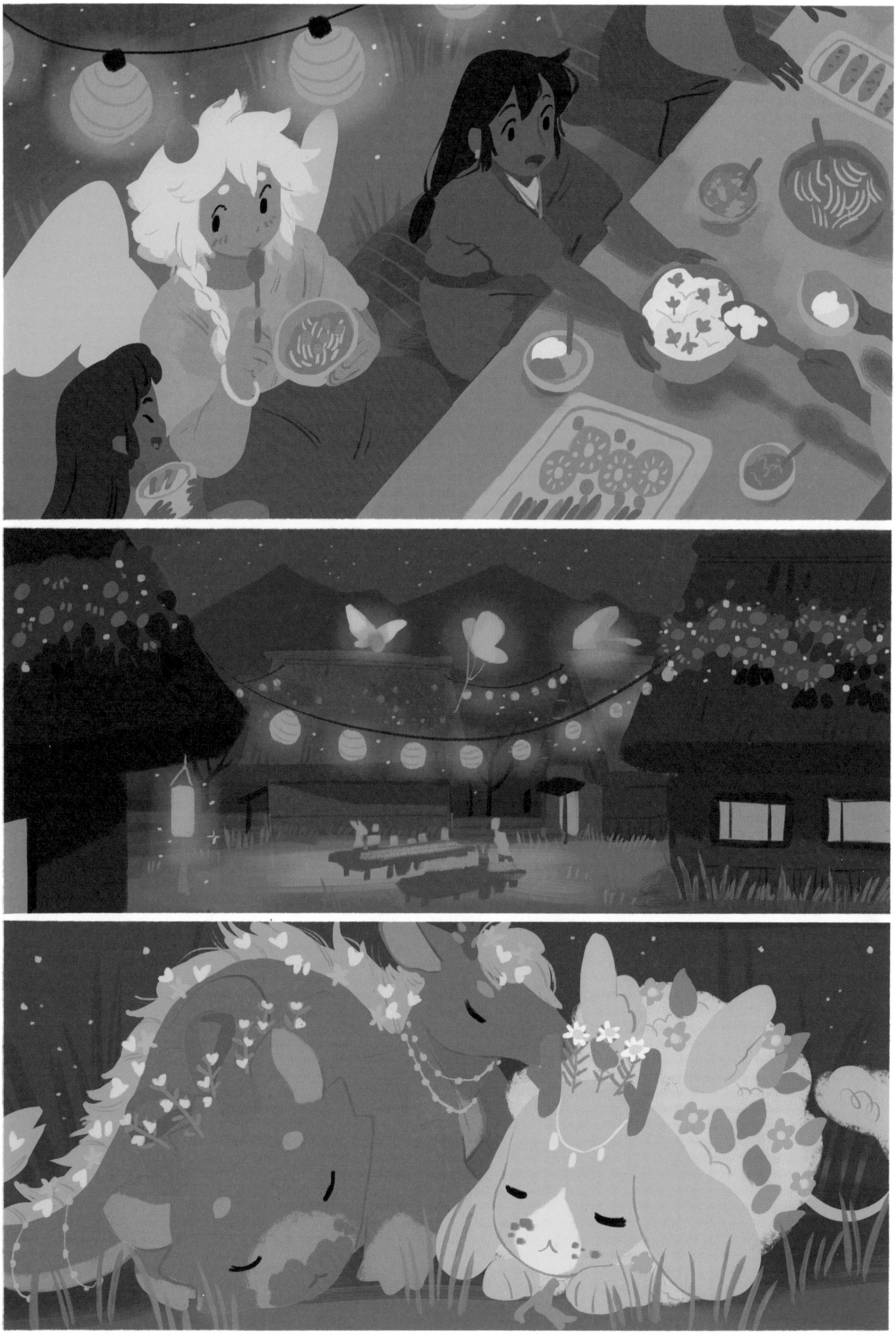

Chapter Seven

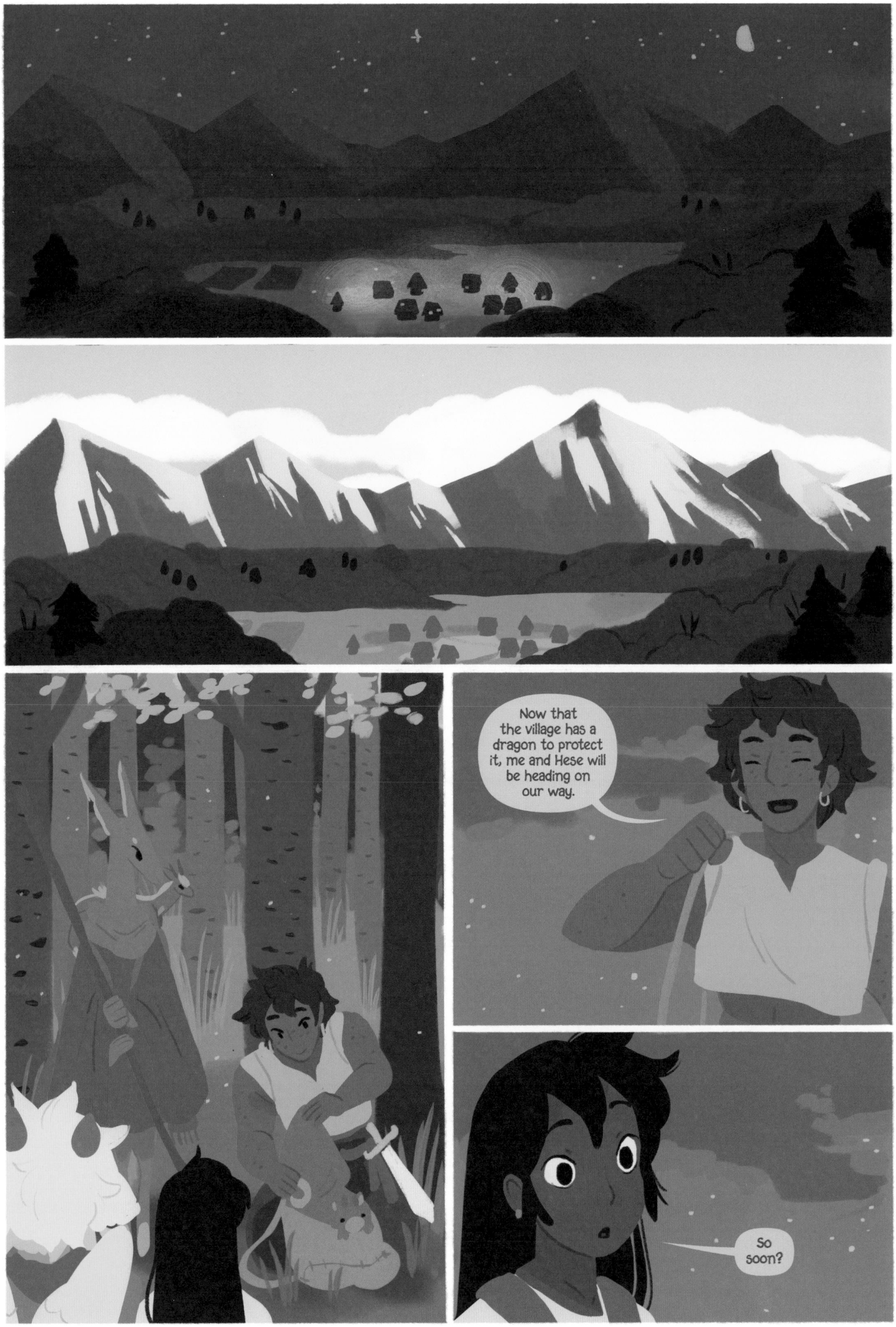
Now that the village has a dragon to protect it, me and Hese will be heading on our way.
So soon?

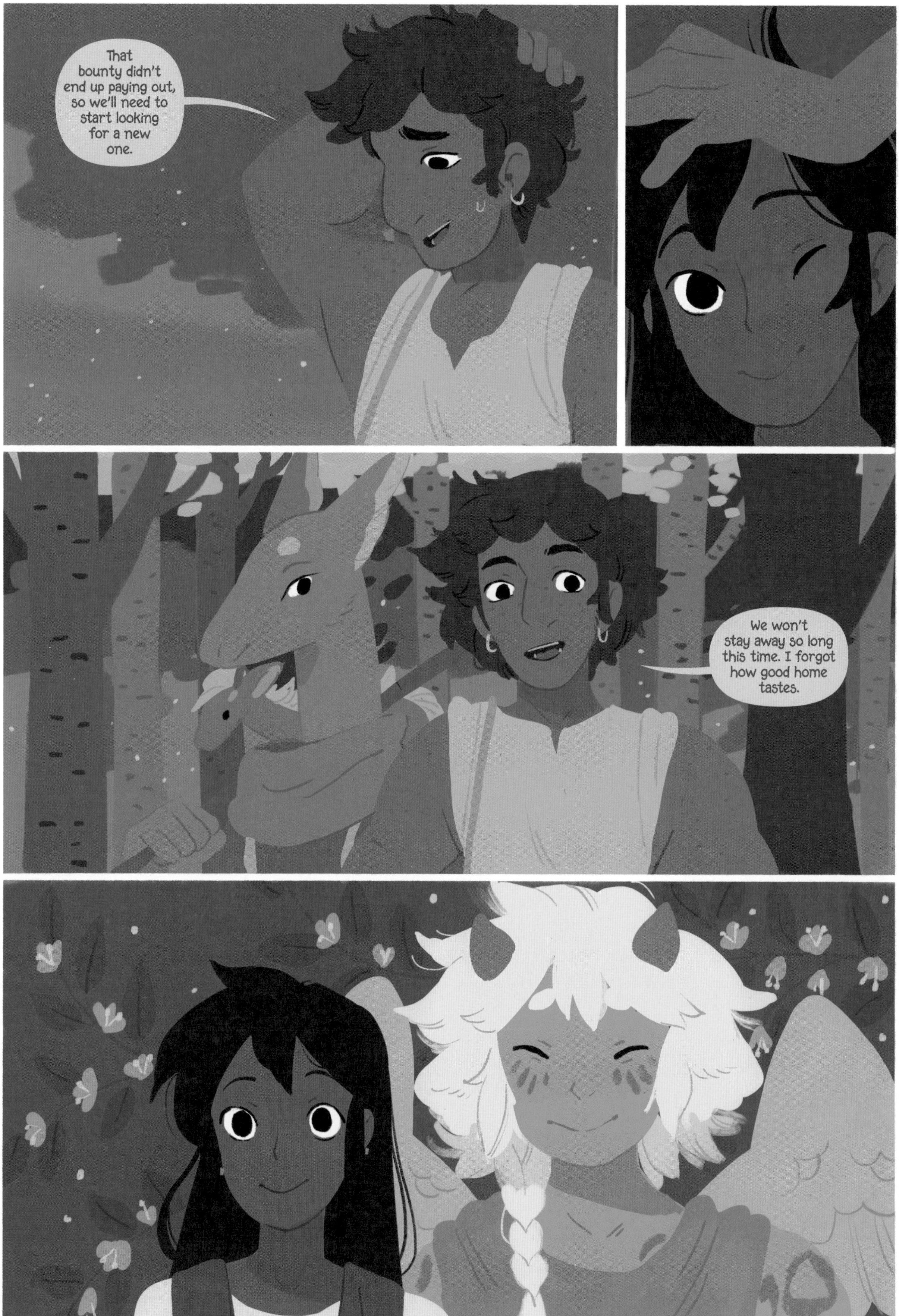
That bounty didn't end up paying out, so we'll need to start looking for a new one.
We won't stay away so long this time. I forgot how good home tastes.

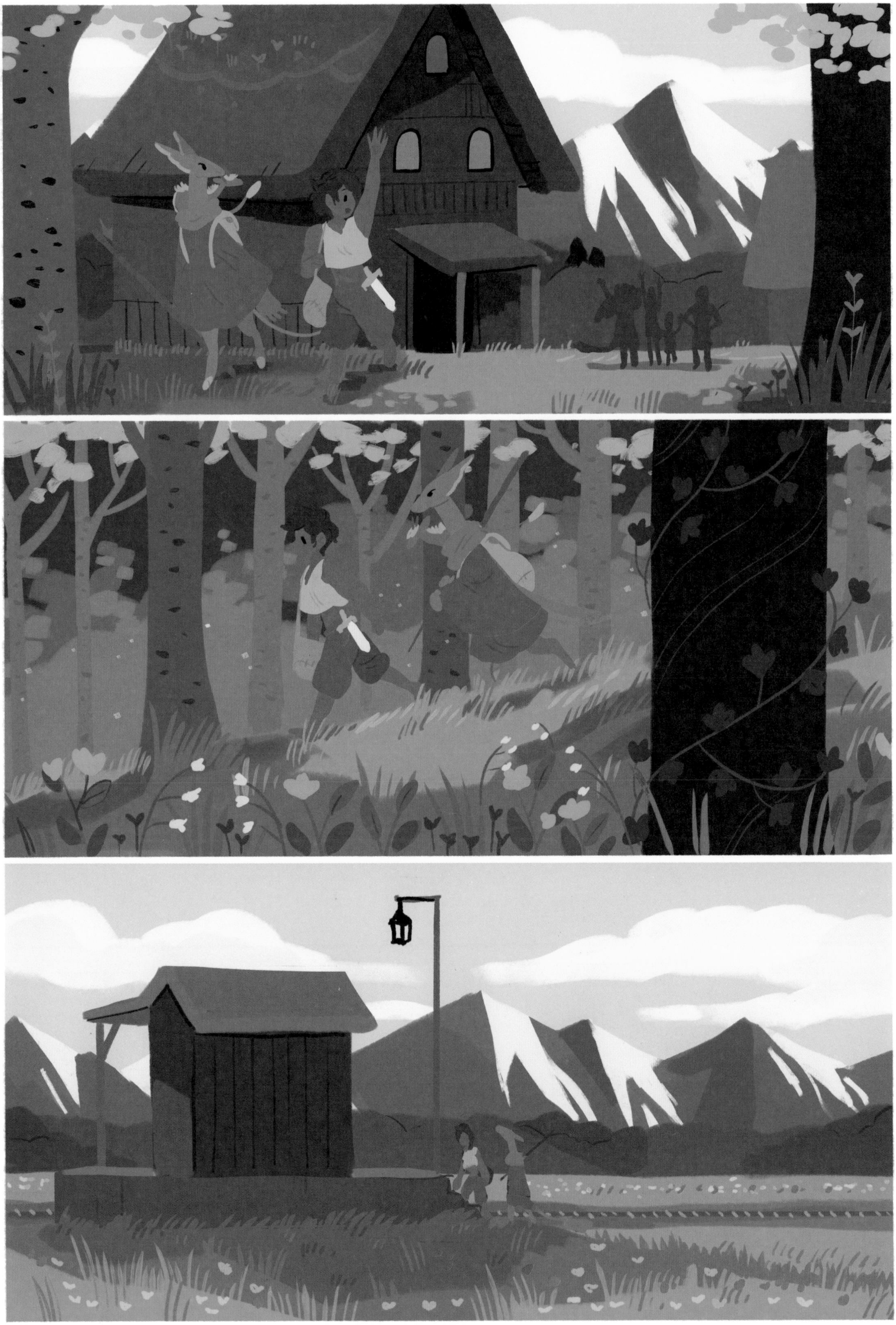

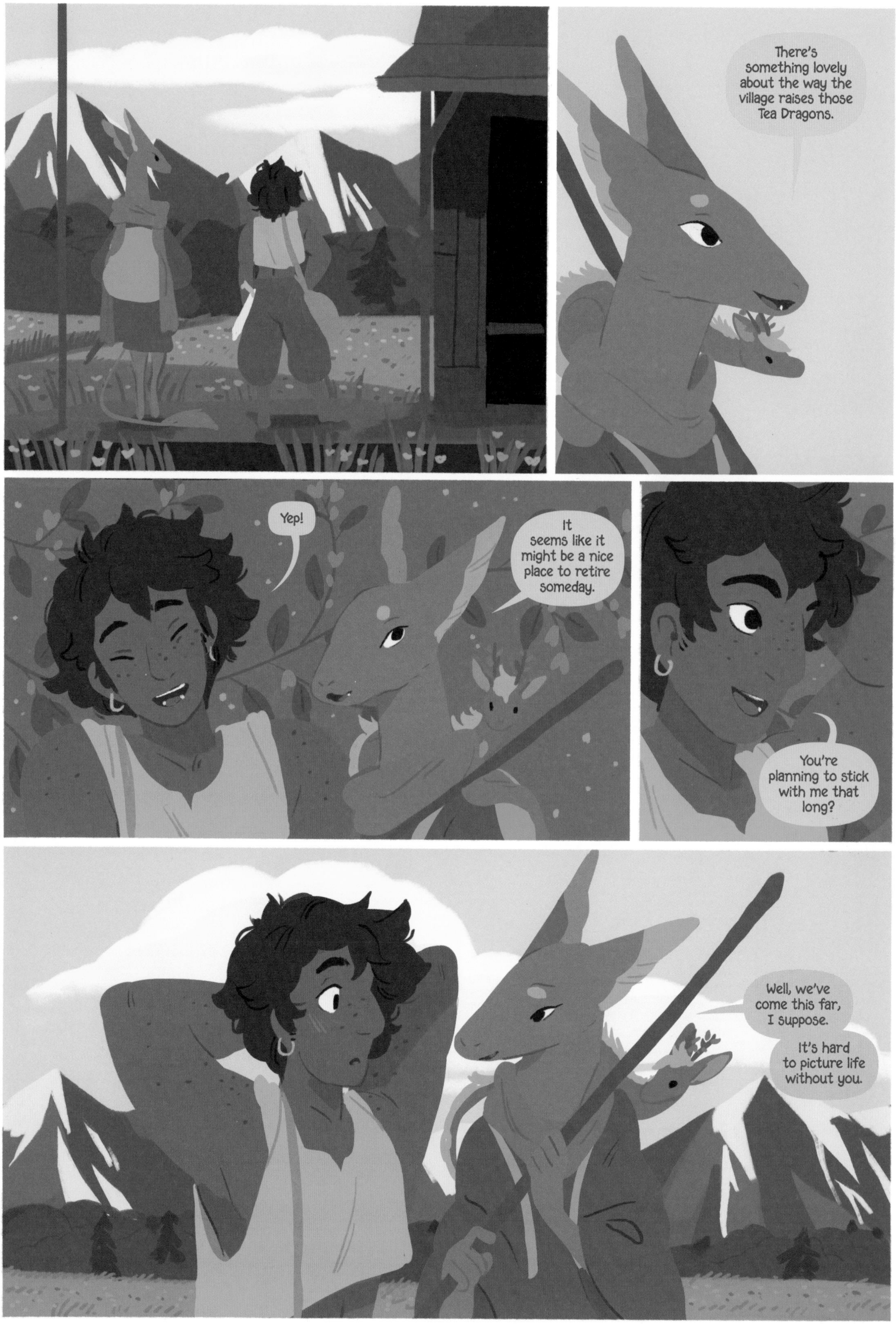

There's something lovely about the way the village raises those Tea Dragons.
Yep!
It seems like it might be a nice place to retire someday.
You're planning to stick with me that long?
Well, we've come this far, I suppose.
It's hard to picture life without you.

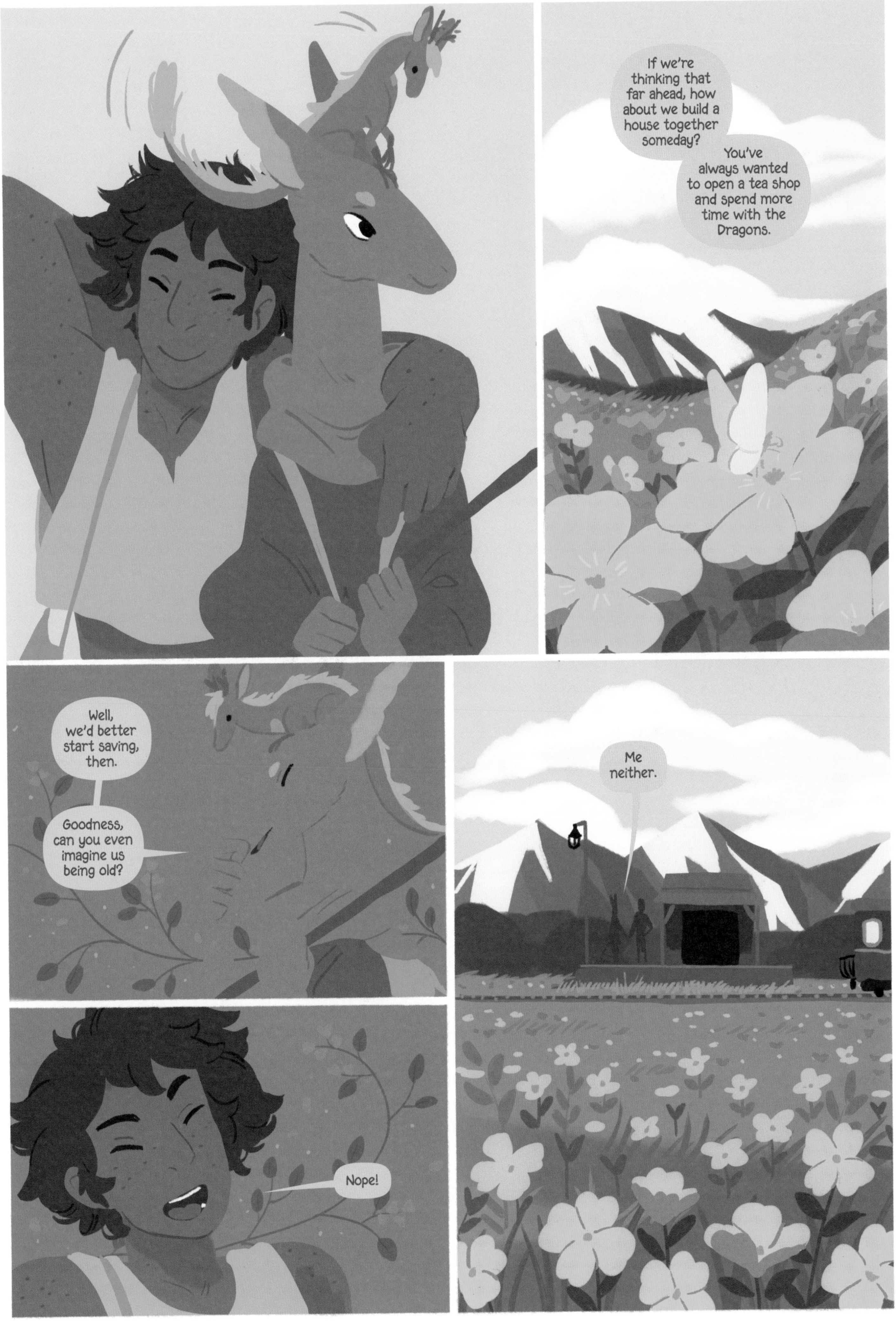
If we're thinking that far ahead, how about we build a house together someday?
You've always wanted to open a tea shop and spend more time with the Dragons.
Well, we'd better start saving, then.
Goodness, can you even imagine us being old?
Nope!
Me neither.

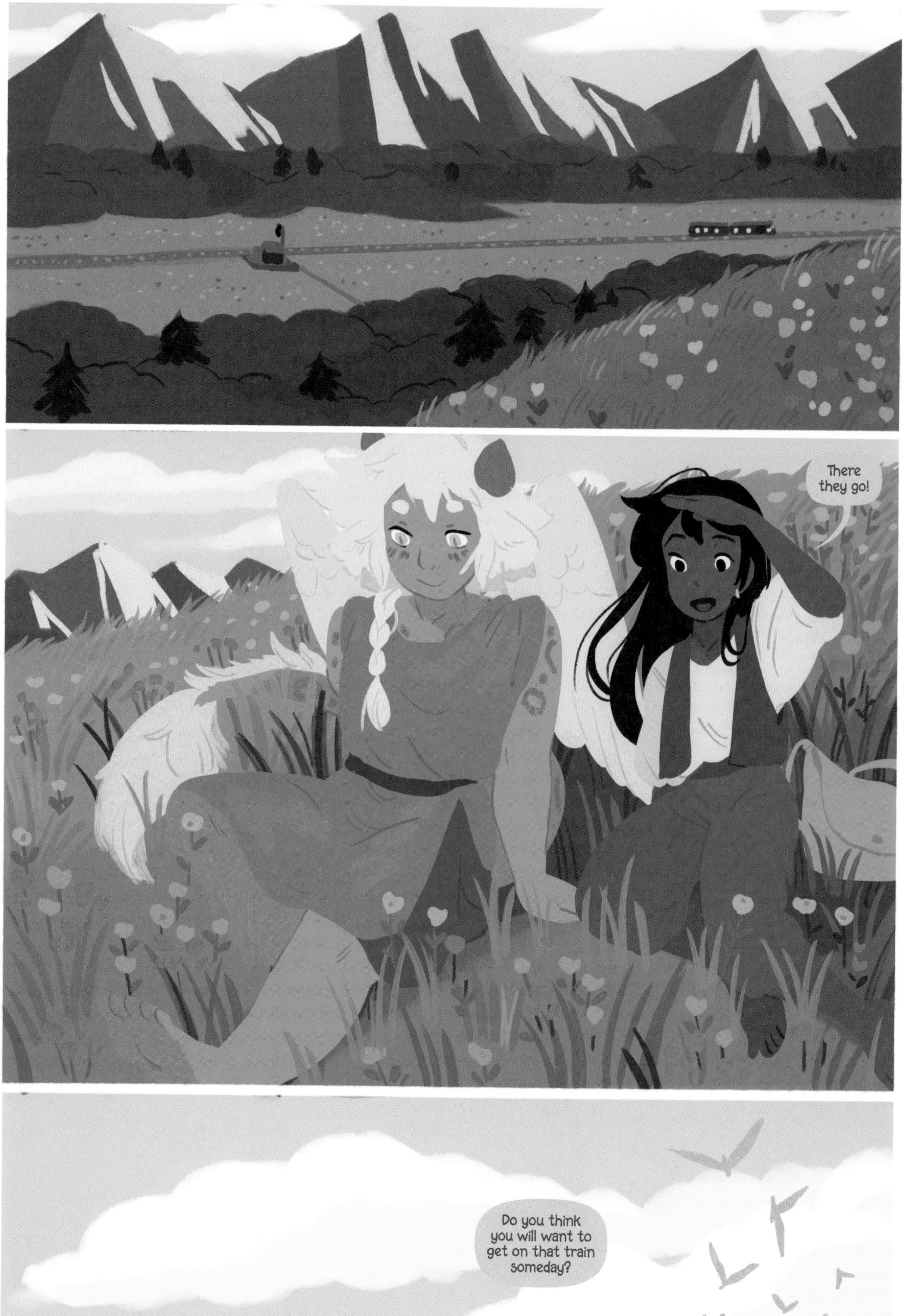
There they go!
Do you think you will want to get on that train someday?

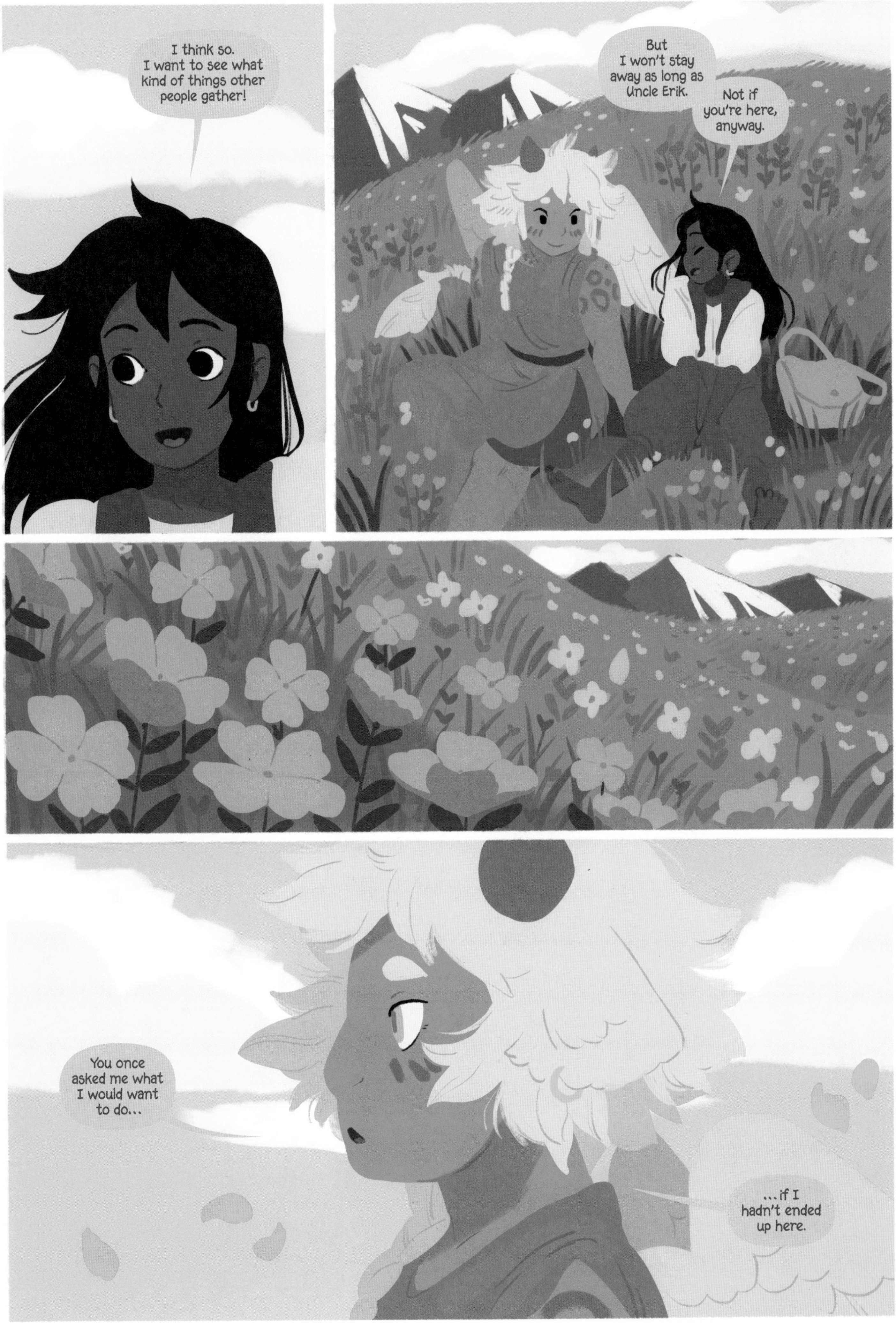
I think so. I want to see what kind of things other people gather!
But I won't stay away as long as Uncle Erik.
Not if you're here, anyway.
You once asked me what I would want to do...
...if I hadn't ended up here.

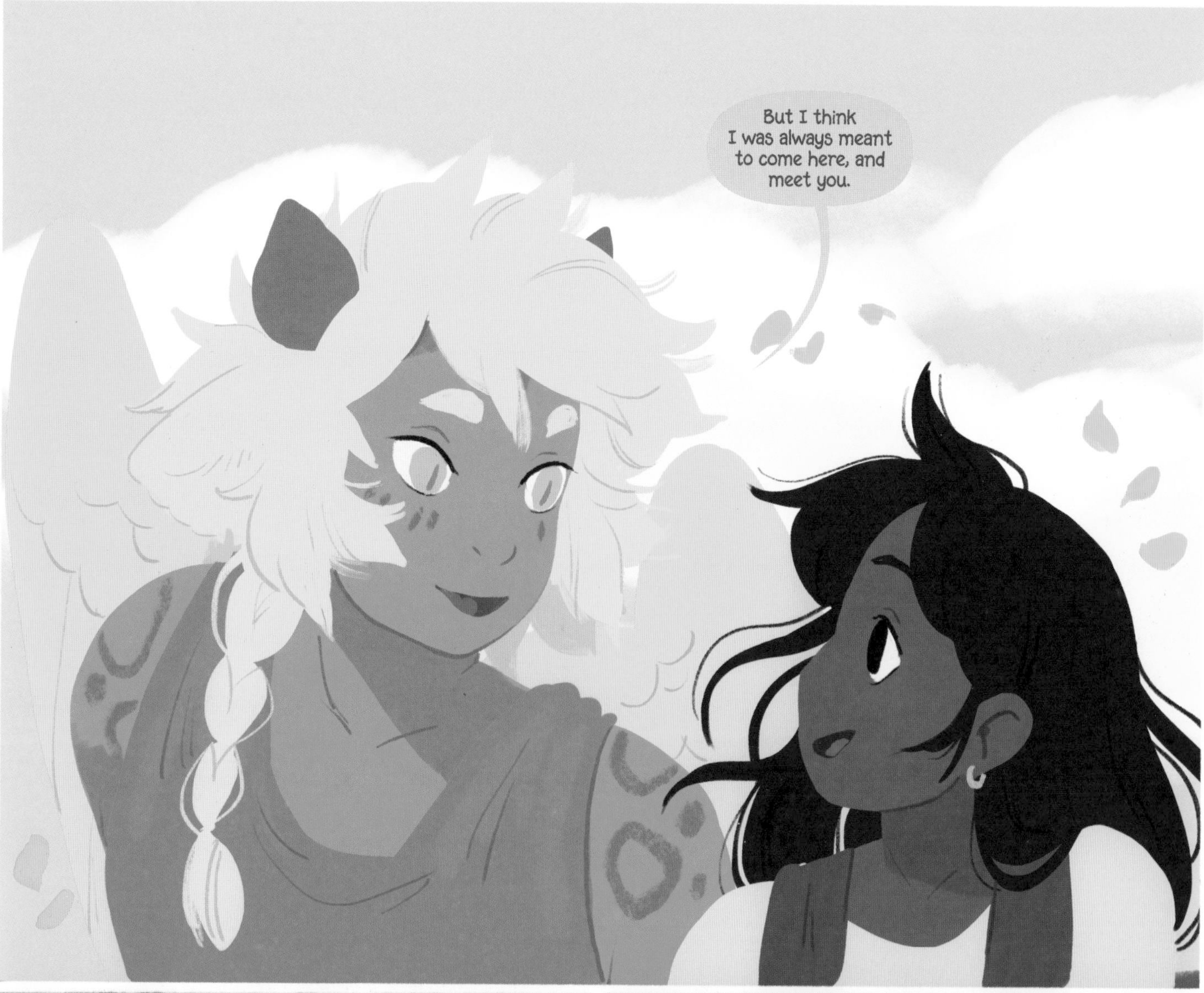
But I think I was always meant to come here, and meet you.

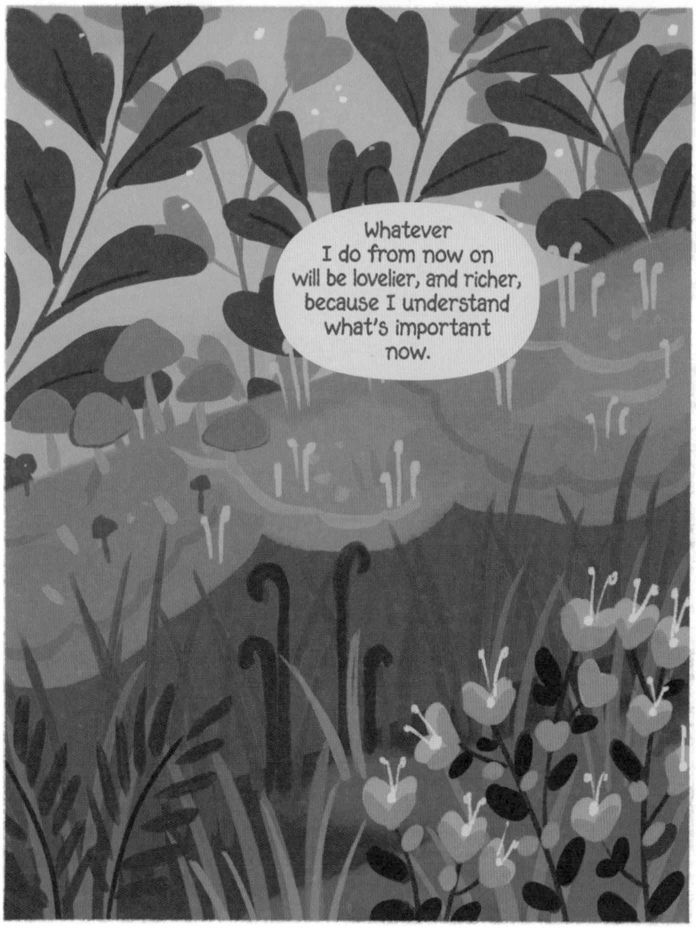
Whatever I do from now on will be lovelier, and richer, because I understand what's important now.

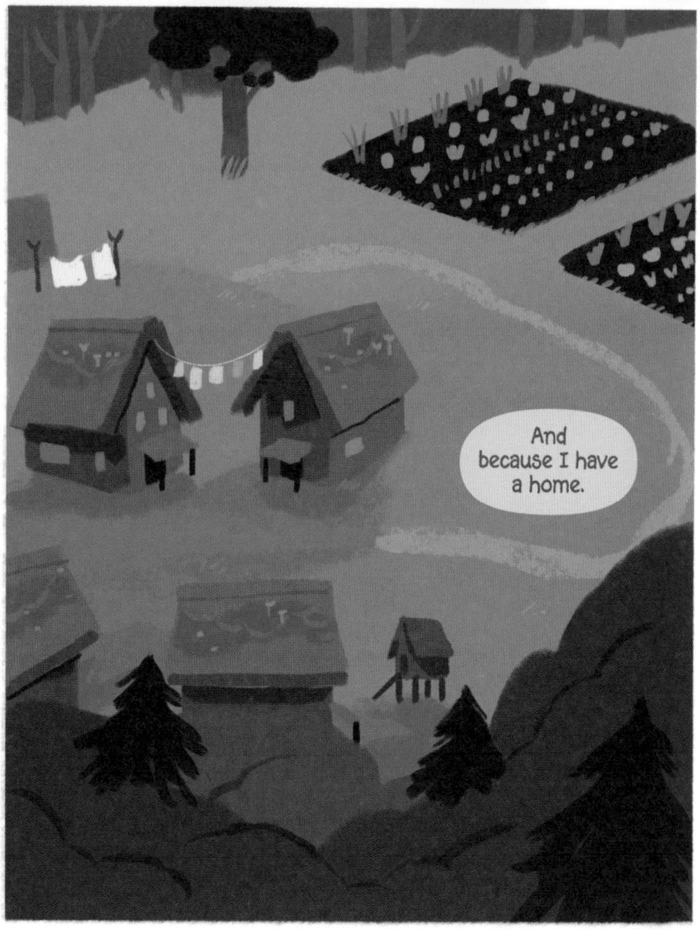
And because I have a home.

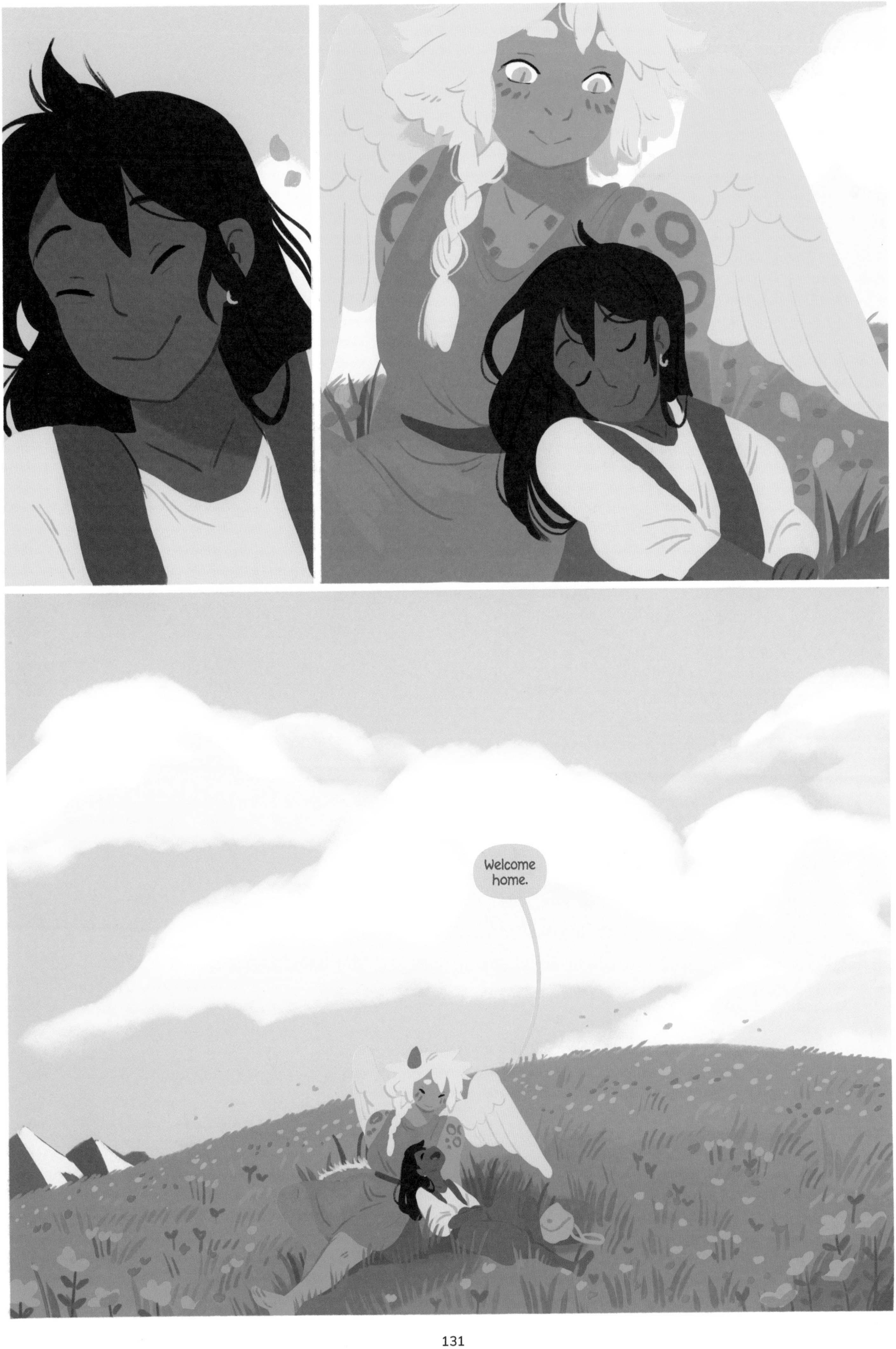
Welcome home.

EXTRACTS FROM THE

Alpine Tea Dragon Handbook

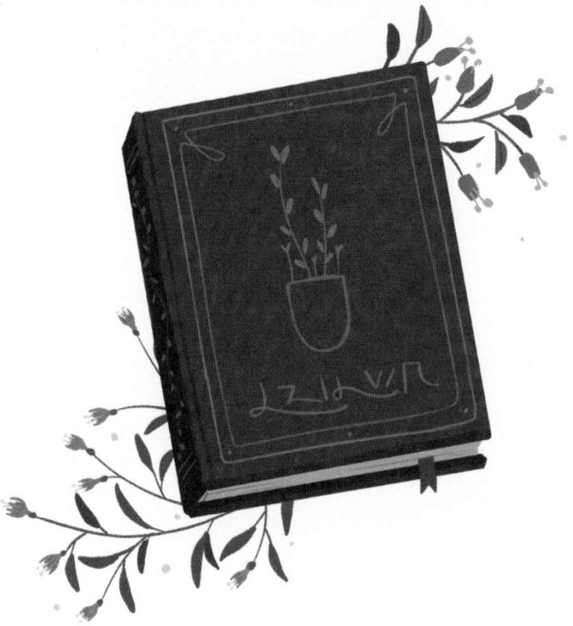

Mountain Chamomile

AVERAGE LENGTH: 40 cm

AVERAGE WEIGHT: 8 kg

TEA BREWED BY: Leaves and flowers

CARE NOTES: Dense wool-like fur requires regular brushing with oils to keep it soft and bouncy.

Despite wearing a perpetual expression of grumpiness, Mountain Chamomile Dragons are not actually that much harder to look after than their relaxed regular Chamomile cousins. It seems they just alternate between wanting attention and wanting to be left alone, but aren't very good at expressing it.

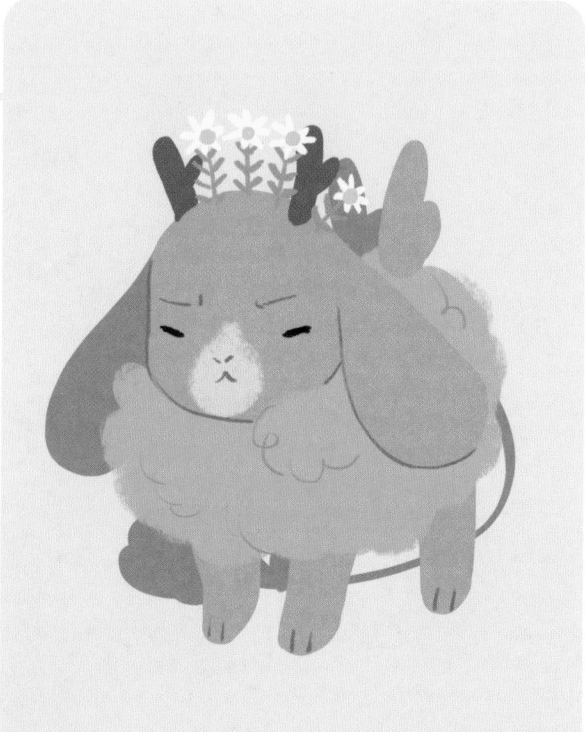

Fennel

AVERAGE LENGTH: 45 cm

AVERAGE WEIGHT: 8 kg

TEA BREWED BY: Leaves

CARE NOTES: Keeps a light coat all year round, so in alpine climates will need to be dressed with scarves and coats in winter.

Fennel are one of the most curious and intrepid varieties, and enjoy a good meddling wherever they can get it. Unlike many Tea Dragons who are cautious and worried about consequences, if a Fennel dragon sees a stack of objects, it will immediately desire to push them over.

Marshmallow

AVERAGE LENGTH: 35 cm

AVERAGE WEIGHT: 10 kg

TEA BREWED BY: Leaves gathered from ruff

CARE NOTES: For summer, trim the top layer of fur only, as the denser layers do not grow back easily.

When the leaves and flowers are brewed, they have healing properties, and complement sweets made from wild marshmallow root extract very well. They are a sturdy variety of Tea Dragon who love the snow, and become more playful and active during winter. They will not consent to wear winter clothing.

A NOTE ABOUT
Tea Dragons
& Dragons

Dragons (Dracona Major) and Tea Dragons (Dracona Domestica) share a common ancestor that dates back hundreds of thousands of years. Dragons like Aedhan and his clan are by far the most evolved of any dragon species, with a complex history, language, culture, and magical abilities similar to or exceeding humans. Tea Dragons are the domesticated result of a smaller sub-species of wild dragon, which is now found only in rare numbers.

Dracona Major are uncommon to find in general society, keeping mostly to themselves—partly a result of never knowing whether a stranger might be seeking the archaic honour of slaying a dragon. However, those that do dabble with the wider world enjoy a certain glamour and respect wherever they go, almost like aristocracy. Some clans, such as Aedhan's, see this as a responsibility to uphold, and are especially protective of villages and shrines that have formed around places that are historically important to dragons.

Dragons live longer than Tea Dragons, but their lifespans are similar. Family lines are the most important relationships within dragon society—some who find this suffocating tend to spend more time in the wider world, amongst other folks. There is a strong sense of duty and loyalty, and it is difficult for a young dragon to question the elders, the most senior of which may have lived for a thousand years.

Dragons and Tea Dragons have little to do with each other—a dragon would certainly never keep a Tea Dragon of their own. When they do cross paths, the reaction usually ranges between bemusement and disbelief.

Kay O'Neill is an Eisner & Harvey Award-winning illustrator and graphic novelist from New Zealand.

They are the author of *Princess Princess Ever After, Aquicorn Cove, Dewdrop, The Tea Dragon Society, The Tea Dragon Festival,* and *The Tea Dragon Tapestry,* all from Oni Press. They mostly make gentle fantasy stories for younger readers and are very interested in tea, creatures, things that grow, and the magic of everyday life.

MORE RESOURCES ABOUT

Sign Language

GENERAL INFORMATION

THE NATIONAL ASSOCIATION OF THE DEAF (NAD.ORG)
A United States civil rights organisation of, by, and for deaf and hard of hearing individuals.

DEAF AOTEAROA (DEAF.ORG.NZ)
A New Zealand organisation that provides services, resources, and advocacy.

WORLD FEDERATION OF THE DEAF (WFDEAF.ORG)
An international advocacy organisation that covers over 130 countries.

ARTS & SPORTS

DEAFLYMPICS (DEAFLYMPICS.COM)
Recognized by the International Olympic Committee, the Deaflympics invites deaf/hard of hearing elite athletes from all of the world to compete.

NATIONAL THEATRE OF THE DEAF (NTD.ORG)
A theatre company comprised of deaf and hearing actors. Each performance is given simultaneously in American Sign Language and spoken word.

KID-FRIENDLY RESOURCES

ASL NOOK (ASLNOOK.COM)
An online hub of videos where a Deaf family teaches ASL in a casual, fun way.

SIGN NINJA (NZSLSIGNNINJA.CO.NZ)
Learn New Zealand Sign Language via a fun online game!

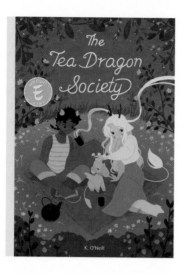

ALSO FROM THE WORLD OF TEA DRAGONS

The Tea Dragon Society
K. O'Neill

THE TEA DRAGON SOCIETY

The Eisner Award-winning gentle fantasy that follows the story of Greta, a blacksmith apprentice, and the people she meets as she becomes entwined in the enchanting world of Tea Dragons.

The Tea Dragon Society
Card Game

THE TEA DRAGON SOCIETY CARD GAME

Create a bond between yourself and your Tea Dragon in this easy-to-learn card game from Oni Games and Renegade Games!

ALSO FROM KAY O'NEILL

"A royal winner." —Kirkus
PRINCESS PRINCESS
Ever After
K. O'Neill

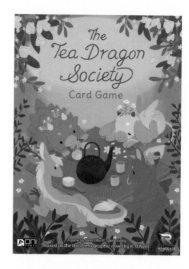

PRINCESS PRINCESS EVER AFTER

Join Sadie and Amira, two very different princesses with very different strengths, on their journey to figure out what "happily ever after" really means—and how they can find it with each other.

DEWDROP
K. O'NEILL

DEWDROP

In this graphic novel for beginning readers, a cheerful axolotl helps his friends do their best in the pond sports fair! Available spring 2020.

AQUICORN COVE
K. O'NEILL

AQUICORN COVE

Unable to rely on the adults in her storm-ravaged seaside town, a young girl must protect a colony of magical seahorse-like creatures she discovers in the coral reef.

The
AQUICORN
COVE
Board Game

THE AQUICORN COVE BOARD GAME

Work with your friends to keep the reef healthy while taking care of your village in this cooperative board game based on the graphic novel!

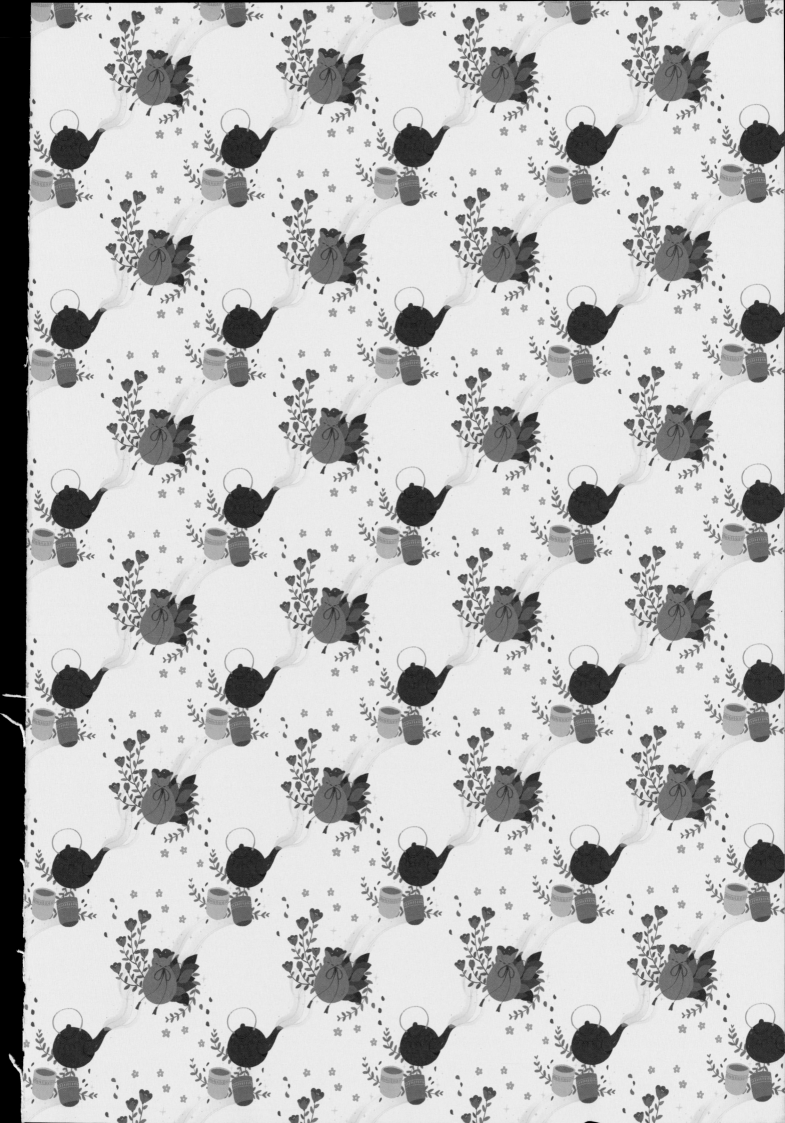

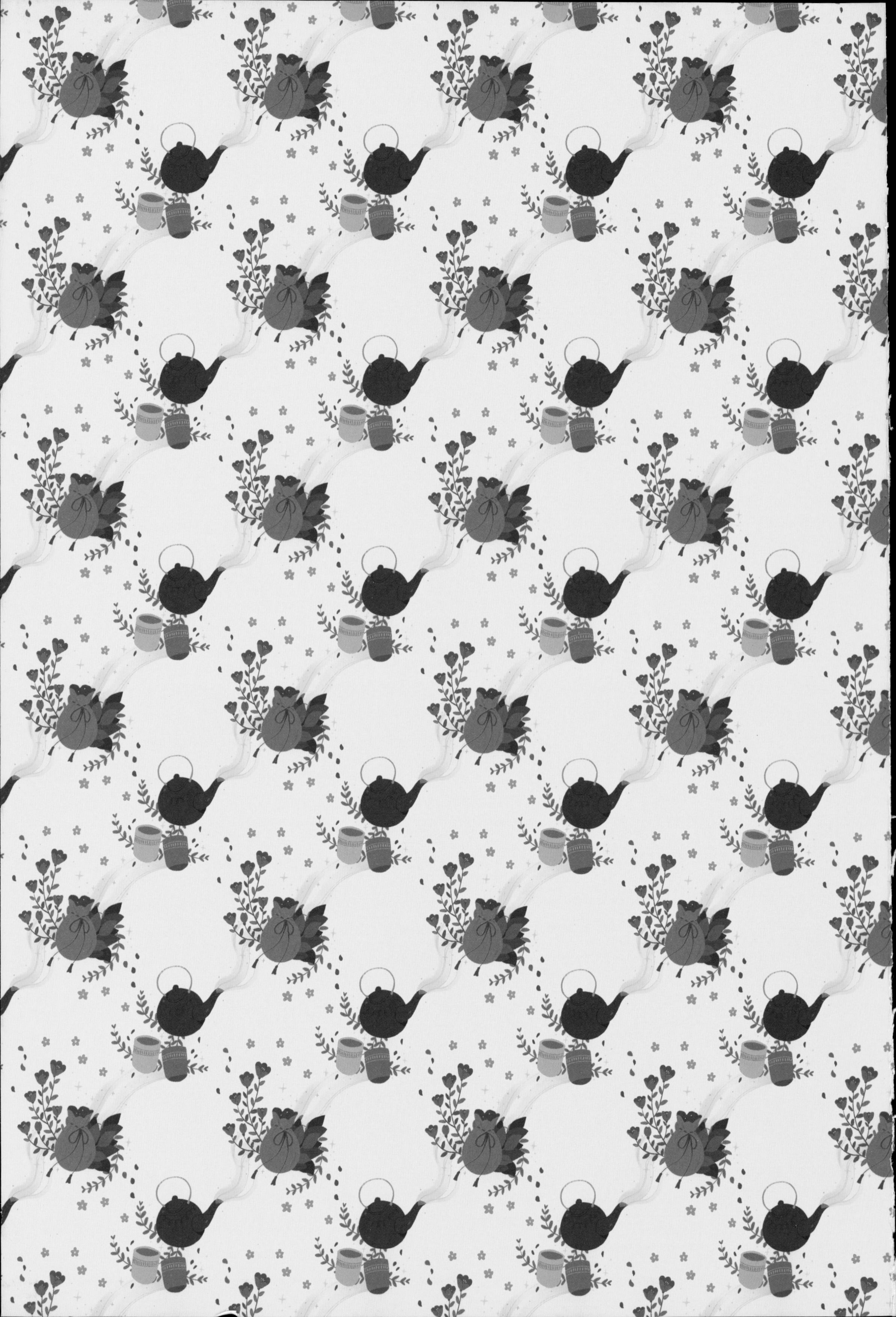